I0633308

Super-Detective!

In the late-1930s, Culture Publications was the leading producer of salacious, under-the-counter pulp magazines like *Spicy Mystery* and *Spicy Detective*. And then the comic books happened. Culture Publications, after having redefined "culture" as "creamy bosoms exposed by torn, lacy undergarments," added a new neo-wholesome imprint, Trojan Publications, and gave the comic-book fans a reason to stay with the pulps. The reason was *Super-Detective*, introduced in 1940, a (near) monthly pulp featuring the novel-length adventures of Jim Anthony, detective extraordinaire, written under the house name of "John Grange." But Anthony was no mere sleuth. He possessed phenomenal physical and mental abilities. Patterned after Street & Smith's Doc Savage, and with the aid of his far-flung Anthony Legion, he battled super-villains bent on the destruction of the United States—no mere whimsy as the dark clouds of World War billowed.

After ten amazing adventures, we may conclude that the comics won the battle for the super-enthused readers, for *Super-Detective*, while retaining its title, transformed the Jim Anthony novels to a hard-boiled detective-story mode. The criminals were less ambitious, and more susceptible to guns and fists. But the stories were no less entertaining.

Here, in this *Super-Detective Flip Book*, a joint presentation of Off-Trail Publications and Reverse Karma Press, are two Jim Anthony novels, one from each phase of Anthony's career. Flip the book and read the other novel. Also included are introductions that explore the dual worlds of Jim Anthony, and the authors who brought him to life. John McMahan introduces "Legion of Robots" (November 1940), from Jim Anthony's high-adventure period, and discusses the author, Victor Rousseau, and the factors that went into creating the series. John Wooley introduces the hard-boiled "Murder's Migrants" (March 1943), and explores the working collaboration between its authors, Robert Leslie Bellem and W.T. Ballard.

SUPER-DETECTIVE
Flip Book

TWO COMPLETE NOVELS
featuring

LEGION OF ROBOTS

Introduction by John McMahan

MURDER'S MIGRANTS

Introduction by John Wooley

A JOINT PRESENTATION OF

Off-Trail Publications
&
Reverse Karma Press

Acknowledgements
The editors are grateful to John DeWalt, John Gunnison, Don Hutchison, John Locke, Stephen Mertz, Will Murray, Phil Nelson, Jerry Schattenberg and Al Tonik, for assistance and invaluable research.

ISBN-10: 0-9786836-9-2
ISBN-13: 978-0-9786836-9-6

OFF-TRAIL PUBLICATIONS
2036 Elkhorn Road
Castroville, CA 95012
offtrail@redshift.com

Printed in the United States of America
First printing: March 2008

Introducing Jim Anthony
By John McMahan

You'll say men like Jim Anthony don't exist in real life—you'll say they're found only in fiction. We're almost ready to agree . . . but wait! Good fiction—and we believe you'll find John Grange writes that very thing—is good only when it's true to life, in spirit and in the human qualities of its characters if not in the smallest details. And—Jim Anthony is human, warm-hearted; an embodiment of ideal American youth.

Of Irish and American Indian descent, he has inherited both immense wealth and tremendous physical attributes. He can see in the dark like a cat, follow a trail like a hound, hear sounds inaudible to other ears . . . perform almost super-human feats of strength. Moreover, he is a scientist—has worked out problems of the future in his laboratory and uses these inventions in solving crimes for the benefit of his country.

No, you won't meet anyone just like Jim Anthony in real life—but again we say, he is real life! for he's the embodiment of young American manhood, with all its ideals and ambitions, its spirit and heritage. That's why we believe you'll enjoy his adventures, month after month, as though they were your own!

— Trojan Publishing promotional copy, 1940

America was little more than a year away from entering WWII when Jim Anthony, Super-Detective, hit the newsstands. Making his debut in a cover-featured tale titled "Dealer in Death," published in the October 1940 issue of a new pulp magazine (technically, a reincarnation of a mid-'30s pulp with a similar title) called *Super-Detective*, Anthony would go on to appear in two dozen consecutive issues. In the series' first ten entries, he and his crime-busting cohorts took on a variety of Fifth Columnists, mad scientists, and would-be world dictators in high-adventure tales containing definite science-fiction elements. Then, an editorial-policy decision recast him as a more down-to-earth character, replacing the over-the-top scenarios with a hard-boiled detective milieu and later bringing in a couple of notable pulp wordsmiths, Robert Leslie Bellem and W.T. Ballard, to facilitate the change. (See "Murder's Migrants," on the flipside of this volume.)

The first three issues of the revived *Super-Detective* chronicled the epic battle between Jim Anthony and master villain Rado Ruric. The two first hooked up in October '40's "Dealer in Death," continued through the next month's "Legion of Robots," and concluded with "Madame Murder," in which Ruric was finally defeated. The novel you're about to read, "Legion of Robots," is the pivotal story of the three-novel arc, and it's chock-full of graphic death, sudden violence—and, of course, robots, although not the metal monstrosities a reader might have found in *Amazing Stories* or other science-fiction pulps of the time.

The book you hold in your hands marks the first-ever reprinting of "Legion of Robots," which has remained unavailable since its November 1940 publication in *Super-Detective*. It's the only story in the three-novel arc that hasn't seen the light of day since 1940; ironically, it may be the best of the trio. ("Dealing in Death" was republished in a pulp fanzine, *Behind the Mask* 45 [December 1998], while "Madame Murder" encored in *High Adventure* 89 [July 2006]).

The remarkable Jim Anthony resided in Penthouse A, high atop the forty-four-story Waldorf-Anthony Hotel in the heart of New York City. When not there, he could be found at his sanctum, the Teepee, located in New York's Catskill Mountains. There, he secretly maintained a large underground living and scientific exploration area. If his endeavors took him out West, he headquartered at a place called the Pueblo. Deep in the heart of the southwest desert, near the Gulf of Mexico, the Pueblo was accessible only by air.

The Jim Anthony stories often mention his parents, unusual in the pulp-hero universe. They were Shean Boru Anthony, an Irish adventurer who amassed an eye-popping fortune later in life, and Fawn Johnson, the daughter of a Comanche chief, who passed to her son an invaluable sixth sense that alerted him to impending danger. As was *de rigueur* in hero pulps and superhero comics of the time, Jim Anthony had sidekicks, beginning with Tom Gentry, a fighting hot-headed Irishmen as close to Anthony as a brother. Gentry was a skilled pilot, chauffeur, agent and all-around man Friday. Also assisting was Dawkins, Anthony's butler, who could drop his cockney British accent at will. "Legion of Robots" reveals that at one time Dawkins was a well-trained and proficient spy. One of the most interesting characters assisting Jim Anthony was Mephito, his grandfather on his mother's side. A Comanche Indian shaman, Mephito practiced strong magic in the Native American way and could foretell the future by use of nine shaman sticks. Love-interest was provided by Dolores Colquitt, the daughter of powerful U.S. Senator Warren Colquitt, the head of the Committee for

Investigation of Foreign Propaganda. He played a prominent role in the debut novel, "Dealer of Death."

If you think this Jim Anthony sounds suspiciously like Doc Savage, you're far from alone. Pulp historians have described the character in terms like "a Doc Savage clone," "a Doc Savage-type hero" or "a Doc Savage knock-off." These descriptions of Anthony, however, don't go quite far enough. While Anthony shared many of Doc's traits, the character is also derivative of Tarzan, Batman, and the greatest comic-book hero of all time, Superman. There are even elements of a couple of real-world celebrities: the Native American athlete Jim Thorpe, a great hero of the early 20th Century, and Olympic swimmer turned action-movie star Buster Crabbe.

Although the author of the Jim Anthony yarns is officially identified as "John Grange," that was actually a Trojan house name (or Trojan house, for you classicists). Most pulp historians agree that the author of the first three Jim Anthony stories was Victor Rousseau Emanuel, who wrote pulp science-fantasy as simply Victor Rousseau.

Born in London, 1879, Rousseau eventually emigrated to America, where most of his fiction was published. Compared by some to his countryman H.G. Wells, Rousseau achieved his greatest success spinning out serialized novels for American pulps of the 1910s and '20s. Emanuel had reached the omega of his pulp-writing career when Trojan representatives approached him about creating a science-fiction-oriented hero character for the reactivated *Super-Detective* pulp.

The original *Super-Detective*, as well as the *Spicy* line of under-the-counter pulps, was helmed by publisher Frank Armer. Interestingly enough, the Spicys, which featured implied sex and rapturous passages describing "creamy" bosoms and thighs, were published by Armer and his business partner Harry Donenfeld, the man who purchased DC Comics from Major Malcolm Wheeler-Nicholson in 1938 and soon unleashed a passel of legendary comic-book heroes on the world—including, of course, the most famous of all, that orphan from the planet Krypton known as Superman.

It's not a coincidence that *super*-detective Jim Anthony was published by the owner of the Superman comic character; the *Super-Detective* pulp and early *Superman* comics even share the same cover color-lettering scheme. In the early stories, Anthony is constantly saving his close friends and aides, Dolores Colquitt and Tom Gentry, from peril, much like Superman protects Lois Lane and Jimmy Olsen. Similarly, both Anthony and Superman (through his Clark Kent alter-ego) are intimately involved with big city newspapers. Both characters have secret sanctums: Anthony has The Teepee, Superman his Fortress of Solitude. Although, technically speaking, he is an alien, Superman is viewed as an all-American hero, fighting the enemies of his adopted country. You could make the case that Jim Anthony was seen as something of an alien in the modern society of the time—in some parts of America in the early '40s, a Comanche Indian wouldn't be considered fully integrated into civilization.

It's not difficult to picture Donenfeld and/or Armer directing the 60-year-old Victor Rousseau to start a new hero pulp, in hopes of profiting from the hero explosion underway in Donenfeld's DC Comics. Perhaps they instructed him to create a character whose strength nearly approached Superman's, with the tricks and crime-fighting ability of Batman and the feral jungle strength of a Tarzan (Anthony is always parading around in naught but his swimming trunks)—at the same time carefully ripping off certain aspects of Street & Smith's very popular Doc Savage. And while the Anthony stories were directed toward juveniles, the Spicy influence would remain in the scantily clad women that graced the *Super-Detective* covers—and, occasionally, the interior line drawings.

While little is known about Victor Rousseau's pulp writing, Jim Anthony, in his first three stories, appears to be a typical Rousseau protagonist. As biographer Peter Lynch blurbed Rousseau in *Contemporary Authors*:

> Victor Rousseau's stories spring out immediately and absorb the reader with global plots and bold valiance. Rousseau's rare talent is to combine medieval values and Louis L'Amour's style in the science fiction context. The result provides sentimental satisfaction. The amusement in reading Rousseau is similar to the *Star Wars* experience in the cinema. . . .
>
> The endearing impressions one gets of Rousseau are staunch traditionalism and faith in a well-ordered universe. Rousseau is good for a cheerful escape from heady ambiguity and the pleasures of a frantic plot with the sugar-coated conclusion never in doubt.

Certainly, the plotting of "Legion of Robots" illustrates Lynch's words. The far-reaching story moves from a daring prison break to a sea serpent terrorizing a Central American country, run by a dictator and harboring a Nazi agent who possesses a secret invention that can bring America to its knees. The tale returns to America for its climactic collision between good and evil, which plays out in the arid desert of the American Southwest.

In contrast, the storyline of "Murder's Migrants" is limited almost exclusively to New York City and involves typical detective-pulp elements: a battle of wits between Jim Anthony (now with only a testosterone-charged Tom Gentry remaining from his original supporting cast); a cutthroat, back-stabbing, magazine staff (an in-house Trojan joke?); and an unknown nemesis seeking to wreak Fifth Column havoc on America's war production. To see the difference in the two approaches, compare the broad, flamboyant brushstrokes of Rousseau in "Legion of Robots" to the narrow focus on a small group of players and suspects, as well as the use of dialogue and other elements from the hard-boiled detective school, that Bellem and Ballard took in "Murder's Migrants."

Two other sources of information on Victor Rousseau are the Sam Moskowitz-edited *Under the Moons of Mars* (Holt, Rinehart and Winston, 1970) and the article "H.G. Wells and Victor Rousseau Emanuel" by Richard D. Mullen, which originally appeared in the magazine *Extrapolation* (v8 #2, 1970). These sources indicate that Rousseau was the son of a Jewish father and a French mother, was in South Africa at the time of the Boer War, and came to the U.S. sometime before 1917.

This worldliness translated naturally into the Anthony Legion of the novels, a large, loose-knit organization of citizens across the United States and the world, all sharing an allegiance to the Super Detective. Bellem and Ballard described it well in "Murder's Migrants":

> In every strata of Manhattan society, from newsboys and lowly char-women, woven up through the middle classes of white-collar workers and even reaching as far as bankers, sportsmen and capitalists, you could find secret membership in the legendary Anthony Legion—a fabulous regiment of the adventurous whose allegiance and devotion can always be counted upon in time of stress. Into the ordinary every-day humdrum of their lives, Jim Anthony had carried the occasional thrill of battle against lawlessness: they were his undercover shock-troops, a heterogeneous army of modern vigilantes banded together to fight crime.

This far-flung band appeared prominently in both Rousseau's Jim Anthony novels, and in the Bellem and Ballard collaborations. In many ways, the Anthony Legion is more closely related to comic-book concepts like Simon & Kirby's Newsboy Legion than to the supporting characters found in the typical hero pulp.

Modern-day pulp luminary Will Murray has placed Jim Anthony, Super-Detective, in the third generation of character-pulp heroes, along with The Avenger, The Black Bat, Captain Future, The Wizard, The Angel, The Masked Detective, Don Diavolo, The Ghost, The Green Llama, The Whisperer and others, many of which could easily have been comic book characters. (In fact, The Green Llama also found his way into comic books, and The Black Bat, because of his similarity to Batman, generated much controversy between the respective pulp and comic book publishing companies.)

To further emphasize the connection between Anthony and the comic-book superheroes of the day, Murray notes that Batman's Bat Cave was very similar to Anthony's Teepee, both featuring an underground hanger and a deserted barn with a grain silo. In later issues, Anthony dons a Batman-style rig, consisting of a set of great black bat-like glider wings that he uses to swoop down on his foes.

In one of those stories, which fall between the first three Rousseau novels and the ones penned by the Bellem-Ballard duo, the author describes Jim Anthony in direct contemporary-superhero terms: "He was Superman and the Shadow and Flash Gordon and the Blue Beetle all rolled into one, for the thin black material was, in reality, a suit of tights, close fitting, which even covered his face."

It seemed important to the *Super-Detective* powers-that-be, and perhaps Victor Rousseau himself, that Anthony—while displaying some of the attributes of comic-book characters—was not a comics-style superhero himself. "Physically," writes Rousseau in "Legion of Robots," "no one man in the world had ever equaled his athletic records. Oh, there is nothing of Frank Merriwell about him! Not about Jim Anthony. Oh, no. He was no Superman, with impervious skin and telescopic eye sight." Throughout the first three novels, he's clearly pictured as a human being; gifted, but still within the realm of the ordinary, albeit one with hyper-developed skills, senses, strength and mental acuity. If there's a comic-book superhero analogue, it's Batman rather than Superman.

While Victor Rousseau has been identified as the author of the first three Jim Anthony novels, there is a dearth of information with regard to the novels published in *Super-Detective* from January '41 through August '42, the issue right before Bellem and Ballard pick the character up and carry him to the end of his run. Because of the similarities in characterization and plotting, Rousseau was most likely the author of the first ten stories before Jim Anthony morphed into a series detective. The timing works. Victor Rousseau quit writing for the pulps in 1941, the year the last Jim Anthony hero-pulp story, "The Spies of Destiny," came out.

The literary style Rousseau uses in the Jim Anthony novels harkens back to his days of writing for such early pulps as *Argosy* and *All-Story*, done twenty or thirty years before his *Super-Detective* assignment. In each of the first three Anthony tales, Rousseau injects certain parallel themes, such as the power of preparation, control of your own destiny and the power of the individual. Rousseau also ably makes use of plot devices: the title of each novel refers to a prominent character or characters within the story. The "Dealer in Death" is a munitions mogul named Sir Basil Mythnos who, through his employment of Rado Ruric, instigates revolutions and encourages war on a global scale in order to sell arms to affected countries and peoples. "Madame Murder" is the beautiful Valeska Hruska, her every move followed by death—including the ultimate demise of Rado Ruric.

"The Legion of Robots" isn't comprised of the familiar metal contrivances, but instead, flesh-and-blood people drugged by Fifth Columnists.

The old Boy Scout axiom, "be prepared," permeates the Anthony novels. Jim Anthony must always plan for all possible contingencies, because things are seldom what they seem. The two novels collected in this book, for instance, feature disguised parties, imposters, Trojan horses, and machines masquerading as monsters from the deep and, in "Legion of Robots," men masquerade as machines.

Beginning with his early science-fantasy work, Rousseau wrote of the power of one man in control of his own destiny to prevail over men controlled by others. In the initial three Anthony stories, Rado Ruric possesses his own powerful organization, but because he is directed by other parties, he is not his own master and, subsequently, is constantly thwarted by Anthony. The very American theme of one man's importance in the outcome of worldly events is repeated over and over in each of those three novels and is even carried forward to a degree in "Murder's Migrants" by Bellem and Ballard. Jim Anthony represents the American ideal of a rugged individualist overcoming impossible odds to achieve the American dream.

Created by an author at the end of his writing career to capitalize on the exploding comic-book market, and derivative of a shopping list of pre-existing superheroes in both the comics and pulps, Jim Anthony appeared at the tail end of a dying era for pulp-hero fiction. Real heroes were rising up out of World War II, and the golden days of the larger-than-life fantasy superheroes were over. Anthony's chances in the pulp market may not have been helped by Victor Rousseau's writing style, which certainly wasn't modern. In fact, the swift Bellem-Ballard storytelling style in the later Anthony tales is far closer to the way Lester Dent crafted his Doc Savage stories.

But let's give Rousseau a little credit. He was, after all, an old pro tapped to write a pulp character aimed at the hearts and minds of American youth, and he gave it everything he had left. If nothing else, his stories were lively and imaginative escapist fiction, and "Legion of Robots"—like all good pulp fiction—is the kind of tale that still makes for a very nice few hours' diversion. It's may not be H.G. Wells, but it surely holds its own, and then some.

SUPER-DETECTIVE

November 1940

It started with a sea-serpent and turned into the greatest plot ever unleashed to undermine the government of the United States. Against the wickedness of Rado Ruric there was only Jim Anthony to save America.

Legion of Robots

By John Grange

CHAPTER I
The World's Arch-Criminal

The warden of the great prison frowned at the excited little man who faced him across the vast expanse of his desk. He spoke stiffly. "Certainly, doctor, I am cognizant of the man's importance. He is a criminal, a dangerous criminal, condemned to die. If you have done all you can for him, I—!" He shrugged.

The doctor's eyes gleamed, his lips twisted angrily. "I, for one, think you do *not* understand! The man is Rado Ruric, internationally known! Let him die in prison and what will the world say? That he was poisoned, that he was done away with purposely, that the American Government is no better than the OGPU or the Gestapo! I tell you I've got to have outside assistance; I am no miracle man! Rado Ruric must live—so that he may meet death in the electric chair, openly and legally!"

Dryly the warden replied, "I thought you were about tops as a doctor. What's the matter with him?"

"I don't know. Frankly I don't know. If I believed a man was capable of suspending all feeling, all muscular activities of his body, I would swear that that was what Rado Ruric is doing. He seems impervious to pain; he does not respond to any treatment whatsoever! He is a living corpse!"

"What do you want to do, whom do you wish to call?"

The doctor said, "I understand this Ruric was once a Tibetan lama and that he understands the mysteries of the Orient. I think we need a doctor as well versed in the occult as he is himself!"

"Why not get Jim Anthony?"

"Jim Anthony is in retirement. No one knows where he is. He certainly did his duty by his country when he put this Rado Ruric behind the bars. Most certainly we should be able to punish the man for his crimes, since Jim Anthony captured him! I would advise bringing in the famous Mahatma Garda."

The warden played with a letter opener on his desk. He carefully weighed both sides of the case. Rado Ruric had been sentenced to electrocution, Rado Ruric must live for the chair. He said, "Very well. I'll assume the responsibility." He pressed a button. A trusty entered shortly. The trusty was a lifer, who had been in prison some thirteen years. "Get Mahatma Garda on the phone, tell him that he is needed to treat Rado Ruric in the penitentiary, and tell him to fly here at our expense. That's all."

The trusty nodded his head and left the room. A moment later he spoke to another trusty who worked on the switchboard. An understanding grin passed between them, two pairs of eyes gleamed with suppressed excitement.

The switchboard man made connections. "State penitentiary," he said, "calling Mahatma Garda." He turned to wink at the first trusty.

There was no mistaking Mahatma Garda. For six years he had practiced psychiatry in New York City. His practice was immense, his income, untold. He was a tall man, with brown skin and great, liquid eyes. His chin was covered by a spade beard, the thin lines of his lips almost obscured by a heavy black mustache. He wore occidental clothing, his single concession to the land of his birth being a great turban of white, wound about his head.

There was no mistaking his limousine, either. It was long and singularly like a miniature cruiser, even to its color of battleship grey. The man behind the wheel also looked Oriental, his eyes slanting toward his temples, his skin slightly coffee-colored. They were, of course, stopped at the gates of the penitentiary, while the gatekeeper called the warden. The delay irked the Hindu doctor; he was extremely cold to the warden, and to the penitentiary doctor who greeted him reverently.

The chauffeur, his eyes submissively downcast, walked behind his master, the black case of instruments in his hand. So haughty was the Mahatma because he had been kept waiting, that no search was made of that black bag. Afterward the warden was to regret this greatly. That failure to search was to cause the loss of the warden's job!

Rado Ruric, isolated in the prison hospital, lay on his back on a white bed. He looked like a corpse. His eyes were open, but the pupils themselves were rolled high, so that only the gleaming whites showed. His long, thin fingers were folded across his thin chest. Those fingers did not stir, because the chest was not rising and falling in respiration!

Mahatma Garda gazed down at him. He put his sensitive fingers on Rado Ruric's pulse—or the spot where pulse should be. To the nervous and awe-stricken little prison doctor he said, "He lives. But he has detached his spirit from his body. He lives as a tree, or a plant. You must leave us. I alone can return him to mortal consciousness."

The doctor's face reddened. He said, "Well, there are certain rules and regulations that—?"

Mahatma Garda bowed coldly. "You may wait outside the door, or you may post a guard. It does not matter."

The prison doctor left the room, stationed a guard at the door of the room with no other exit, hurried down the corridor to tell the waiting warden what was wrong with Rado Ruric, the world's greatest criminal.

The guard tilted his chair against the wall, picked his teeth thoughtfully. Tomorrow was his day off. He was planning where he would go, what he would do. The door opened. The Hindu doctor said, "You will help me a moment, please."

The guard nodded, stepped into the room. The chauffeur moved from behind the door and swung a blackjack. The guard never knew what hit him.

Rado Ruric, smiling, was sitting up on the hospital bed. The black bag of Mahatma Garda was open before him. From it he took a mirror, some brown stain, a life-like mask of himself, a rubber football bladder, crepe hair, and various other objects.

After awhile someone tapped on the door. When it opened slightly, the warden said, "Where is the guard who was out here?" The chauffeur said courteously, "The master is not yet ready. His condition is critical. You shall be summoned, please." He put a lot of s's in the "please," and in the word "master," sibilant, hissing.

The warden and the prison doctor drew back, frowning, but waited patiently. Presently the door opened wide. Mahatma Garda stood there, the chauffeur behind him, bearing the black bag. Mahatma Garda said, "This man must not be disturbed for two hours, do you understand? There must be absolute quiet, serenity, if you would save him."

Over the doctor's shoulder the two men saw the thin body of Rado Ruric still in bed, his head on the pillow, a towel partially obscuring it. The chauffeur closed the door, so smoothly that neither had thought to inquire again for the guard. Accompanied by the awed prison doctor and the thankful warden the mahatma and chauffeur went down the steel and stone corridor; they went out into the courtyard; Mahatma Garda and the chauffeur entered the battleship-grey limousine. The gates of the great prison opened and the limousine went through them—to freedom.

It was the guard who returned to consciousness first. He staggered to the door, he gave the alarm. They found Mahatma Garda unconscious in a corner, his clothes stripped from his body. They found sheets and blankets in the hospital bed, cunningly formed to resemble a body, they found a rubber bladder on the pillow, with the mask of Rado Ruric upon it.

Mahatma Garda could tell them nothing. He had been leaning over his patient, he claimed, when the blow that felled him came. He knew nothing more. The mask? He had no idea where it came from. The chauffeur? The man had been in his employ only a few months but had seemed absolutely trustworthy. The warden swore. Obviously the chauffeur had been an accomplice of Ruric's. And he, the warden, might as well have been!

At the Tepee, that semi-concealed hideout of Jim Anthony, all was confusion—for a moment. But for a moment only. The news of Rado Ruric's escape came to Jim Anthony over the radio. In three minutes he was broadcasting on his own wave length to his ring of co-workers. In twenty minutes fast planes driven by Jim Anthony workers were scouring the country. It was one of these workers, one of these sworn cohorts of the great Anthony, who spotted the burning car. But when motorcycles ridden by state police got to the spot, they found only the smoking, red hot ruins, and the body of one man! The chauffeur.

Jim Anthony pondered well. Aloud, to his grandfather, Mephito, who was the father of the Comanche princess Fawn Johntom, Jim's mother, Jim Anthony spoke. "That is Ruric's work, all right. If we assume that Garda was an innocent victim, then the chauffeur had to be the accomplice. Rado Ruric's way of closing mouths is death! The chauffeur met his reward at the hands of the man he had saved." Anthony paced the room, his great stride eating up the yards, his step as soft and soundless as that of a prowling jungle cat. He went back to the radio, opened the key, picked up the mouthpiece.

"Jim Anthony calling, Anthony calling. Come in K5X, K5X, come in, Anthony calling."

The voice of K5X, Anthony's best shadower and trailer, came floating back over the ether waves.

Anthony snapped, "This Mahatma Garda. He is to be followed, day and night, every minute, and every second. Do not let him out of your sight for a minute. Report back. You can pick him up as he travels from the penitentiary to New York City. Do not fail. That is all."

Back and forth, back and forth, Jim Anthony paced in his instrument-lined study. He cursed himself. He told himself he had played the fool, that he had not given Rado Ruric, the world's greatest criminal and Jim Anthony's arch-enemy, credit for his brains or his organization. He was not, to be sure, positive that Mahatma Garda had been in the plot. But that strange heritage of the forests, that great prickling of every muscle, that fast, hot flow of blood that came to him from generations of Indians, was working. It was like the seventh sense of a jungle beast who, on his appointed way to a water hole or a feeding ground, suddenly turns off and hides for a scent that has struck his nostrils, a sound that has come to his ears. But because that unnamable something warned him that danger was at hand!

Strangely enough K5X called back three hours later to say that Mahatma Garda had somehow been lost. Anthony's trailer hated to report failure, but it was the truth.

For seven days then the house of the Hindu doctor was kept under surveillance, a watcher brooded over every haunt Garda had ever been known to visit. Garda seemed to have vanished from the face of the earth. Out of it all came only one peculiar circumstance that convinced Jim Anthony that Mahatma Garda was in the plot to liberate Rado Ruric, the greatest criminal the world had ever known.

Before going to the penitentiary to treat Ruric, the Hindu doctor, they learned, had paused long enough to close out a bank account and visit a safety deposit box in the same bank. The amount of his withdrawal had been well over two hundred thousand dollars. No one knew, of course, how much money he had tucked away in the safety deposit box.

One thing was certain. Rado Ruric was once more free. And sooner or later, Jim Anthony knew, Rado Ruric and his great organization would strike! And, Jim told himself grimly, wherever or whenever the arch-criminal struck, no matter where it might be on the face of the earth, Jim Anthony would be there to thwart him!

CHAPTER II
The Sea Monster

Ramon Perez, Dictator of San Rosario, was a man of few words and those words, hard. Ramon Perez was a tyrant. In a way he was a benevolent tyrant, for he built roads through his backward country, he built schools, he even allowed *peons* to vote—for politicians selected by Ramon Perez.

San Rosario was a country rich in natural resources. For the past seven years, Ramon Perez had been exploiting those resources with the aid of a bit of foreign capital, gringo, German, Italian, and—others. Oil made San Rosario, and the signs of its progress, the great tanks, went clear down to the water's edge of San Rosario City, or Ciudad San Rosario, in Spanish idiom. The derricks, however, didn't stop at the water's edge. They extended outward into the bay, in some places, as far as half a mile.

Ramon Perez loved his people. If you did not believe this, all you had to do was ask him, he would promptly tell you it was so. Of course, if you did not choose to take the dictator's word for it, you might find yourself rubbing your shoulders against a 'dobe wall some fine morning, waiting for the first rays of the sun—and the lead from the rifles of a squad of San Rosario soldiers.

All of this is leading up to those three oddly shaped rocks which thrust themselves up out of the sea some four miles south and west of San Rosario City. None of the three was large, none totally devoid of vegetation, covered more than a square city block. The first was called Cabeza Grande, the second Cabeza Media, and the third, Cabeza Chica, Big Head, Medium Head, and Little Head, for in truth, viewed from a distance they greatly resembled rocky profiles, each of them.

The Tres Cabezas belonged to the government, that is to say, to the tyrant Perez. They were valuable—not as valuable as San Rosario's oil, but still worth many *pesos*—because for millions of years the seabirds had nested on them, brooded on them, until they were great and immense rocks of guano, the finest fertilizer known to man. Not only that! On Cabeza Media, the battering sea had drilled and plucked and eaten and gnawed, until the whole island was a labyrinth of caves—bats had spent millions and millions of nights! Consequently, the caves were filled with bat guano.

Now Ramon Perez, the dictator, was not a hoggish man. Already his income from oil and the like was enormous. But he was a careful man, a trifle on the Scotch side; he did not like to have anything go to waste. Consequently, once a month a puffing and decrepit tug steamed for the Tres Cabezas, towing several even more decrepit barges, loaded with San Rosarian political prisoners, whose task it was to fill the barges with guano.

The barges and their puffing tug set off bravely that particular morning on their noisome task, with Capitan Anastasio Bustamente Eufemio Garcia standing bravely forward on the tug, twisting his mustachios, patting the heavy gun at his side, and swearing by the eternal that these dogs of *politicos* would shovel until they dropped!

When the barges and the tugs failed to return that night—the sea was a bit rough—*Presidente* Perez did not think much of it. But on the morrow the sea was smooth as glass—and still the guano-loaded barges did not come back. Through his spy glasses in the turret atop the presidential tower Ramon Perez could see the three gaunt rocks, not too many miles away. But there was no tug, no string of barges clustered about them.

He cursed long and well. For it came to him that *El Capitan* Anastasio Bustamente Eufemio Garcia had no doubt been reached by crooked gold, and had taken his politicians and put out to sea—and liberty. Whereupon the San Rosarian navy was called into action with a great to-do. The San Rosarian navy consisted of an old pleasure yacht, once belonging to a Mexican millionaire who had fled with Diaz, a gunboat once owned by the Republic of Texas and sunk in a storm off Yucatan, from which watery grave it was raised and purchased—eventually—by *El Presidente* Perez.

With colors streaming and bands playing, the San Rosarian navy steamed out of the harbor in search of the *politicos* who had bribed *El Capitan* Garcia and made their escape. Presently, however, they disappeared beyond the three mile-distant islands. They made no sound. The band music died away. There was no sound or noise of firing guns. Once, indeed, those watchers on the modern docks of Ciudad San Rosario thought the landward breeze brought them the screaming of humans, but of course they could not be sure.

The Santa Nova returned first. The Santa Nova was the converted yacht. She steamed into harbor so fast that she almost wrecked her dock, and, while she was several feet from anchorage, men cast aside their guns and leaped overside to get the good earth beneath their feet again. Some knelt on the dock and prayed. The hair of others had turned white in that short while; they were as old men, those men who had been in their prime but a few hours ago when the Santa Nova steamed proudly away!

The dockmaster wormed the strange story from one of the men. The Dictator, Ramon Perez, hurried down to see with his own eyes. And his great voice rang out, "*Silencio!* Let no man speak! It is commanded." Then he had the stretcher that bore *El Capitan* Gil, commander of the Santa Nova, brought up the steep hill to the presidential palace.

And strange things went on happening during the next few days. The gunboat from Yucatan never came back. And one by one, before they had a chance to talk, the sailors on the Santa Nova disappeared, deep into dungeons, never to be heard from again.

Dictator Ramon Perez was a shrewd man. He knew how panic-stricken a country could grow overnight. He knew it was not good for his people to learn the horrifying truth! That the tug and the barges and the gunboat would return no more. *That a great sea-monster had crushed them like eggshells in its great jaws, and even now hid in wait for more victims, somewhere behind the three guano rocks that jutted from the sea.*

El Presidente was a man of the century. He was an army man, he had been an exchange student with the great colossus of the North, the United States, and there, at Kelly Field, had learned to fly. Secretly he entered his own fast scouting plane, and secretly took off for Tres Cabezas.

It was just past dawn and the breakers slashing against the three heads were like white cotton froth. Down, down, dove *Presidente* Perez, and realized with a little surge of horror, that those black things pounding against the western rocks were bits of wood, were all that remained of the small boats attached to his gunboat, his barges and his tug. Flying even closer he saw something white, and gleaming, like the exposed hoops of a barrel, only this thing had a grinning skull atop it that flashed in the sun like a million-faceted jewel.

Perez' passage frightened the scavenger crabs. They scurried away from their gruesome feast with the peculiar scuttling motion of their ilk. But of a sea monster, Perez saw nothing.

The sun came up in the east and the water turned pink, then red. Higher went the sun, and now the water that lapped the white-covered rocks was golden, almost like oil it seemed, so thick and viscous. To himself Perez said, "Bah! Sea monster! There have been no sea monsters since the dinosaurs crawled out of the prehistoric and primeval slime, then turned around after one look and crawled back!"

And then he saw it.

It was slightly to the south and west of Cabeza Media. There was no sound of broaching, no spouting such as a whale makes. First the sea was black and bare, then, suddenly there was a strip at least thirty feet long, and equally wide, that looked as though a scaly rock had thrust its way through. The scales were as large as great dinner plates, and gleamed like metallic spots sewn on a dancer's costume.

Perez was so startled he went into a dive and was almost in the water before he could pull himself out! The plane zoomed upward just as the tail of the thing emerged, a broad flat thing at least half again as wide as the body of the beast. Up it came, and up, as if it were reaching for the plane, and Perez zoomed for safety like a frightened seabird. The beast—if beast it was—dropped its tail then with a great, flat splash, a splash that sent water a full hundred feet in the air. And up came the head!

Presidente Ramon Perez was not a religious man, and yet he crossed himself. His eyes almost popped out of his own head, perspiration was like water from a shower bath on his own features.

The thing raised its head and glowered at him out of the green fastnesses of the ocean. In a way, it was like the head of the dragon slain by the good Saint George, except, if anything, it was more fearsome. It opened that great cavern of a mouth to yawn, then the spotted red and mottled throat could be seen in it, the great moving tongue, the fangs, some of them, the jaw fangs, all of four feet in length and gleaming in the early sunshine like spikes of chromium-plated steel.

Over all, Perez estimated the serpent, undulating through the nearly still water, was at least one hundred and twenty feet in length, and to him, the head itself seemed half of that, with a jaw leverage of perhaps fifty feet. No wonder his barges had disappeared, and his gunboat, and his tugs! Fifty feet!

Ramon Perez was no coward. He fingered the triggers of the twin Thompsons mounted on his cowling and glowed at the answering burst of tracer bullets. Looking back over his shoulder he saw that the noise had made the monster curious, that it was casting a pair of great, baleful eyes, red and gleaming, aloft! It closed its mouth, sank its noisome snout into the sea until the great nostrils alone protruded! They were as large as the entrance to a ballroom through double doors! And from them, suddenly, as Perez banked to turn back, issued great clouds of steam, smelly, terrible to look upon, steam that did not readily evaporate, as it should, but shot toward the charging aviator and hung motionless in the air, like a suspended blanket.

Instinct alone made Perez climb well over that gas. Once above it he dove again, coming in from the tail end of the thing, and less than fifty feet above it, raked the monster fore and aft with machine gun bullets. He could see the tracers, see them crash against the scaly hide of the beast. He circled again, came back the same way, and this time, disaster almost overtook him. For he flew too low. The beast seemed to have vent holes in the top of its head, just as a whale, and when he was right over it with his plane, the beast blew.

Water? Gas?

Perez did not know at the moment. He knew only that the plane suddenly became heavy, almost unmanageable, and that he, too, became drowsy. Only some instinct made him able to hold that plane from the ocean and above the beast. Somehow, with his senses reeling he went into a climb, heard a motor miss, cut in another motor and winged, like a crippled bird, for Ciudad San Rosario.

His servants came running when he landed at his own flying field, and marveled as they lifted the dictator from his plane. The wings looked as if they had been subjected to the fire of an acetylene torch. Much of the fuselage, seemingly damp only, burned and blistered like fire when an unwary examiner touched it. Perez, miraculously, was quite all right, except for a few burns.

But Perez knew this: He knew that out there by Tres Cabezas lurked a monster the like of which no mortal eye had ever before seen!

CHAPTER III
A Job with Jim Anthony

When little Linda Tabor of Tall Corn, Iowa, was down to her last dime, she got a break. She remembered afterward that she had climbed out of her bed that morning and dressed quietly, taking the hose she had washed the night before from the hanger on the bedroom door and pulling them, oh so carefully, onto her long slender legs. Carefully, because she had washed them exactly twenty-six times, and after twenty washes even the best of hose sometimes go to pieces. Very carefully she had scraped the last of the powder and lipstick from their respective containers, and applied them to the fresh loveliness of her face. One hundred times she had brushed the honey colored loveliness of her hair, then she had donned her trim little Tall Corn, Iowa suit and her basement bargain pumps, taken a handkerchief from where it had been pasted on the window, and hied herself forth.

She was hungry. For, as a roving dog sometimes will, she had gone to bed early the night before in order to save supper money. For a dime, she thought, I can get some doughnuts—two, in fact—and either a cup of coffee or a thin glass of fruit juice, presumably orange juice. So she walked in the direction of the nearest stand.

She was not thinking about tomorrow or tomorrow. She was not wondering what would happen to her after the dime was gone. She knew her room rent was due, and that the landlady's heart was as cold as a stepmother's kiss. She knew she had not a single, solitary thing left to hock. But she did not worry. Practically her only worry was her indecision whether to take the coffee or the thin glass of juice.

Habit is a marvelous thing. For seven weeks, ever since she had been in New York searching for work, she had made it a point of coming this way—past the magnificent black and white and chromium structure of the Waldorf-Anthony Hotel. It gave her a little thrill just to see the doorman outside the main entrance with the heavy gold embroidery over his left pocket, W-A, and to realize that the A, that wonderful letter, stood for Jim Anthony. For, to her as to countless other girls throughout the world, Jim Anthony was a hero. He was Cyrano de Bergerac and Richard the Lion-Hearted and Hector and Aeneas and Jason! Yes, and even Errol Flynn! And anybody else who might be worshiped, depending on the time, the place, and the girl!

Linda Tabor knew practically all there was to know about Jim Anthony! What American girl did not? She knew that his father had been Shean Boru Anthony, that wild Irishman who had moulded the destinies of half a dozen South American countries, that explorer of unknown lands from the tundras of the Antarctic to the hot steamy hell of the tropics. She knew that his mother had been Fawn Johntom, the last princess of the Comanches. And she knew that all the better traits of two civilizations had come into being with Jim Anthony.

Physically, no one man in the world had ever equaled his athletic records. Oh, there was nothing of Frank Merriwell about him! Not about Jim Anthony. Oh, no. He was no superman, with impervious skin, and telescopic eyesight. True, his vision was better, far better than any one with whom he had ever come in contact. His hearing was so acute that often he had solved crimes by hearing conversations in another room inaudible to any one else without a stepped-up dictagraph. One of his hideaway rooms at The Tepee, which was only one of his many mansions, was devoted to cups and trophies won in competition in every sport known to man, from jai-alai to fencing, from judo to pole-vault!

Jim, usually, was a bit reticent. He was not, strictly speaking, a handsome man. He was too craggy, too jutting, for that. His nose, like the beak of a hawk, was too large. And his eyes were too deep, and his mouth too wide, but, in spite of all that, well—women invariably turned their heads to look at Jim Anthony.

Added to his splendid physique, added to those keen attributes he had inherited from his father and his Indian mother, was the Anthony brain. When Jim had been but three years old his father had noted his precocity. Tutors were brought in; not dried, hidebound professors, but young men, wiser than their years. At fourteen Jim Anthony had the brain of a Phi Beta Kappa man—and was not aware of it. His Comanche grandfather, Mephito, taught him things which could never be learned in books. The greatest savants of the Orient, the finest teachers of the Continent, all contributed to his education.

Reticent as he was—there were some things Jim Anthony could not keep out of the papers. From time to time, after the completion of some phenomenal invention, or the wind-up of some successful campaign against evil-doers—such as his recent wiping out of a world-wide plot to loot the United States of billions for munitions—on such occasions Jim's picture had been published in the newspapers and flashed upon the silver screen.

Whereupon, all over the country, countless romantic little girls sighed deeply and clenched trembling hands to their bosoms, swearing fervently to themselves that no other male under the sun ever enthralled them like the mighty Jim Anthony.

Linda Tabor was one of these.

So she walked down Fifth Avenue that morning, toward the juice and coffee and doughnut stand, intent at the time on one thing only. She meant to pass the big Waldorf-Anthony Hotel. For not only could she see the attendants, with the name Anthony emblazoned on their uniforms with gold thread but by passing the marquee and looking back, she could see that great bronze figure that was the emblem of the hotel, poised on one slender foot, the muscles of his mighty calf, the thews of his mighty body tensed as he seemed to be running with lightning in one hand, emblemizing service! For its guests, the Waldorf-Anthony would bring the lightning down out of the sky!

So, she walked beneath the marquee, smiled condescendingly at the two majordomos, one of whom worked the revolving door while the other waited at the curb for the string of arriving guests. Past the marquee she turned the slender column of her throat graciously to glance back at the huge bronze figure. It was wonderful. She never looked at those mighty muscles or that stern visage without thrills coursing through her supple body. She butted into someone, she didn't even bother to excuse herself.

She was vaguely conscious of being in a sea of humanity, but paid no attention until a white gloved hand was placed firmly on her shoulder and a good Irish voice said, "Here, now, miss, and it's waitin' yer turn ye'll have to be and no shovin' wid ye! It's form a single loine for the loikes of ye, and that broth of a lad, Jim Anthony will soon be a-seein' of ye!"

The name, perhaps, brought Linda back to reality. Jim Anthony would soon be a-seeing of her! Hers not to reason why, hers not to question why! Just stand in this line, this line that was nearly a full block long, and pretty soon—*she'd see Jim Anthony!*

Minutes ticked by. She looked at her neighbors. There were old women and young women, and fat women and skinny women! Women who might well have been scrubbing floors, others who just as well could have been working with Billy Rose at the Aquacade! All of them intent on shuffling slowly forward, until they passed through that service entrance a hundred or so yards away.

She didn't ask what was wanted. Hadn't the copper said they would be seen by Jim Anthony? If she thought anything at all about it, she probably thought all these women were autograph hunters. Minutes passed. No one spoke to her, she spoke to no one. As a matter of fact there was no conversation whatsoever, along the whole serried rank. This was too important to speak of.

From time to time someone in the hotel uniform came to the head of the column and in peremptory tones told the assembly to count off. Number one said, "One," number two, "Two," and so on. And always, as soon as the number *fifty* was reached, the counting stopped and the fifty women so selected were ushered into the service entrance of the Waldorf-Anthony Hotel.

At last, at long last, Linda Tabor was number 49. She found herself with forty-nine others being escorted through a door, past a bisecting hallway, and into a magnificently appointed waiting room. Hardly had she composed herself to wait for she knew not what, when the entire room began to rise slowly. Grimly she clung to her chair. And seconds later, the one entrance door opened and a uniformed flunkey announced that they had arrived.

Linda Tabor was only twenty. She might live to ten times twenty and never have anything odder happen to her. For, in groups of ten the women were led into separate compartments and handed what seemed to be the mouthpiece of a dictaphone. A small blank screen at one end of the room suddenly became illuminated with letters. Out of nowhere came the pleasantly modulated voice that said, "Now, please, ma'am, push the button by the mouthpiece and read the lettering on the screen into that same mouthpiece. Not too loudly or too slowly, simply in your ordinary voice."

Linda shrugged. She read all about Peter Piper and about the pickled peppers that Peter picked. The reading on the screen changed and she told the mouthpiece that a Burma girl was waiting by the old Moulmein pagoda. After awhile the voice said, "That will be all, and thank you, please."

A little frightened at the whole thing Linda emerged from the booth. A smiling young lady hurried forward, her eyes shining. This young lady looked like a Greek goddess, her hair was as blonde as that of the girl from Iowa, her eyes as shiny, her lips as red.

"My dear, my dear," she breathed, "you were wonderful! Of course I can't tell for sure, but I really think you're the best by far! Now—but of course, how stupid of me! My name is Dolores Colquitt." Linda felt a surge of envy. Senator Colquitt's daughter—the fiancée of Jim Anthony. "Won't you step this way?"

In spite of the fact that Linda immediately envied the girl's closeness to Anthony, they were soon on a friendly basis. Dolores Colquitt spoke truly when she said she was Jim Anthony's fiancée. She was as near to a sweetheart as the man would ever allow any girl to be. Dolores had been trained by Jim in his remarkable work and she was, in her own right, a trained psychiatrist.

Hardly had Dolores talked with the girl from Tall Corn, Iowa, more than ten minutes until she understood her thoroughly. She knew that there was an unassuming naiveté about Linda, a depth that more than balanced her lack of worldly polish, that equipped her to be a capable and trusted member of

Jim Anthony's staff.

So, presently there was a tap on the door. An attendant handed Dolores a sheet of paper, Dolores read it, looked pleased, and burned it carefully in an ashtray. Then she turned to the wondering girl.

"My dear," she said simply, "the position as advertised in Mr. Anthony's paper, the New York *Star*, is yours. You are to be congratulated. You will receive all your expenses and one hundred dollars a week."

She held out her hand.

"But I don't understand! I didn't see any advertisement! I didn't—!" Almost overcome, Linda sank down on a lounge, Dolores laughingly beside her. And Dolores explained everything.

Every woman who had come in answer to the advertisement had had her voice measured by the vocometer, an invention of Anthony's. Just as the lie-detector makes a graph, a jagged line denoting heart reactions, the vocometer recorded the harmony, the clearness in the human voice, the cadence.

"Here is the situation," said Dolores. "It is absolutely necessary, right now, for Mr. Anthony to keep up with all the odd situations in the world. You can readily see how impossible it would be for him to read all newspapers. He is searching for a man, the world's arch-criminal. He has, at his estate, hundreds of readers, whose business it is to read every newspaper published in the world. And to clip from those newspapers those odd items which may or may not have some meaning in connection with his search for this man. Items of catastrophe, accidents, uprisings, in every nation under the sun!"

"But where do I come in? I don't see—?"

"These items are pasted in a strip and given to you. Because your voice, fortunately, causes not one bit of fatigue on the part of the listener, you have been selected to read these items onto wax!"

"And he listens to them played? Why can't I just read them to him?"

Dolores smiled knowingly. "Jim Anthony is one of the busiest men in the world. He has no time to sit and listen. You will read the items onto wax and when Anthony is exercising, doing something physical that leaves his mind free—horseback riding, for instance—he can flip the radio switch of the small receiving ring he wears on his finger. This starts the record going in his laboratory and without wasting time he receives all the oddities in the news of the world! Come, you will not need to get your clothes. Costumes are included in your expense account. We are going to—The Tepee."

CHAPTER IV
GOD HELP SAN ROSARIO!

IN THE CATSKILLS, Greene County is an area of deserted farms. Once, years and years ago, hardy settlers grew corn and flax and pumpkins on the sides of its rugged mountains, in its fertile valleys. But, as the land became overworked, more and more of the settlers loaded their ox teams with their families and belongings and moved westward. In this particular section the undergrowth and the forest had long since overcome all lanes and roads. It was simply a tangle of virgin timber.

Old Mephito, the grandfather of Jim Anthony, squatted in a small clearing over a nine stick fire. Only God knew Mephito's real age. He was as toothless as a crone, as wrinkled as a mummy, and his ribs stood out on his skinny torso like barrel staves on a broken cask.

So he squatted over this little fire, his beady eyes half closed, feeding monstrosities, dried frogs, adder's tongues, mandrake roots and the like to the flames, while a strange chanting mumble jumble issued from his blue lips. Dawkins, Jim Anthony's cockney valet squatted on his skinny haunches across from the old man and alternately watched the fire and the sky, holding his nose at the same time, for the fire and its monstrosities did not produce a very pleasant aroma.

"H'I'm more than sure, h'old one, that the mawster will not be pleased h'at this. And h'ennyway, h'I do not believe h'it!"

Mephito wore a breechclout of buckskin. Dawkins was the epitome of what the well dressed footman would wear. Dawkins went in for uniforms. They made him feel fine; and this was the best of all, the one that now graced his skinny body. The breeches were of yellow satin, the tailed coat was plum-colored, and the vest was canary yellow. The trousers of course, came but to his knees, and the silk stockings on his spindly shanks were of a flesh tint. Great silver buckles adorned his patent leather shoes.

Mephito closed his eyes, arose, began to sway and stomp. "He comes, he comes, we have prayed that he come back to cheer an old man and he comes! Listen, listen, Mephito has summoned him!"

Dawkins, too, arose. Dawkins wasn't exactly superstitious, but the old shaman, the old chief and medicine man, sometimes got queer results!

Dawkins had tried to talk him out of this session, for, if truth be told, there was nothing at all the matter at The Tepee. Jim Anthony had been gone three or four days and the old man had gotten lonesome! Dawkins had told him that Jim would be back in good time, but the old shaman would have none of it.

"The devil map, white man," roared Mephito, "the devil map. Your master comes!"

Behind the two men loomed a ramble-down house. To all appearances, this too was a deserted farmhouse. In reality it was a turret for The Tepee, Jim Anthony's underground castle. Into this deserted appearing place hurried Dawkins. He went directly to a fireplace, pressed a button. Into the gaping black hole came a small elevator, and into the elevator stepped Dawkins. After all, there might be something to what the old man said!

A second later Dawkins was poring over a huge relief map of this section of the Catskill Mountains. While he looked, far to the southeastern edge suddenly there appeared a dot of light, no larger than the point of a lead pencil. The old man was right! Someone was coming! Dawkins kept his eyes on the map until he was positive the parachute net of the Anthony estate was indicated, then he hurried back the way he had come.

"H'I sye h'old one," he called, leaping into a tremendously fast tractor kept for such emergencies, "you 'ave brought the mawster. 'E comes! What 'o!"

Mephito, grinning with his toothless gums, approached on a dead run and together the men boarded the tractor and rumbled off through the primeval forest toward the landing stage.

No one came to The Tepee except by parachute. Over the tops of the trees, disguised by cunning green undergrowth, was a great springy net, more than a block square. There were ladders leading up to the net, and the net itself was electrified, so that once it was stepped on, it made an electrical connection on a net-chart in the house, showing the progress of the lander.

The two men neared the net. Already they could hear the drone of the airplane. Already the white mushroom that was the white parachutist seemed to be suspended in midair, above the net. Down, down, floated the white flower. Dawkins grew suddenly tense. He reached for Mephito, but Mephito had faded away into the shadows. Mephito, too, had sensed it—this was not Jim Anthony.

The man landed, cut himself loose from his parachute. Through a periscope-like contrivance Dawkins viewed him, saw the swarthy, almost black face, the thin, cruel mouth and the jutting cheek-bones. He saw the sky blue of the stranger's uniform coat, the bright red of his trousers, tucked into shiny boots. And most of all he saw and noted the two heavy automatics at the man's hips and the glistening saber by his side.

The man glared about for a moment, then noted the golden arrow that pointed toward the exit ladder. Down he came, backing down, grunting. He whirled there, and almost fainted at sight of the overdressed Dawkins. Dawkins was weaponless, but Dawkins was unafraid.

Dawkins said, "What do you want?"

The man thundered, "Who are you?"

Dawkins answered, "I am the valet of Jim Anthony!"

"Then get your master! I do not deal with underlings!"

Perhaps it was his supercilious attitude that caused the trouble, perhaps it was because his brown fingers lingered too closely to the walnut butt of one of his guns. Whatever it was, from the underside of the net Grandpa Mephito dropped like a great spider. His thin, but wiry arms wound about the man's thick throat, his legs locked themselves about the man's middle!

After awhile, the man lay very still, breathing, but breathing hard. They loaded him aboard the tractor and took him back to The Tepee, where they disarmed him and locked him very carefully in an air conditioned room. Both Dawkins and Mephito were a little worried about what Jim Anthony would say.

By four o'clock that same afternoon, Jim Anthony and his friend Tom Gentry were high in the air over the Catskills in an immense Douglass plane. This plane, had it been in use as an airliner, would have had a seating capacity of forty-two passengers. But Anthony had revamped it, rebuilt it, so that the fuselage bore what was nothing less than a luxuriously appointed efficiency apartment.

Now the two men lounged at ease in this apartment, talking over their trip. Up front, in the pilot's compartment, a small black box, an invention of Anthony's, steered the plane and held it on its course more efficiently than a flesh and blood pilot. This was the Anthony robot.

Tom Gentry lay on a deep divan, his hands clasped back of his head, staring upward at the ceiling of the cabin. He sighed. Tom was tired. For the past seven days the plane had been almost constantly in the air, landing, of course, occasionally, just long enough for Jim Anthony to contact one of his men. The freckles on Tom's honest face stood out like deep brown spots.

"Well, Jim," he sighed, "we've tried Tokio and Manila and Singapore and all stops in between. We've uncovered plenty of screwy criminals—but no Rado Ruric. Maybe the guy is dead!"

Jim Anthony lay on a similar divan clad only in a breechclout. He sat up suddenly, moved across the plane's cabin with all the grace of a jungle beast, the magnificent muscles rippling beneath his satiny skin. He leaned over a metal table, twisted a switch and illuminated a map of the district over which they were flying. A tiny spot of light moved with the plane, showing exactly where they were,

"Tom," he said to his pal, "you fly the Douglass back to the Anthony Airport. I'm going to take the pick-a-back glider and see what I can accomplish at The Tepee. I want you to go over to the Anthony Shipyards and get the sub in working order. We've tried the east, now I think we'll try closer to home."

In a moment Jim Anthony had slipped on a pair of slacks and a sweat shirt, had crawled to the roof of the big Douglass, stepped into the little glider and taken off.

Down below him he saw what looked like a green glade in the forest, but which he knew to be the parachute landing net of The Tepee. Moments later he brought the frail craft to rest upon the net. From a concealed roller he tugged a green blanket, with which he covered the glider, so that it would not be observed from the air. Then, down the ladder he went—and Dawkins was awaiting him!

Now right from the moment of his arrival Anthony knew that Mephito and Dawkins were doing—or had been doing—something that lay on their consciences. But he was like a father with a pair of recalcitrant children. He watched them smilingly, knowing that sooner or later they would confess.

In the meanwhile, Linda Tabor and Dolores Colquitt, in another wing of The Tepee, were sharing tea and experiences, as women will. Upon her arrival a long roll of clipped news events had been handed to the girl from Tall Corn, Iowa, and all of these she had read into an apparatus that recorded them in her well modulated voice. There had been news of revolutions, news of crimes, news of explosions, of catastrophes of all kinds. And all of these were duly read and recorded.

Jim Anthony came out of the shower room into the great room that housed the swimming pool. He wore a pair of yellow trunks that accented the healthy brownness of his body and the narrowness of his hips. He adjusted an odd-looking swimming cap over his ears, went to the diving board. He touched a button with his toe and the board began to rise, hydraulically. When it reached approximately twenty feet, he released the button and the board paused above the lapping green water. Then, suddenly, Jim froze. For the tiny microphone in the odd-appearing swimming cap began speaking, in a clear, pleasing voice.

"San Rosario City, San Rosario, Central America. It has been established here today beyond doubt that some sort of prehistoric sea serpent is preying upon local fishermen at Tres Cabezas, the three guano islands some miles from the mainland. The city and the surrounding country is in a superstitious uproar. As an added horror, President Ramon Perez seems to have totally disappeared from his palace. The Vaterland Oil Company is threatening action unless its newest leases are upheld, and the nation of Costaduras is threatening war."

Anthony froze because that inexplicable thing that worked in him as a hunch works in other men—than unnamable something that he had inherited from thousands of years of forest ancestry was at work. Just as surely as if he actually saw the man, he saw the bearded face and the slotted eyes of Rado Ruric, the arch-criminal! Sea serpents! Foreign oil control! Disappearing dictators! Threats of war!

Suddenly the end door of the pool room opened. A man backed in. The man was a bit grotesque, because he wore a sky blue coat and red trousers tucked into high polished boots. Two empty holsters flapped against his hips, an empty scabbard almost tripped him. He was looking back the way he had come, as if he had just, somehow, broken out of the place where he was held prisoner, and was now making good his escape.

He closed the door softly behind him, leaned against it, his black eyes encompassing the room. Suddenly he saw the man on the diving board. He drew himself up imperiously, he thrust out his chest, his right hand dropped to the empty scabbard.

"Who are you?" he thundered.

"I am Jim Anthony," said the man in the trunks, amusedly. "And you?"

"Jim Anthony? Thank God! I have come half across the world to beg your help! Who am I? I am Ramon Perez, president of San Rosario, God help my country!"

He saluted.

CHAPTER V
TRES CABEZAS

JIM ANTHONY DID NOT LIKE RAMON PEREZ, the arrogant dictator of San Rosario. There was something about the man, something right from the start, that made Jim—well, not suspicious—but something that went a bit against Jim's tastes. On the trip south to the tiny country so near the equator, Tom Gentry, at the controls of the giant Douglass, had a hard time covering his own dislike.

Aside, he said to Anthony, "Gee, the guy thinks he's a combination of Napoleon, Hitler, Il Duce, and maybe a touch of Julius Caesar. Heck, I never heard of this comic opera country of his."

Jim grinned at the indignation on Tom's honest face. He shrugged, answered, "No man's native country is comic opera to him. I've promised him help, and we'll do what we can." He looked through the windows of the plane at the thick fleecy clouds ahead of them, and he saw there, not clouds alone, but the malignant, taunting face of Rado Ruric. He left the control room and went back into the apartment to his guest.

Ramon Perez half sat, half lay, in a great padded chair, a taboret covered with liquor bottles at his elbow, a glass in his hands. Already his eyes were red-rimmed, liquor inflamed, his voice thick. He gestured with a hairy hand, said, "Anthony, the world will be grateful for the assistance you render my country. We are a great and grateful people. You shall be amply rewarded." He pulled his lips back from his teeth and smiled.

Like a wolf, thought Jim Anthony, and dropped down on a settee across from the man.

"Ah, yes," repeated Perez, raising his glass, "the great Jim Anthony will be rewarded for what he is doing!"

Jungle instinct, forest instinct arose in Jim Anthony! The same instinct that warns the beast when the trap is near. But he smiled, although the smile was only on his lips and never in the bleak depths of his eyes.

He said, "It will be well, Perez, if you go into greater detail concerning some of your country's affairs. What's this war threat from Costaduras all about?"

Jim Anthony already knew what that war threat was, all about it. He already knew what the threatened suit of the Vaterland Oil Company was about as well. His private espionage system reached right into the heart of the American Black Chamber, and before he had even boarded the plane and headed for Central America with this dictator, the voice of Linda Tabor had brought to him all the detailed affairs of the tiny country.

Perez glared at him. He said, "My affairs are my own, Anthony! I come to you in the interests of humanity! I have asked you merely to destroy, like the good Saint George of history, this great sea serpent, that threatens the happiness of my people."

Anthony could have said that this, indeed, was a change of front, that Perez had spoken at The Tepee of other things as well. But he did not. He merely wanted to study the man who aroused so much antagonism in him.

Softly he said, "You know, and I know, Perez, that there are no sea serpents, no prehistoric monsters!"

Perez glared. He put down his glass, sprang to his feet, slapped his thick chest. "You doubt the word of Ramon Perez? I with these very eyes have seen the monster. Did he not almost kill me? Has he not destroyed ships of mine—ships and armed men?"

And before the smiling Anthony could answer, the radio broke into voice.

It was tuned to a Mexico City station, and the announcer spoke excitedly in Spanish. "Presence of a sea serpent off the coast of San Rosario has absolutely been verified. The monster lives. According to latest dispatches just received from Costaduras, neighboring country, the natives of Ciudad Rosario have fled from their city into the mountains. Refugees report that the monster has crawled up out of the sea breathing fire and gas fatal to all who come in contact. The city is absolutely deserted!

"Eyewitnesses and observers estimate the beast or serpent at from one hundred to one hundred and fifty feet in length! Members of the San Rosarian Gold Shirts, the elite guard of the mysteriously missing Ramon Perez, dictator, stood their ground, firing at the serpent with machine guns. The bullets made absolutely no impression on the serpent. It wound through the city streets, the inhabitants fleeing before it, made its way south of town to the plantation of one Hans Guttmann, where it spent the dark hours.

"The city is now emptied of all inhabitants. Aerial observers, however, report that shortly before noon the serpent went back the way it had come and slipped off the national docks into the sea. Known dead are forty-one, crushed to death or choked by the serpent's breath, some sixty or seventy burned severely by the same breath, and over a hundred shocked into a form of insanity."

On and on raced the excited voice, telling of the horror that had visited itself upon the tiny country. Jim Anthony watched Perez. Perez stared imperturbably out the window, raising his well filled glass from time to time. He sat stiffly, erectly, and because his head was turned, Jim could not tell whether the man was thunderstruck, or frightened.

Anthony said, "Perez, this Guttmann. Who was he?"

Without turning Perez said, "Some foreigner, I was not well acquainted with him. He had a plantation of some sort." He shrugged and continued to listen to the eyewitness reports coming over the radio.

Anthony left the apartment on soft feet, went back again to Tom Gentry. Gentry's wide eyes showed that he, too, had heard the newscast, and that he, too, was more than startled. Anthony shook his own head, sat down to a radio and began calling The Tepee on his own wave length.

Soon the high-pitched, cockney voice of Dawkins came to him. " 'Ello, 'ello, Jim Anthony, Dawkins answering Jim Anthony, come h'in, Jim Anthony."

Jim answered, "Dawkins, I want everything you can find out about a Hans Guttmann." He spelled it out slowly and distinctly. "The man operated a plantation of some kind in San Rosario. I want his background, I want to know all about what he raised. That is all."

Back at The Tepee, Dawkins' eyes sparkled. He liked his job. And all too often, he many times complained to his employer and friend, there was not enough for him to do. So now he scurried about and found Dolores Colquitt and Linda Tabor, swimming in the marvelous pool. He explained just what Jim Anthony wanted. In a matter of minutes Linda Tabor was in the file room and reference library, literally diving into the immense indexes. Dolores Colquitt was already at the phone talking to Gibbons, managing editor of the New York *Star*, whose major stockholder was Jim Anthony. And Dawkins himself, via radio phone, was instructing agents of Anthony to go to Yorkville and other German sections of the city and find out everything possible about Hans Guttmann. Thus did the agents of Jim Anthony function, like a huge and well oiled machine, once the master's hand was on the controls.

Back in the apartment of the plane, once again Jim Anthony regarded the arrogant man who had come to ask his aid. Perez glared at him, and Anthony could not tell whether the unusual tone of his voice was a jeer or the deep, black echo of superstitious fear. "Now do you believe?" asked the man. "Bullets do not harm this thing! How then, will you destroy it?"

Anthony grinned. "We'll come to that, Perez. First, we're going to land. Maybe the city isn't as deserted as the radio would have us think; perhaps there were, after all, a few men and women who didn't flee from the monster. We'll work something out."

And Perez said a strange thing. He said, "I am not yet ready to appear in my country, Anthony. Do not ask my plans, for I must not disclose them. I must ask you, once you land, not to reveal that I came to America for your aid. After all, the glory—"

Jim watched him through narrowed eyes. What was the man implying? Evidently he meant to imply that when the proper time came he intended to reappear as the savior of San Rosario, the Saint George who slew the dragon. Just a cheap, tinplate hero who wanted all the glory while others took the danger!

"As you please," Anthony said coldly. "You may stay in the plane once we land. If the town is deserted, you have nothing to fear. If it is not—I shall show you a couple of hiding places in the plane that you evidently have not suspected."

Perez nodded, well pleased. The plane flew on into the south. Over the couch where Jim Anthony sprawled at ease on his back, a statue of the Discus Thrower was set in the wall. Suddenly the discus itself glowed for a brief moment. Just the fraction of a second, but it was observed and noted. It meant that The Tepee was calling on the radio phone in the control room. Perez was pouring himself another drink. Jim murmured something about seeing how things were going, and left the compartment.

Tom Gentry greeted him. "They're on the phone, Jim, waiting for you." Jim picked up his radio phone, signaled a go ahead and waited. The pleasing voice of Linda Tabor came to him. Across many thousands of miles it floated through space, softly modulated, yet loud enough to be distinct, every syllable coming plainly to him. Even as she spoke and he digested the meaning of the message, his subconscious self was glowing at the perfection of that voice. He remembered that it had sounded wonderful enough off a wax recording, but here, over the radio phone, it was a living rather than a canned voice, and it was doubly enhanced.

Linda Tabor read aloud from the paper in her hand. "Hans Darwin Guttmann, born in Saxony, 1872." Swiftly she read on, how the man had obtained, through hard work, a wonderful education with several master's degrees. Botany had been his major study. For years he had been in the employ of the government as an economic botanist, ranging the world for beneficial plants which could be brought back to Germany and cultivated to advantage. To him were due several of the *ersatz* products that now enabled the Axis Powers to carry on the war.

"Doctor Guttmann," continued Linda, "has operated a plantation in the Republic of San Rosario for the past eight years. Much of his work has been secret, but rumors have issued forth from time to time of strange plants that he has taken from the Central American jungles, bred and cross bred with other strange or stranger plants to produce miracles in botany. Rumor has it that he now specializes in medical plants, herbs and the like." She paused for a moment, then, "That is a condensation, Mr. Anthony. Should you require details, they can be furnished concerning his life and his early work, but not his work in later years." She clicked the radio phone off.

Jim Anthony removed his own headset and stared unseeingly at Tom Gentry. Gentry said, "Well, what is it? What'd you want to know about a German named Guttmann?"

Instead of answering, Jim said, "How much farther?"

Gentry looked at his wrist watch. "Another hour. But listen, Jim, what should I do, land, or should we circle the guano islands and try for a look at the monster?"

Jim nodded, still as if he did not hear him. He raised a hand in goodbye and went back to the efficiency apartment that was the body of the Douglass. Dictator Ramon Perez was asleep in his chair, his hands clasped over his paunch, his mouth open beneath the black of his mustache. For a moment Jim stood staring down at him, his own brow knit. And again he felt that strange feeling—distrust, or a warning?

His feet made no sound as he moved to the kitchenette of the Douglass, and the section of panel that came out of a seemingly solid wall was just as soundless as it slid up in answer to the knowing touch of Jim's fingers. The small cabinet thus revealed was filled with tiny bottles of concentrated chemicals. With the aid of a small test tube, Jim blended two of them. Where one had been yellow in color and the other a dirty brown, once blended, the resulting liquid was as colorless as water.

From the same cabinet he took a small rubber syringe. The contents of the test tube were soon in the syringe. Carefully Jim closed the cabinet's steel, protecting door, touched the button that slid the panel back into place, and went, soft-footed, from the kitchenette.

Dictator Ramon Perez still slept the sleep of the conscienceless, faint rasping sounds issuing from the red-black cavern of his mouth. Jim was not trying to approach his passenger surreptitiously. One of the reasons for his great success as a battler for the right, as a super-detective, was that he never underestimated an enemy. The situation was this: The man aroused something in him, a feeling of distrust and a feeling of danger. Call it hunch if you will, but all his life Jim had possessed that seventh sense and it had never failed him. It followed then, that Perez was watching Jim Anthony as shrewdly and thoroughly as Anthony was watching Perez, at least so reasoned Jim. Then it was altogether possible that the man feigned sleep for some ulterior purpose. On the other hand, worn out by two fast air trips of thousands of miles, he might really be asleep. Jim Anthony never took chances.

He lifted the bottle from the table with his left hand, drew the cork with his right hand, and poured a short drink into a clean glass. In recorking the bottle he seemed to have a bit of trouble. When he put it back on the table, the syringe in his hand was empty. Ramon Perez did not open his eyes. It was half an hour later before he did awaken.

He yawned, never bothering to cover his mouth. He stretched like a bulky beast of the jungles, he grunted. Presently he and Anthony were again engaged in conversation. Jim again worked it in. He said, "This Guttmann, this plantation where the serpent spent the night. You didn't know him?"

Perez grunted again, waved a fat hand. "I knew of him. He paid his taxes. I had no need to send for him."

And that was the end of that.

Presently the center of the Discus Thrower's body glowed redly. Jim Anthony flipped the switch that made it a communicator now. Tom Gentry's voice said, "Want to come up here? I've sighted the Tres Cabezas!"

Jim said, "Okay!" He turned to his guest.

Ramon Perez was half up from his chair, his face ashen. He gasped, "No! No! Not yet, I tell you, not yet!"

Anthony's slotted eyes watched the pompous dictator gain control of himself. Watched hairy fingers pour another drink from the bottle and swallow it so fast that drops of liquor dripped from his lips and ran down onto his chin.

Anthony said, "Thought we'd look them over on the way in. Want to come up front?"

Perez' eyes rolled whitely from side to side, his brow, sweat covered, was corrugated. He babbled, "But you do not understand! I have seen this monstrosity! I have nearly died before its wrath! I—I—beg of you, let us land first! Then you and *Senor* Gentry can return. I—I—I am afraid!"

Anthony thought, This man the dictator of a country! This man wading to power through blood and bones, afraid! Aloud he said, "Suit yourself," curtly, and left the apartment. A second later he was beside Tom Gentry, who was peering interestedly through the windows toward the three guano islands, not five hundred feet below them.

Anthony said, "Cabeza Grande, there in the middle. The one to the west will be Cabeza Chica, the one to the east, Cabeza Media. Go lower, Tom, we'll have a look at them."

The plane passed the island, banked sharply and circled back. The door to the cabin crashed open, a hoarse mad voice shouted, "Turn back, you fools, back! Damn you, I'll shoot!"

Both men turned their heads. Every muscle in Jim Anthony's body was taut. For Ramon Perez stood in the door like a madman, a great automatic in his hand.

"What—?" began Tom Gentry.

"Back," screamed Perez, beside himself with fear! "I will not die, I am afraid to die! I—"

Jim made a gesture with his hand. So long had he and Tom Gentry been together that Gentry understood the command and acted in split seconds. The big plane veered sharply over, practically stood on its left wing. The automatic exploded, the bullets spattering against the bullet proof glass. At the same time the dictator was hurled sideways, the heavy entrance door banged shut. Banged shut on the gripping fingers of Perez. His screams filled the room.

Quickly Jim Anthony leaped for the man, jerked him to his feet. Perez did not even look at him! He seemed paralyzed with fear. His eyes were wide and stark, his mouth flecked with white spittle. Those eyes were staring out the window as the ship leveled out over Cabeza Media, the furthermost east of the three guano islands.

"No! No!" he screamed, and his heavy body thudded to the floor. Jim Anthony and Tom Gentry, too, looked through the glasses of the plane.

The sea serpent was crawling from the water upon the sheer, rocky slopes of Cabeza Media!

CHAPTER VI
TWO SMALL SAMSONS

TOM GENTRY GIGGLED, BUT THERE WAS NO AMUSEMENT, no hilarity in his giggle. A woman might have screamed. Even Jim Anthony breathed hard and tightly through his nostrils at sight of the utterly unbelievable thing that *was*.

The great nose and snout came out of the chopping sea water first. Red eyes, as horrible as those of a tarantula, enlarged a thousand thousand times, roiled upward at the plane as it passed overhead. The great mouth opened slowly, almost indolent with power, like the mouth of a great alligator of the southern swamps. Up, up, it went wriggling onto the rocks of the guano island, and the red rays of the descending sun danced viciously off the great plate-like scales of its back.

It had no legs. It crawled on its belly like a great and primeval snake from the Jurassic slime, writhing, slithering on and on. Now, as the plane circled and turned again to pass over the monster, it lay with a full hundred feet of its immense body out of the water, as if it were sunning itself on the rock. Its great head was raised from the rock, like the weaving head of a viper about to strike, and those red, red eyes seemed to follow the swiftly moving plane in its flight.

As they were almost directly over it, something issued like a sudden immense jet of steam from both nostrils, and, the plane being but a few yards above it, the steam, for only a moment, enveloped the lower surface of the fuselage and the wings. The plane swayed beneath that blast as if an antiaircraft gun had rocked it!

Gentry worked at the controls. His face was white, his freckles were dark brown spots, his eyes frantic. Hoarsely he said, "Now what?"

Jim was looking backward over his shoulder at the serpent. The flight of the annoying plane seemed to enrage it, for it raised its great head even higher from the rock; the great red and black cavern of its mouth gaped for a moment. What appeared to be a forked red tongue thrust itself forward out of the mouth! And suddenly the air about the serpent was filled with a black, dust-like stuff that floated up and up and up in unbelievable volume. It was as if the serpent were laying down a smoke screen, like a battleship, or a battling plane!

"Now what?" repeated Tom Gentry again. But there was no need to ask. One look at Jim Anthony's face and Tom knew what to do. Gentry was scared, as frightened as he had ever been in his life. Perhaps Anthony was frightened. Most certainly he was not a man without fear. Perhaps it was only that his curiosity was so much stronger than his sense of fear! And Gentry, knowing Jim so well, banked the plane. He banked it so sharply that the body of Ramon Perez thudded off the padded seat on which it lay and rolled like a log clear across the cabin. Jim Anthony did not even look at the unconscious man.

Back into the heavy and arising blackness plunged the plane, the Thunderbird II. Jim Anthony peered with slotted eyes into the blackness, said aloud, "It's crawling back into the sea, backwards, Tom!"

Then they were through the black smokelike stuff and into the clear air again. But strangely enough, the cabin seemed murky, as if someone had recently been burning oily rags. Tom Gentry sneezed. Ramon Perez rolled over again, fought his way to his hands and knees—and sneezed three times.

Jim Anthony felt a prickling at his nostrils. For a brief second he did not sneeze, he did not move, for he was listening to the motors. Again they missed, both of them! He leaped toward the instrument board, sneezing as he did so! He cut in the other two motors. Both turned over half a dozen times and began to conk out.

"Head her down, Tom," he commanded, "keep her out of a dive! She's going, it's that damnable dust!"

As Tom headed her toward the choppy sea, now not over fifty feet below them, Jim fumbled for a moment at a small compartment, came out with a handful of what appeared to be ordinary black silk. Quickly he slipped one—it was shaped as a tight sack—over Tom's head, another over his own head and face, then approached Ramon Perez.

Perez was praying on the floor, tears streaming down his face. He did not look up, he did not cease his babbling, when Jim leaned and jerked the black sack, which was a special gas mask, over his head. Nor did he change posture.

The motors had stuttered their way into oblivion, and Tom Gentry was setting the pontoons of the plane down on the ocean when Jim Anthony finished. Thickly, through the mask, Tom said, "What is it, Jim? What made us conk out like that? I don't understand."

"Dust," said Jim laconically. "The dust of our reception committee." Behind his mask Tom looked dumb for a moment. Then suddenly he stiffened, his hand on Jim's arm tightened. Jim too turned.

Not fifty yards behind them the malignant head of the sea serpent was rising from the sea, its bloody red eyes gleaming malevolently, its great cavern of a mouth gaping open to seize them as it swam steadily, as steadily as a boat, toward the marooned and apparently helpless plane.

Jim, in turn, seized Tom's shoulder. "Hold it," he cautioned, "I want to see. When I give you the word, cut in the compressed air!"

As he spoke, he was dragging a Tommy gun from a rack overhead, and as he finished speaking, he loosed a stream of tracer bullets into the open mouth of the beast. He could see them enter, could see them spend against the thing; the forked tongue lashed out and a stream of the dust-like stuff again enveloped the plane! Jim roared, "Now!"

Tom Gentry pressed a pedal, manipulated a lever. Inside the gigantic pontoons of the Thunderbird II were immense tanks of compressed air. The pedal and the lever released this air in a million fine streams, released it against the weight of the sea water so that the plane shot forward at high speed, like a darting fish! The whole operation was based on the same principal that an octopus uses in swimming, the emission of a solid stream against the water.

Unbelievably fast, the Thunderbird II shot forward and out of the dust. For a moment it slowed, as Tom controlled the air at a gesture from Jim. They waited, poised like a bird awaiting flight, waited for the monster to reappear. He did, in a matter of seconds. The great gaping jaws appeared from the mist of dust, they opened and closed with a great snap, and all three men in the plane shuddered, realizing what it would mean to them to be caught in that trap.

But the serpent seemed to realize its inability to catch the plane. For after that one immense snap—as if it were showing these puny mortals what it *could* do—the great mouth remained closed, a greater amount of steam than ever issued from the nostrils, and slowly, slowly, like a settling alligator, it went down below the surface of the water.

"Let's go," said Jim softly to Tom, through his thin mask. Tom turned on the air. The Thunderbird II headed for Ciudad Rosario, visible across the horizon, some four miles eastward in the twilight.

Jim opened all windows, turned on all ventilators, and soon an immense cross-current of air, created by those powerful fans, dispelled the remainder of the smoke-like dust from the cabin. Jim took off the mask, promptly sneezed, thrust his head out the window and breathed deeply of the clean sea air. A few moments later, Tom took off his own mask, sniffed cautiously, and grinned.

Jim Anthony fumbled at his belt for a moment. Around his waist, protected by the belt, ran yard after yard of a special fiber substance he had invented himself in his own laboratories. It was as fine as ordinary twine, yet its tensile strength was as great as that of a steel cable a hundred times its diameter. The spring in the belt buckle held it, worked like a reel, so that at a touch of the button as much of the stuff as Anthony wanted unwound slowly into his hand. This time he took little more than a foot before he pressed another button that drove a special blade into the fiber and cut it short.

Ramon Perez, still in an epilepsy of fear that immobilized his muscular body, that glazed his eyes, was still praying on the floor. Jim murmured, "A bad time to do this, but it must be done."

He took the mask from the man's head. The man kept on praying, the palms of his hands still pressed together before him. Jim took the cord, wrapped it twice about the man's thick and hairy thumbs and turned away. Ramon Perez did not move, did not seem to notice that he was firmly and inescapably held as if he were handcuffed.

The plane came nearer and nearer to the deserted docks of Ciudad Rosario. They passed a deserted fishing smack rocking at anchor in the evening swell. They taxied up toward the dock, and Jim noticed that the far end of it was broken down, as if some immense weight had crushed it into the sea. This, he assumed, was the path the sea serpent had taken when it went ashore, right up over the end of the dock.

There was no sound or sign of life for a moment. Tom brought the plane into a vacant spot, far down the pier, turned off the air with the pontoons tapping gently against the piling, and opened the door to go out and tie up. But he paused. He said, "Gee Whillikins! That's the first time I ever saw—"

A wide cobblestoned street led down to the dock. Around the comer, from the first cross street, issued a flat-bedded Ford truck. At first sight it appeared to be floating through the air. For its wheels were a full four feet from the cobblestones! Steadily it floated toward them, and as it issued from the shadows of the white buildings, both Tom and Jim grunted in surprise and amazement. For the heavy Ford truck was being carried! Absolutely carried down the street. Not by a great crew or gang of men—but by two men! A pair of legs and a back for the front of the car, a similar pair of legs and a back for the rear!

On they came, like a pair of ghosts bearing a ghost truck. They disregarded the plane, they walked steadily to the edge of the pier, the men in front wheeled aside, the man in the rear came up to him, and the two men dumped the truck overboard, into the sea with a great and resounding splash.

Tom Gentry wiped the sweat from his brow. He said, "Gee whiz, gee whiz, gee whiz," over and over. Jim went back in the plane for a moment. When he came out, a pair of egg-shaped objects hung at his belt. He was releasing the cord from about his waist and looping it in his right hand as it unwound. Attached to the free end were two brass balls, no larger than the egg-shaped objects at his waist.

"Masks," he said.

Tom turned, saw that Jim was once again wearing one of the black gas masks. He took his own from his pocket, donned it. "Some more of the reception committee," said Jim laconically.

For a moment he watched the two brown-faced *peons* on the dock. They were standing quietly staring downward at the spot where the heavy truck had disappeared.

They wore the ordinary cheap white clothing of the tropical *peon*, though both were hatless. Their feet were bare, their arms, exposed almost to their elbows by their short sleeves, were reedlike and thin. Both pair of shoulders were stooped and hunched, the average shoulders of the average *peon* who has spent all of his life carrying and packing. The amazing part to both Jim and Tom was that both were so small, so puny in appearance, yet they had carried the heavy truck down the street and dumped it into the bay!

"Come on," said Jim through his mask, and together they walked toward the men. Neither paid the slightest attention to them! They were within twenty feet of the two skinny natives. Jim said, "*Buenas noches, senores.*" The two men turned and looked at him.

Their eyes were as dead as black buttons of gunmetal. Both coffee-colored faces were absolutely immobile. Neither answered the greeting. Instead, both started plodding away the way they had come. Jim plunged after them, Tom at his side. "Let's stop 'em," said Jim.

Tom Gentry put a hand on a skinny shoulder. He said, "Hey, you!" He tugged. His hand came away. He stood silent and unbelieving, for the *peon* went on exactly as he had gone before, with not a twitch of a bony shoulder! It was as if Tom Gentry had walked over to a solidly built house and tried to pull it down with his bare hands. Jim put no finger on his man, rather he walked beside him talking rapidly in Spanish. And that too was as successful as talking to the same house that could not be pulled down!

Gentry hastened past the two stolidly plodding peons and paused some six feet in front of them, his jaw set. As they neared him he spread out his arms, said belligerently, "Listen, you guys, you can't—!"

But they could. They walked over him, literally over him, knocked him down by the irresistible force of their slowly moving bodies. They were like a pair of tanks advancing over rocky country and Tom Gentry was one of the rocks! The laughter was Jim Anthony's.

Jim allowed them to go on some thirty or forty feet before he swung the thin cord with the brass knobs attached about his head. The knobs shot through the air, to the right of the plodding *peons.* When the knobs were well past, Jim moved his arm and hand slowly but precisely, the brass knobs shot to the left with terrific velocity, like a cracking whip. The *peons* tumbled into the dust, the knobs having encircled their ankles, the steel-like cord binding them.

"That got the Samsons," chuckled Tom and started forward.

The *peons* arose as one. For a moment they both swayed, like slender saplings tormented by a heavy breeze. *And they continued their stolid walk up the street!* The cord that would support such a terrific strain and weight lay in tangled bits in the dust. Jim Anthony grinned without mirth as he picked up the twin brass knobs. He said, "I hate to do this, the poor fellows." He took one of the egg-shaped objects from his belt, pulled a pin and tossed it directly ahead of the slow-moving *peons*.

There was no smoke. There was nothing at all visible. But the two *peons* quit walking. Again each swayed. Then, as if they had rehearsed the action many times for a stage production, each crumpled slowly into the dust and was motionless and inert.

Tom Gentry, standing over the two men, said, "Gee whiz! Gee whiz! What do we do with them now?"

Jim answered, "We'll carry them aboard the plane first."

They did. They found Perez staring down at his thumbs like a crazy man, muttering to himself. Jim put a hand under the dictator's chin, flipped on the overhead lights. He said something that sounded to Tom like, "I thought so!" But when Tom looked, the only thing out of the way he noticed was a few white lines running from Perez' mouth down onto his chin.

Anthony cracked, "Now listen closely, Tom. You've got a lot of work to do and no one to help you. I'm inclined to think the motors quit quickly enough to save scarring the cylinder walls." At Tom's questioning look he explained, "The dust, that chemical dust. Haven't you figured yet why we conked out? Don't tell me you believe that was a sea serpent?"

"I saw it," began Tom stubbornly, but Jim's laughter stopped him.

"Never mind. You keep these two Samsons locked up, and every couple of hours you toss in another gas bomb. It won't hurt them and it'll keep them sleeping. You go to work on these engines, and you'll find them dust-clogged, all right, with a chemical dust. I've heard of the stuff before, conks out all gasoline engines. And—wait. Before you do that, you assemble the motor plane and have it ready. Keep an eye on the two Samsons and a good eye on Perez." He grinned. "Keep his thumbs the way they are, he can use his hands. Snap him out of it if you want to, and make him work!"

"A dictator?" Tom's mouth was open. Jim nodded with amusement. Tom went on, "Where you going?"

Jim answered, "I'm going to make a social call, although I doubt if anyone will be at home. I'm going out to the *hacienda* of one *Herr* Doctor Guttmann. I want to find out why a sea serpent went to all the trouble of crawling out of its boudoir to visit a particular plantation. There must be a reason."

He was still choking as he left the plane and set off up the cobblestoned street of Ciudad Rosario.

CHAPTER VII
Liquor from the Serpent's Egg

Ciudad San Rosario, once a city of fifteen thousand people was now like a city of the dead. Except, thought Jim Anthony wryly, that there weren't any corpses! In the downtown area the shutters used during closing hours were neatly up, as if the owners were simply home taking a temporary *siesta* rather than having fled the city because of the sudden appearance of a prehistoric monster. Panic might have overtaken the city, but it was an orderly panic.

The marks of the monster as it crawled through the main street were plainly visible. Several times Jim stopped to examine them, but because the serpent had used the same route for his return, it was difficult to make them out exactly. One thing was certain, they closely resembled the tread marks left by a caterpillar tractor.

Twice Jim stopped to enter cars standing at a curb with their keys in the ignition, and each time he had to abandon the idea, for neither motor would start. He knew the reason for this, of course. They had failed for the same reason the plane's engines had failed. Because of the chemical dust emitted from the forked tongue of the sea serpent.

He stood in the main plaza scratching his head and wondering if he were going to have to walk the entire distance to the *hacienda* of the German botanist. There was no question of finding it. All he had to do was follow the tread marks of the serpent. But getting there?

Miraculously, with customary good fortune, a solution presented itself. Leaning against an adobe wall he found a bicycle, abandoned by its owner. Evidently the dust of the serpent had no effect on a bicycle, for the gears worked perfectly, and he was soon mounted on the leather seat and peddling along the track left by the serpent.

By now, night had descended, and the tropical moon overhead was soft and silver and luminescent, like an incredible balloon released in a wide blue bowl. Night birds called from the leafy palms, a cooling breeze swept down from the not-too-distant hills to rustle the leaves. The scent of night-blossoming flowers was so redolent as to be almost too sweet, almost sickening. But Anthony pedaled along the road in the wake of the monster, oblivious to all that was around him.

Jim Anthony was a scientist. He knew the last of the sea serpents had died a million years ago. He was certain, positive in his own mind that the serpent was nothing less than a mechanical marvel. Inside that serpent, he knew, were men, mortal men, able to direct its coming and going. It moved, he was positive, by caterpillar tread, operated from the inside by a human man. Instruments controlled the opening and closing of those gigantic jaws, gave them immense leverage through the use of gigantic motors. The steam could be actually that, steam impregnated with a new gas, perfected by mortal minds. And the dust, that chemical dust, mixed with a lighter than air gas capable of great lifting power, was also the product of a mortal mind.

Why, however, he asked himself, was the serpent off San Rosario? And for that he had an answer—a guess, of course, but a guess that he hoped to soon verify.

He pedaled on into the moonlight, his agile brain afire with his thinking and—call it hunch. For again that inheritance of the forests passed down to him through his mother, Fawn Johntom, was at work. He recalled how for weeks, ever since the escape of Rado Ruric from the death cell, he had watched for the man. Perhaps, to others, his way of watching might have seemed peculiar, for he looked not for a man, but for a deed, an act.

Rado Ruric, he knew to be a psychological abnormality. The man's brain was the epitome of all criminal brains. He could no more stay away from crime—huge, vast, enveloping crime—than a fish could stay away from water. Ruric possessed an organization. He and that organization were for sale. He had sold it to Mythnos, the late munitions king, in order to send orders for billions of dollars worth of munitions to the unscrupulous Greek. Before that he sold his services and the services of his organization to the Communists, and Jim Anthony had waged war with his forces on the Tibetan plateaus for the control of the Chinese Empire.

On the disappearance of the arch criminal, Jim had not wasted time looking for the man himself. He had simply had his own organization report unusual deeds, unusual actions, throughout the world. The result—this! For, knowing there were no sea serpents, the phenomena had aroused his instant suspicion, had plunged into being that forest-hunch, that primeval-foreboding. In other circumstances, he reflected, while his muscular legs speeded the bicycle over the sandy road, he might have attributed the serpent to the superstitions of a backward people, the *peons* of San Rosario. But that didn't explain the sudden appearance of Dictator Ramon Perez at The Tepee! Ramon Perez and his dramatic request for aid for a stricken country!

Jim smiled to himself again. That Perez! That schemer! Most assuredly Jim saw the hand of Rado Ruric in this thing. The possibilities were so great with this serpent that no mind but that of Ruric was capable of—

He ceased his reflections, for the road had topped a knoll and passed through a grove of trees. He crossed a modern culvert with a stream trickling loudly and happily beneath it, paused to look at the *hacienda* to his right, perhaps a city block ahead. His eye followed the track of the serpent until it disappeared to the right, through the gates of Guttman's place.

The white house of the plantation gleamed in the moonlight. But behind it, some hundred yards, was a long series of buildings that gleamed even more. A quick glance showed them to be hothouses. Hothouses in the tropics? that didn't make sense. Still *Herr* Guttmann had been one of the world's leading botanists. If he saw fit to grow tropical plants under glass—? Jim shrugged, and rode on.

In the *patio* of the *hacienda* he paused and called aloud. A parrot in a papaya tree answered him; only that and nothing more. He entered the house. Automatically he flipped the switch and was not too surprised when the place was flooded with light. He was standing in the living room of a well-furnished place, bright with the colors of the tropics, comfortable with all the chairs and cushions and hangings a man might gather who had roamed the world.

He crossed the room. There was an open fireplace in the room, another whim of Guttmann's, for the white tiles of the floor showed it had never, of course, been used. But Jim wasn't interested in the floor. He was interested in the picture in the heavy beaten frame that stood on the mantel itself. He leaned closer to examine it, read the inscription, written in Spanish across the lower left hand corner. It said, "To my faithful friend and true, Herman Guttmann." It was signed, "Ramon Perez."

Jim grinned again. What was it Perez on the Thunderbird II had told him? That he didn't know Guttmann personally! Had never been to his plantation! Yet here was an inscribed picture from the dictator himself!

He went on through the house, noted that volumes of books were missing from the well stocked library, apparent because of the vacant spaces, noted that the drawers and compartments of an old fashioned desk were open as well, and the papers ruffled. Either some one had searched for something—or the owner of the desk had hurriedly selected whatever papers he wanted from the jumble and had taken them with him. Jim went to the closets of the bedrooms, found each stripped of clothing, only discarded, torn and useless articles left. Herr Guttmann, of course—and Jim grinned wryly saying this to himself—might, of course, have been eaten, devoured by the so terrible sea serpent, but it looked rather like he'd simply packed up, taken what he wanted, and vanished!

But it was the greenhouses that were the final and greatest surprise. The electricity worked there, too, and the same switch that turned on the lights set semi-concealed fans blowing. The smell of dank and fertile humus filled the air, hot sweltering, wet heat filled the first greenhouse. Suddenly from overhead came tiny drops of water, so many of them that they were a fine spray. But they dropped downward on empty beds, for every plant had literally been lifted from its dirt by the roots. The greenhouses—for all the others were exactly like this—were empty, absolutely void of anything alive.

What had *Herr* Doctor Guttmann been growing?

Beyond the last greenhouse were bushes and trees, planted in orderly rows. But what he saw there did not surprise Jim Anthony; he had been expecting it. Rather than growing lushly and verdantly, as tropical trees and shrubs should be growing, they were stripped of their leaves and their tender shoots. They looked like the long ago dead shrub forests of the northern tundras, stripped and killed and blighted by the unrelenting wind and cold!

There was no way to recognize their species. As a matter of fact, although Jim had studied some botany, a few brief glimpses showed him that only an expert would be able to classify these growing plants even when alive. Cursory examination proved that every shriveled trunk had been the result of grafting. Grafting what? What had been carefully spliced into what? So that the life of one blended with the life of the other—to produce what?

Around the roots of each tree and shrub the earth was still spongy looking and wet. Tentatively Jim picked up a clod and dropped it with an expression of pain. The dirt burned like fire! He knew then what had happened. An acid of some kind had been placed there, at each and every shrub and tree, in order to eat out the roots. So that no curious person could ever determine just how the grafting was accomplished, or to which species each root and each stalk belonged!

Jim went back the way he had come, paused long enough to tuck the silver framed picture beneath his sweatshirt. Out in the moonlight again he mounted the bicycle and pedaled slowly and thoughtfully back toward town, once again wrapped in thought.

Three men now, he was saying to himself—and perhaps four. Three men! Rado Ruric, the arch criminal. Mahatma Garda, who had disappeared from New York after helping Ruric escape from prison. And *Herr* Doctor Guttmann, the botanist. The fourth? He shrugged, that was yet to be proved.

A sea serpent, three keen and criminal minds. Step by step he reasoned as he rode along in the moonlight. Why the sea serpent? To make the thing utterly fantastic, of course. And because, in spite of its fantastic appearance the serpent was a damnably practical weapon and submarine! And why its visit to the *Hacienda* Guttmann? Easy. To pick up Guttmann and his plants? Why then hadn't they simply shipped his stuff out? Because the use of the serpent was infinitely more spectacular. It left Guttmann in the clear, for his disappearance would be laid to the monster. The point remained—why Cabeza Media as a base? And already Jim Anthony thought he had a reason for that. The morrow would tell.

He entered the outskirts of the town, soon turned into the business district. He paused. Not far from the dock where the Thunderbird II was tied, the street was illuminated by the lights from an unshuttered place of business. The sign over the street proclaimed that this place was the *Campagna de Plata*, the Silver Bell. It was a *cantina*, or saloon, and a pair of voices, raised in song poured out into the dirty street with the light.

A second later Jim Anthony was off the wheel and peering into the lighted saloon. What he saw widened his grin. Two *peons* were bellying the bar, each with a bottle in his good right hand, their voices raised in song, a Spanish-American tale of a girl who was none too faithful, and a lover who evened the score.

They were the same two *peons* who had carried the Ford truck down the cobblestoned street of San Rosario and tossed it into the water at the foot of the dock. Now, however, they did not look doped or drugged, they seemed entirely human, enlivened by the liquor they were drinking. He wondered how they had gotten out of the Thunderbird II.

Jim entered. The *peons* quit their singing, eyed him suspiciously but without much fear, as if they had never seen him before. He wondered that neither questioned how he had come there. It took but a moment for him to enter into conversation with them, and to gain their confidences. Jim Anthony could do that when he wanted to. Already he had decided they were too simple-minded to be curious about his business in the place.

Of a certainty they had seen that serpent! At first Pablo, seeing it, had sworn a great vow never again to touch the *aguardiente*, but soon, when the people fled the town, Pablo and his friend Jose both knew the serpent was a fact, and so they hid!

"And why," asked Jim, "did you run, *senores*?"

They grinned at one another, they grinned at Jim, and evidently decided to trust him, for with affability and good fellowship they wondered if he did not know how it would be in a deserted city? How there would be much to eat and much to drink! So here they were, alone, in the great city of Ciudad Rosario, and this *cantina*, where they had so often been thrown out before was now theirs for the taking. Were they not brilliant to have hidden and stayed behind?

Jim agreed that they had been brilliant. And had they seen the great dragon of the sea go back to his fastness?

"*Senor*," said Pablo crossing himself, "right down this street he comes creeping and crawling. Frightened? I am a bit unsteady, you see, what with so much food and *aguardiente*, and so I can but run to the side of this very building!"

"And I," proclaimed Jose, "am even unsteadier than my friend Pablo. I cannot flee as far as he! It was I who saw the serpent egg in the dust of the street when the thing had slid into the water." He patted his chest in satisfaction.

Pablo, unwilling to surrender the spotlight mocked. "And such a small serpent egg from such a large serpent. I tell you, my friend, it was ridiculous!"

"Where," asked Jim cautiously, "is the egg?"

Jose went out into the darkness and returned a few moments later. The egg was egg-shaped, true enough. Jim took it in his hand and was surprised at the weight of it. It was silver, and later he was to find that it was lead lined. There were two small holes in it.

Jose explained this. "Never," he said modestly, "in all of my life have I ever had enough eggs. And Pablo is the same way. This one we could not break, and so we punctured it with a sharp nail and drank its contents."

Jim said, "And how did it taste?"

Pablo leaned toward him earnestly. "*Senor*, in this very *cantina* I have sampled liquor from many countries, all of which was pleasant to my palate, and more pleasant to my senses. And I will tell you this—none of them can hold a candle to this liquor from the serpent's egg!" He smacked his lips. Jose rubbed his stomach and rolled his eyes.

"The things you did," said Jim politely, "they were pleasurable?"

The *peons* looked at each other a bit vaguely. It was Jose who broke the silence. "Truly, *senor*," he said uneasily, "I do not remember quite all." Pablo agreed by shaking his head. "I drank," went on Jose, "and a sudden glow filled my body! From my heels to the top of my head I positively glowed! It was like I was placing my arms about the most beautiful of living women, like she was about to become mine and mine alone!"

Pablo took it up. "He is right! And for her I wanted to do something big! I felt strong, like a hundred oxen. I wanted to push over a building! I wanted to uproot a tree!"

He babbled on about his great feeling of strength, and Jim, remembering how these same two puny mortals had picked up a Ford truck and carried it for blocks, did not smile.

Eventually he said, "It must have been wonderful, that feeling. But those bruises on your faces, those cuts. You fought, perhaps?"

Pablo said, "We have spoken of that. We do not remember. I will tell you the truth, *senor*. I do not rightly remember doing all these things of which I spoke. The juice of the serpent egg made me very sleepy for a few moments. I remember *wanting* to do them, and at the same time recalling that it was *siesta* hour and that to sleep in the shade of a mango tree is also nice. And would you believe, that when I awakened, I was beneath that mango tree!"

"And it was likewise with me," said Jose, sighing at his *aguardiente* bottle, tossing it aside and reaching for another at his elbow. "The very same." He made a wry face after his drink. "*Senor*, compared to the liquid in the serpent egg, this is vinegar!"

Jim, suddenly anxious, hurried away toward the dock. His fears were riding high for a moment. For although he saw the Anthony motor plane riding on its tiny pontoons beside the giant Thunderbird II, there was a gaping hole in the great plane's side, and when he leaped aboard and raced to the control room he found Tom Gentry, unconscious, the ear phones of the radio still in place.

It took but a few seconds to revive his friend, who rubbed the bump on his head and moaned, gazing unbelievingly at the debris of the stool which had been broken over his head. "What happened?" he asked. "I was listening—listening—" He reddened.

"Sure," said Jim, grinning, "you were listening to the most beautiful voice in the world—don't blush, I've heard it myself, it belongs to my new reader—and while you were listening, one of the Samsons walked in and busted you with a stool!"

Tom nodded. "But where are they? I'll admit I forgot to keep them gassed, but I did have the plane locked tight as a drum. You had to use a key to get in, so they must still be here." He arose, as if to go to get the Samsons personally.

"They're down the street drinking *aguardiente*," said Jim dryly. "They beat out the steel sides of the plane and got out that way. How about Perez?"

They found him sitting lonely and disconsolate and frightened in the efficiency apartment. He did not speak to them. He kept on regarding his tied thumbs in wonder, reaching both hands to the bottle that stood beside him on the taboret. Jim shrugged. Tom said a bit bashfully, "This reader of yours, the one with the beautiful voice. Is she as beautiful as she sounds? Gee, I could listen to her all night! I could—?"

"Go ahead and listen," snapped Jim. "But be sure you get these engines fixed to take off in twenty-four hours. The motor plane is ready to go, sealed and ready?"

Tom looked a bit ashamed of having fallen for a voice that came to him over the air. He assured Jim Anthony that the tiny motor plane was absolutely ready to go in every respect. He went to work on the engines with such purposefulness that Anthony took pity on him, slipped into a pair of greasy unionalls and helped him. Far into the night they worked, while Jim told Tom from time to time what he had found at Guttmann's, his suspicions.

At last they retired, Jim trusting to his extraordinary senses to rouse him if any enemy approached. Perez was stretched on a couch, snoring.

They slept in the darkness, the tide gently rocking the Thunderbird II at anchor. Jim was saying sleepily, "—and so that's the way I believe it is. All we can do is wait—wait and watch to see where they strike their first blow. This Guttmann has evidently perfected a herbal fluid that gives its drinker supernatural strength, a blank mind—hence open for suggestion—and—"

"Look, Jim," broke in Tom, "is she blonde or brunette, this Linda Tabor that reads that stuff?"

Jim groaned in derision and relaxed utterly. With Jim, to relax was to sleep. Every muscle in his body loosened and sank into repose. In split seconds he was sleeping, deeply and dreamlessly. It was as if his nervous system was a system of electric lights, and he had suddenly turned the switch that cut off the current.

CHAPTER VIII
THE VAULTS OF SAN ROSARIO

BEFORE THE TROPICAL SUN HAD SHOULDERED ITS WAY over the mountains of the east, Jim Anthony was up and about. He stood on one of the great pontoons of the Thunderbird II and watched the town. A flock of parrots flew toward the forest, screaming and whistling. Furtive dogs began appearing, one at a time, like skinny shadows to nose about the gutters hopefully. By sunrise, Tom Gentry was awake, and the two friends had eaten their breakfasts, leaving Ramon Perez to sleep off the tremendous amount of liquor he had absorbed the night before.

Another half hour passed as the men smoked in silence, staring out across the choppy waters of the bay. And suddenly both were aware of the churning approach of a fast motor boat. Swiftly Jim arose. "Take Perez and lock him up," he snapped. "I want him kept out of sight. This is probably the first of the San Rosarians returning to their native land."

Tom said, "Keep him out of sight? I don't get you! Gee whiz, he's the ruler of this country, he'll want to see who's been killed and who's—"

"Hasn't bothered him so far, has it?" interjected Jim, and Tom disappeared into the plane just as a resplendent motor boat swept into view from down the coast, the flag of San Rosario flying smartly at its mast. Jim remained where he was, sucking thoughtfully at his pipe.

The boat throttled down, the hand at the wheel nosed into the slip that was marked with the San Rosario coat of arms. A barefooted man in a pair of ragged trousers and nothing else, sprang out and tied up the prow. A fat, swarthy fellow, resplendent in a uniform of blue and scarlet, stepped carefully to the pier, stood with out-thrust chest, twisting one end of a heavy mustache as he glared about the scene like a conqueror who has laid the country in waste. One pudgy hand rested on the hilt of his sword. A great diamond gleamed on the ring finger of that hand.

Jim kept down the amusement in his eyes, kept the smile off his face at sight and actions of the *opéra bouffe* figure. Then as if noticing it for the first time, the uniformed man allowed his eyes to rest on the silver seaplane. He stiffened. He threw back his shoulders, his long mustache seemed fairly to bristle. Then he was approaching on the wooden pier, his military boots resounding, his jowls trembling at every step, his medals swinging like pendulums.

He glared at the grinning Anthony. "Sir," he thundered, "I am General Rafael Augustano Joselito Gomez!"

He waited.

Jim said, "Morning, mister. Just get in? Stranger here?"

"Stranger," roared the man, aghast at such impertinence. "I am the General-in-Chief of Ramon Perez, the beloved president of this country! Who are you, where is your master?"

Jim answered, choosing to disregard the latter question. "Then perhaps your president has sent you on an errand? You have been away, no?"

"I have been away on affairs of state! That has nothing to do with you. Who owns this plane? Where are your papers? Where—?"

"Why," said Jim, "I own the plane, as a matter of fact. My name is Anthony, Jim Anthony. I heard you had a sea serpent down here and came down to look it over, but I reckon it was just a rumor."

"Rumor!" General Gomez almost jumped up and down in his rage. "A rumor, when I have risked my life these past twenty-four hours searching the seas for this monster, to kill him with my sword, so that the good people of my country shall have no more to fear?"

It went on and on, and the principal word used was a capital "I." Jim sucked on the pipe with amusement. And behind the general, one by one, returning San Rosarians began to gather. Some had their meager belongings on their backs, others were plainly foot-weary. For the past day and a half they had been hiding back in the hills, and now they were home.

It all ended up by Jim accompanying the general to the government palace, where he found out many things, by adroit questioning. But one of his first acts was to ask the general to commandeer any mechanics who might be in the town, to help Tom Gentry clean the engines of the Thunderbird II. Then, over a bottle of *aguardiente*, Jim began probing for his information.

Yes, Ramon Perez, it was to be admitted, had left San Rosario a few days before, with the intention of gaining some such needed aid for his country. What aid and why? Ah, the *senor* would understand it was impossible to reveal state secrets. It did have to do, however, with finances. What was that? The *Herr* Doctor Guttmann? To be sure, a very good friend of Ramon Perez!

"This Guttmann," went on Jim, contemplatively viewing the half filled glass in his hand, "I have been up to his *hacienda*. I heard over the radio in a dispatch from Mexico City, that this so famous sea serpent paid a visit to the plantation as well."

The general's eyes gleamed with excitement. "It did, *senor!* Right over the edge of the principal dock it crawled, up the very street outside the door and out the road to Guttmann's. I with my own eyes saw it." He seemed to get the general idea then, and flushed. "Naturally I and my brave men fired thousands and thousands of shots at it, using rifles and artillery such as we have—all to no avail!" He said this stiffly, as if expecting Jim to make some comment concerning his apparent lack of courage.

"Oh, naturally," agreed Jim, struggling to keep down his laughter, to keep his face straight. "This Guttmann now, he had a large plantation. He worked many *peons*, he had overseers?"

General Gomez agreed that he worked many people—and he passed on information that meant a lot to Jim. For, according to the pompous general, the only San Rosarians working there were a cook and two men who kept the stables clean. Guttmann, it seemed, was a lover of horses. The other help had been—of all things—Hindus!

"Men," said the general, "who walked the streets like cats when they came to town, great dirty towels wrapped about their arrogant heads, and the fiery look of a thousand devils in their eyes and their supercilious bearing! As if we were dirt beneath their feet!"

"And their names? Doubtlessly you knew the names of the most important?"

"There was one who called himself Das Sinha, a great ruffian. Another called Chakravarti. But the proudest of all, the one who sneered openly in our faces when he honored our fair city with his presence, was a tall slender man, with a square cut beard and a bristling mustache! One who wore the clothing of a westerner and the white turban of the Hindu." The general turned and spat into the collected dust at his feet. "This one," he continued, "I think to have been a guest of *Herr* Guttmann, rather than a worker."

"And his name?" Before the man said it, Jim Anthony knew.

"Garda, he called himself, M. Garda!"

So, thought Jim, his theories were working out. Mahatma Garda had somehow managed to get to San Rosario, to join Guttmann. A sea serpent—which could have been conceived by no other brain than Ruric's, even though the conception happened in jail—appeared, the *Herr* Doctor and all his Hindus disappeared!

"And how did Guttmann live? What did he ship from his plantation?"

"Mmmmmm, that was a peculiar thing. He grew a great deal of *yerba mate*, and often he shipped bales of this great and enervating tea. What he grew in those houses of glass I can only guess."

Jim arose. He said, "General, you were trusted by Ramon Perez." Gomez nodded. "Then I would suggest that you look in the vaults of your country at once and see if Ramon Perez has left anything to conduct the government. You will find me at the plane. *Adios*."

He stalked out, leaving General Gomez staring suspiciously after him. And before he was out of sight he was conscious of movement behind him, he heard, "Santos, Jesus, Federico! Come, we go to the vaults." Jim grinned to himself, out in the street.

CHAPTER IX
More Powerful than Hashish

Anthony was alone in the room with the man who called himself Ramon Perez. There was sweat on Perez' brow, his nervous tongue dabbed at his thick lips. He spread his hands, he said, "And so, do you not understand, Jim Anthony?"

"In a way, yes, in another way, no. It seems to me that you could do your country more good at the moment by reassuming your place, helping to rebuild the morale that has been destroyed."

The man who called himself Perez shook his head. "You do not understand, *Senor* Anthony. A dictator must always be the man on the white horse! I must reappear when the serpent is gone, I must reappear in a blaze of glory—or I lose prestige. And a dictator, *senor*, must have that."

Jim nodded as if in agreement. "What makes you think the serpent is gone? Perhaps he is still lying in wait around Cabeza Media."

Perez looked at him through slotted eyes, laughed. He laid fat fingers on his heart. "It is something that I feel, *senor!* It is what you call hunch in your country."

Jim leaned forward. "But we must make sure, Perez! Today we go to search for the serpent, you and I!"

Perez breathed hard through his nose. And, to Jim's amazement, he agreed. "You and I," he boomed. "We shall arm ourselves! We shall fly out and over the sea, and we shall seek this serpent!"

He thrust out his hand. Jim grinned inwardly as he took the fingers in his own. They were moist and clammy it seemed to him, but they were steady.

And at the same instant, both men looked out the window of the Thunderbird's cabin and saw the mob approaching. In the van, walking like Napoleon, strode General Gomez, his face as black as a thundercloud. He approached the plane, he called, "*Senor* Anthony!"

Jim grinned at Perez, who was suddenly cowering in his chair, peering wide-eyed out the window. "Your public," he said dryly. "Well, stay here, I shall meet them."

He left the plane and met the indignant Gomez on the dock.

• • •

Moments later he was back; the crowd—and the general—having dispersed. "It seems," said Jim, "that you took the greatest part of the San Rosarian treasury with you when you came north, Perez. General Gomez is highly indignant. He is, as a matter of fact, thinking of proclaiming your guilt and calling the legislature to make him president."

Perez sputtered denials, he raged, he ranted, but there was a wild look in his eye. At last Jim arose. "It seems to me, that if we should go search for this serpent, Perez, if we should succeed in killing it, you and I, that you could again—as you say—be the man on the white horse."

And this time, he was not at all surprised when Perez assented.

Shortly they stole away from the Thunderbird, unobserved by the mechanics helping Tom Gentry clean the chemical dust from the motors.

A moment later they were safely in place in the queer-appearing little motor plane that had been carried in pieces in the baggage compartment of the Thunderbird II. Jim sat in front, with Perez riding tandem behind him. It was very odd, considered the man who called himself Perez, that the motors were so silent in this little bug of a plane. And odd, indeed, that the air inside the stuffy cabin was so cool. But oddest of all, was the fact that he could talk to Jim Anthony, in the forward seat, and that Anthony could talk to him!

Why was this odd? Because between the two seats was a substance exactly as clear as glass, so clear that at first the man who called himself Perez had thought there was no obstruction whatsoever. And only when he reached forward did he find the glass-like stuff. Clear as glass, yes, but not so rigid. It gave slightly to the pressure of a man's fingers, and for this Perez was glad. Anything as soft as that could be penetrated. . . .

"You see," came Jim's clear explanation, "this plane, Perez, is the work of Tom Gentry and myself. We call it a motor plane, because it operates from concentrated batteries rather than from a storage tank of gasoline. I think we shall find that useful."

"Useful?" Perez was fumbling at his leg.

"Yes, considering the fact that the plane is absolutely air tight, that you are now breathing oxygen rather than air. He paused for a moment. He peered down at his own feet, on the controls of the motor plane. A light glowed as he pressed a button. The light glowed behind a magnifying lens no larger than a silver dollar, and Jim grinned. For the contraption worked like a doctor's cystoscope, like an improved periscope. In it he could see all of Perez' movements in the tiny rear cockpit.

"You see," went on Jim, disregarding Perez' movements at his pants leg, "the motors of the Thunderbird conked out because the dragon or the serpent," he put great emphasis on those two words, but it was lost on Perez, "fouled them with the chemical dust emitted from its forked tongue, and the acid steam from its venting nostrils. In this motor plane, the batteries and the motor itself are enclosed."

"Then," said Perez, "we can safely seek the serpent!" He seemed to be gloating within himself. "But you are going the wrong way! To the west, my friend!"

Jim said, "First, I must talk to you, Perez. I wonder why you said you did not know *Herr* Doctor Guttmann when I found this picture at his *hacienda*." He held up the picture he had taken from the mantel. Perez' face worked and contorted.

There was a fumbling explanation concerning the popularity of a dictator, how a secretary signed such pictures and he, Perez, did not rightfully know how many citizens of San Rosario had them. The plane sped on. Jim watched in the periscope and the muscles of his jaws ridged so tightly as to gleam white.

Suddenly he said, "And what is your real name? How much did Ruric pay you to come to me in the States?"

Perez' eyes gleamed like coals, again his tongue flicked toward his lips, like the tongue of a snake.

"I do not know what you are talking about."

"Indeed you do. You are not even Spanish, my friend. You were frantic with fright when we flew over Cabeza Media yesterday. Should I tell you why? Should I tell you that with the aid of Guttmann, you learned of Ramon Perez' proposed visit to me? That you imprisoned him—or killed him—you, and Guttmann and Ruric and Garda and others—looted the treasury, then made you up to resemble Perez, knowing I had never seen him in person."

"Go on!" There was madness in Perez' eyes now. Glancing down in the periscope device Jim could see his brown hairy hand tightly gripping an automatic, which had been concealed in the leg of his trousers.

"Your plan," said Jim calmly, "was to get me down here to investigate this man-made serpent. Only, you were to stay behind. Gentry and I were to seek it out, and the serpent's chemical dust would conk out our motors, we would land in the sea, and the great jaws of the mechanical serpent would do the rest. We crossed you inadvertently. You were frightened hysterical because you thought you were going to share the death meant only for us. No doubt we all would have died except for the compressed air we used in the Thunderbird's pontoons. I—" He paused.

Behind him, turning his head slowly, as if he could not see in the periscope, he saw the man who called himself Perez pointing the gun directly at the back of his own head. He managed to look frightened—though he wanted to laugh.

There was no fear in his passenger's voice now, only gloating mirth. He said, "They warned me you were a very extraordinary young man, Jim

Anthony. But, as you say in your country, so what? I have cautiously felt these dual controls back here and find that they work perfectly. There is no reason why I should spatter the instrument board with your brains, is there?"

The silent little plane flew on toward the southwest. Jim looked properly taken in, though he could hardly fight down the smile on his lips. He tried to appear very frightened indeed that his brains would soon be spattering the instrument board.

Gloatingly Perez went on. "You are right as far as you went, you poor fool, but you did not reckon with Nanda Jaini!" He went on with his bragging, his boasting and his crowing, while Anthony was thinking: Another Hindu! Nanda Jaini! "Now you will turn and fly me northward, fool. Perhaps I shall have you carry me all the way to the meeting point. The others naturally think I have been overcome by you! I wonder how Rado Ruric's face will appear when I bring you to him!"

He seemed perfectly willing to talk now, the words fairly fell over themselves emerging from his moist mouth.

Jim put in, "No doubt he will reward you, and then you will cease being a mere servant."

"Servant!" howled Nanda Jaini. "I, a servant? By Allah, I have never served! It is true that Ruric has placed my intelligence below that of Garda, or Guttmann, or some of the others. But when I bring the great Jim Anthony to cower at his feet—!"

"That is what he wanted then? I really play no other part in his plans?"

"Since you will soon die, I do not see why I should not tell you the truth. The serpent was the idea of Ruric, conceived when he was in a Yanqui prison. He knew the superstitions of these poor Central Americans, the abysmal ignorance! Guttmann and the others built it and had it ready for his coming. He—"

"But I do not understand," wailed Jim plaintively. "Why should he go to all the trouble to—"

"Because Guttmann, the botanist-chemist, has evolved the greatest herbal mixture the world has ever known. Have you ever heard of hashish? Have you ever read the history of the Old Man of the Mountains, and the Assassins? The Assassins were fed with hashish, the men of our ring shall be fed on—never mind!"

Jim Anthony knew! He remembered the two San Rosarian *peons*, skinny and underfed, weakened by the ravages of disease and drink. How thirstily they quaffed the milk of the serpent egg—and became as twenty men each!

"I see," said Jim. "And you were afraid it would make too much commotion if *Herr* Doctor Guttmann's discoveries were lifted bodily from San Rosario and—"

"Exactly, exactly. The serpent drove people away from the city. Dr. Guttman's plants and his finished products could thus disappear. You," there was scorn in the voice, "were brought like a sheep to slaughter, simply to please Rado Ruric. For some reason he wishes to experience the subtle pleasure of killing you an inch at a time, of making you die a thousand deaths."

Jim said, "I didn't see any laboratory out at Guttmann's, I—"

"Fool. I was on the island, Cabeza Media. Cabeza Media is like an inverted bowl. The inside of the rock is hollowed out by nature. There stayed the crew of the serpent, there the leaves of the grafted plant were distilled to make a concentrate of psythrium."

"Psythrium? Is that what they call it? Is—?"

"You're too far west, damn you! There are the three Cabezas!"

True enough, looming on the horizon were the bulking guano islands!

"Well," said Jim mildly, "it won't hurt to look at them, will it. And—" The time was at hand now. His voice grew hard and stern. "You, Jaini, you haven't fooled me at all. Your makeup threw you. The moment I grew suspicious of you, I put a harmless and tasteless acid in a bottle from which you were drinking. You drank nervously, the liquor ran down your chin and left telltale streaks of white behind it! The finding of the picture at Guttmann's of the real Perez, verified my suspicions. I think the time has come to bring this farce to an end. I have all the information I need for the moment. Suppose you and I take a look at the haunt of the serpent."

Jaini's eyes glowed red, his trigger finger tightened. He growled, "Head north by east, my friend, and follow the coast. Do you understand we have a trip of some three thousand miles before us? Do you understand that I have a .45 caliber automatic ready to blast your brains out and that I can control the plane from where I sit, and that it is merely incidental whether I take you to Ruric in one piece—or half a dozen?"

Anthony said, "Pull the trigger and take the plane, great fool!"

Jaini pulled the trigger, he held it down for a moment. The roar of the heavy gun filled the tiny compartment. Suddenly he screamed and the gun dropped from his fingers. He had been hit twice! Blood dripped from a split over his left eye. His right shoulder felt as if some giant had hit it with a sledge hammer. The cool amused voice of Jim Anthony came to him.

"Try again, fool, you've missed me. I thought you could shoot as well as you talked?"

With a roar of rage the Hindu snatched the automatic in his left hand. He emptied the magazine. The plane kept serenely on its way, though leaden hornets buzzed and roared around Jaini's ears. He was not hit again. There was madness in his face when he sat back nursing his shoulder and dabbing blood from his eye and regarded the calm shoulders of the man ahead of him.

Jim's sarcastic voice floated back. "The partition, my friend, as you might have observed by now, is bullet proof. I happen to know you had a full gun—and no more shells. Have you any gloating to do now? How will your master, Rado Ruric, treat you when he finds what an opportunity you lost?"

The voice that came to Jim was very faint. "Where—now?"

"Cabeza Media! I am interested." The plane nosed over in a dive for the farthest east of the three guano islands almost directly below.

"No, no!" screamed Jaini. "They would not leave unless they laid a trap! You'll kill us, kill us both. The island must be mined! They wouldn't leave! You'll kill us—kill us—!"

The silent plane kept on in the dive.

CHAPTER X
Anthony Summons the Clan

For a moment there was silence. Then Jim's answer snapped the man erect in his seat. "Coward! I have a button on the dash before me, I can press that button and release a gas that will render you unconscious. I—"

"Press it! Press it! I cannot stare death in the face like this! Let it be easy for me! Press it!"

"You're going to face the tortures of the damned, for once in your life," said Jim grimly, and leveled the little plane out over the bowl-like guano island. Jim himself wasn't quite sure just what was going to happen. Jaini's confession that the island had been mined—or something—was not surprising. For Jim never discounted the ingenuity of his opponents. The man's words, that is, the words of Jaini, of course had simply pieced together the definite pieces of the jigsaw that Jim already held, they had helped him to put the thing in its right perspective. All he lacked now was—reason. The why of the thing.

They passed close over the highest peak of the rockgirt island. Impulsively Jim stiffened. He would not have been at all surprised to find himself blasted high and wide by a great explosion. Instead, from what seemed to be nowhere, great clouds rose, of the same dark, chemical dust that had wrapped itself about the Thunderbird II the day before. Jim sighed with relief, knowing that the dust could not hurt the sealed mechanism of the motor ship. But behind him the voice of Nanda Jaini rose to a high crescendo, a quivering scream of terror! He had forgotten how safe the ship was!

A split second and the ship was out of the cloud. Quickly Jim wheeled, headed back the way he had come, directly over the island. He was thinking of the fishermen and the guano gatherers who might set off the mines of chemical dust sometime in the near future, and meet their collective dooms! He knew how they were fixed, for he had used the same principal many times. There were simply a thousand electric radio eyes casting their invisible beams into the air, vertically, at a target, horizontally. Any foreign object crossing those beams set off a mechanism that released the death-dealing clouds of the chemical smoke! To Jim there was but one thing to do, and that was to cross and crisscross the island until no more dust-mines exploded.

Back and forth, back and forth, flying half by instinct and half by instruments. No sooner was he out of the dust than he wheeled and dived back in. The dust was released, of course, by compressed air, and the very swish, the very force, of the emission, was noticeable in the plane. Nine separate jets were loosed before the little motor plane dove through successfully without more dust. Again and again Jim went through grimly, until he was absolutely positive that all dust mines had been set off.

He growled, "You, Jaini, I can open that compartment so that you'll breathe a bit of that dust on the next trip. Should I?"

Jaini's screams of terror filled the plane, reverberated from stepped up magnavox to magnavox. "Ask me, ask me anything! I'll tell! To breathe that dust is to die a death of horror, of torture and pain. Ahhh! Tell me, what is it you wish?"

Grimly Jim banked the plane again in the clear sky. There was no kindness, no mercy in his voice now. "What are Ruric's plans? With the aid of Guttmann and his psythrium, what does he intend?"

The words, once again, fairly fell over themselves coming out of the Hindu's mouth. "Sabotage! The brew of the serpent, as we call it, gives the drinker phenomenal strength! Nothing but a bullet reaching a vital spot—ahhhhh!" The long shrill yell came from his horrified lips as the little plane once again disappeared into the smoke.

Through the blackness the voice of Jim Anthony cut like a knife. "Fool. I know that! I know what he has to fight with! I want to know where he is going to fight! Quick, my hand is on the opening lever that admits horror to your compartment. Quick!"

"Sabotage, I tell you! He will lead the greatest Fifth Column of spies and counter spies, of organizers and saboteurs the world has ever known. In the United States. He is in the employ of a foreign power. He—"

The little plane came out of the dust. So, thought Jim bitterly, Ruric again plays with international crime.

"What power?"

"Before God, I do not know. We Hindus, all of us, we have worked with him and for him because we have his word to see to it that munitions and help are sent to our own country, Mother India. I do not know who pays Ruric! His workshop is beneath the island! Could we land there with diving helmets I could show you! The serpent was built there. The inner side of the island is hollowed out, it is like a cone! Let us go back, let us obtain diving helmets, let us—Mother of God! The wing! The wings, both of them!"

For, now that the motor plane was approaching water level in a steep dive, the wings seemed to be shrinking inwardly, collapsing in the same manner as a jointed fishing rod, or a folding camera, the first section sliding into the second, the two of them into the third. At the same time, though Jaini could not see it, the small pontoons had folded back, leaving the plane shaped like a bullet. Vanes or fins had slid out of the motor plane, and once again the reverberations of the screaming Jaini filled the plane from side to side, from front to back! The black water swallowed the little plane. And suddenly the water was no longer black. An immense light, set in the body over Jim's head, sent its sunbright rays through the water. He swerved the plane in time to miss a looming rock, and a moment later, leveled off, sensing that he was near the bottom.

Jim couldn't resist the boast. "Has your master," he called, "any such contrivance as this? Now, where is the entrance to this diabolical cave or laboratory?"

His answer was a moan. A swift look over his shoulder, aided by ceiling lights he had flashed on, showed that Jaini, alias Ramon Perez, had found the merciful arms of unconsciousness! The smile that drew Jim's teeth back from his lips was not nice to see. So! Sabotage! A Fifth Column! There was not much time to waste. He did not know the speed of the submarine-serpent constructed by the followers of Rado Ruric. But there would be time enough to find that out when the frightened Hindu returned to consciousness. That, and the first scene of action. Then back to the States, back on the wings of the gigantic Thunderbird II to thwart the world's arch criminal once again.

Jim circled the island warily, cut through a school of multicolored fishes, through a forest of magnificent seaferns. A great squid wriggled its loathsome body close to the cruising sub and shot away in a cloud of "ink" when Jim speeded the motor to make the propeller throw a stream of water at it.

A moment later he found the opening, wide and black, a great conger eel waving its snakiness in and out among the weed-covered rocks that guarded the entrance. Jim throttled down the motor, cut down the speed of the boat and looked over his shoulder again. The Hindu was snapping out of it.

In answer to his query, Jaini admitted this was the entrance. He seemed overjoyed at being alive. The passageway was narrow, but not too narrow for the plane, although once or twice Jim was afraid—almost—to risk it, and true enough, much to Jaini's annoyance, rocks scraped the side. Jim concluded that the serpent-submarine must have been brought to anchor at the mouth of the cave, and the crew released in diving helmets to make their way up the passageway on foot.

Far ahead of him, after long moments in the tortuous passage, Jim saw the light growing even brighter, and knew the sub was about to emerge. A second later he leveled off, on the surface of the black water. A touch of the lever pulled down the windows automatically. It was as if they rocked gently at sea level—except that they were enclosed on all sides by rock, damp, sticky rock, slimy and repulsive.

"Water! Water! Ah God, water! Mother of God, bring me water!"

Jim stiffened at the voice from the depths of the cavern. Jaini made animal noises in his throat. Jim cast the light about the great cavern, saw that it was absolutely empty, but saw the black entrance to another chamber nearly straight ahead. He started the motor. Atop the surface the craft nosed its way toward that black entrance, and again that raving, hopeless prayer for water came floating out of the black entrance and into the chamber, to echo and re-echo in their ears.

The plane came to rest against an improvised landing.

"Out," said Jim. Whimpering in fear, Jaini left the ship, and Jim followed him, a gun in one hand, the great light in the other. "Down the passage," snapped Jim Anthony.

Jaini dropped to his knees. "There will be a trap, I tell you. We will die!"

"There's already someone down there dying," snapped Jim. "We're going after him. Go on, before I beat you before me like a dog."

Somehow Jaini got to his feet, began stumbling, fear stricken down the passageway, the light illuminating its vaulted corridors. Again that voice, "Water, water! For the love of God, water!"

Jaini whimpered, slowed. The gun prodded him onward. The passage turned and they were in the workshop of Rado Ruric and his crew! Benches ranged the wall, there were immense tanks, there were bins, there were pieces of abandoned steel and iron, a complete forge. And all were abandoned, their promise fulfilled!

But only for a second did Jim glimpse them. For once more the scream, the agonized prayer for surcease from suffering came to him, and the light quickly picked out the location, the source of the prayer.

It was a niche, perhaps six feet deep, cut into the far wall. There was a man in the niche, bound by his wrists to a ring in the far wall of the niche. Bound so high that his stretched toes barely reached the rock floor, so high that only the cord, cutting into his wrists supported his sagging body. His head was on his chest. He sensed the light, he raised his head, he peered hopefully into its rays.

"Water, water!" he moaned.

The man was the same man whose picture had decorated the mantel of *Herr* Doctor Guttmann. The real Ramon Perez, dictator of San Rosario. And this is what his friendship had led him into. Jim saw it in a flash. How he had confided his plans to Guttmann, perhaps even to Ruric. How they had taken him prisoner, looted his treasury, and sent Jaini, made up to resemble him, to lure Jim Anthony into the trap of chemical dust prepared for him! And what had Ramon Perez received? Horrible, lingering death, left here alone in this under-island cavern, to die slowly and by degrees. A wave of horror at the human animals who could conceive such torture swept Jim Anthony!

"Cut him down, take him down," he grated at the still cringing Jaini. Slowly, a step at a time, the impersonating Hindu moved toward the tortured man. He was afraid. There was a fear in every line, every nerve, and every muscle of his body. He did not know what he was afraid of. And Jim Anthony? His hair prickled at the base of his skull, his nerves were tense. He too, with that primeval sense of his, sensed hidden danger.

It struck like lightning.

Jaini, inched forward a step at a time, reached out a reluctant hand for the bonds that tied the real Perez. He touched a bit of down-hanging cord. He jerked. To jerk meant death. For from the side of the wall swept a horizontally contrived guillotine, a great, flashing blade of steel, like a gigantic scimitar, to slice through the air and separate Jaini's scheming head from his body, before he could utter a single scream.

The man tied aloft kept on moaning for water. Blood gushed and spewed from the neck of the Hindu's torso. The head lay face downward, as if ashamed. Jim stepped over the body as if it were a log. He felt no pity for the decapitated man. No pity whatsoever. For, partially through his contriving, it well might have been Jim Anthony lying there inert and dead on the floor.

A second later he pushed the spent, bloody blade aside and carried Ramon Perez from his appointed place of death. It took the dictator of San Rosario some ten minutes to revive. And during that time Jim searched the underground workshop meticulously. There was nothing to be found. A few broken tools, an empty food locker, and an empty bottle. Jim's nostrils told him the bottle had held liquor, alcoholic liquor, and not the stuff he desired to find—the brew of *Herr* Doctor Guttmann.

At one o'clock President Ramon Perez, dictator of San Rosario addressed his followers from the balcony of the palace. At his back stood General Gomez—and Jim Anthony. He told in a ringing voice how he had been overcome by the enemies of the country, how the treasury had been looted by these same robbers, how he, Perez, had been left for dead. And how he had been rescued by—General Rafael Gomez!

Jim grinned as the strutting little general stuck out his chest and acknowledged the plaudits of the crowd. Perez said, *sotto voce*, to Jim Anthony. "Why you should wish it that way is more than I know. But I have lied, as you wished."

Jim nodded, gripped the man's hand. Perez went on to tell how with all shoulders to the wheel, San Rosario would soon again take its rightful place in the international scheme. He said nothing of the serpent except that it would no longer molest his people. If Jim was right, already the monster had moved north.

By three o'clock the Thunderbird II was winging north, totally repaired. The robot pilot was holding the course, Jim and Tom were at ease in the great efficiency apartment that was the body of the plane. Jim said, "We've got a lot ahead of us, Tom. There were things I meant to ask that Hindu. Where the blow was to be struck, and how, exactly. I meant to force the truth out of him concerning the country backing Ruric's Fifth Column of agitators. I meant—"

He paused. Tom sat upright, his eyes glowing. For he had been fooling with the stepped-up radio phone and he had an answer. The voice that came floating into the apartment thrilled him to his fingertips.

"Calling Jim Anthony, Jim Anthony. The Tepee calling. We are ready, Jim Anthony."

A click. Jim grinned at Tom. "Want to talk to her?" Tom nodded. "Then repeat what I say, after me."

"Tom Gentry speaking for Jim Anthony. Are you there, Miss Linda Tabor?"

Miss Linda Tabor was there. Tom flushed again, hearing her cool, breathtaking voice.

"We shall land at the Anthony Pueblo sometime tonight, Miss Tabor." He liked to say her name, to roll it off the end of his tongue like a sweetmeat. "You are to assemble Dolores Colquitt, Dawkins, Mephito, Gibbons of the New York *Star*, and arrange to meet us there as soon as possible." He paused, worried. "And you too, of course," said Tom anxiously, and Jim smiled, went on speaking softly to Tom.

"Gibbons is to get in touch at once with Carlton Thames. He is to tell him that Jim Anthony desires his presence at once at the Pueblo. He is not to take no for an answer. Tell him that Anthony has positive information concerning Fifth Column activities in the U.S.A. that have to do with bombing, with sabotage, espionage, in all nefarious phases. Be sure you have it right. Carlton Thames, ex-member of the FBI, one time Attorney General. That is all."

He sat staring at the instrument in his hand, grinning like a love-stricken schoolboy. In love with a voice! The next move was impulsive. He thought she had hung up. He said, "Good night, Linda, sweetheart."

He reached with the phone for its hook. And a voice came out of it! The voice said, "Goodnight—Tom!"

Jim Anthony rocked with laughter.

CHAPTER XI
Dead—and Buried!

Stronger men than Jim Anthony might have broken under the strain of the days that followed, and even as it was, toward the last he was running on nerve alone, using up that magnificent reserve that was stored in his muscular body, as a pilot taps a reserve tank of gasoline when the main tank has taken him as far as it can. Jim Anthony wore out Tom Gentry. He sent him back to The Pueblo to recuperate. He wore out half a dozen other pilots, who might well have been listed in the category of right hand men. He wore out a score of G-men. He even wore out the seemingly inexhaustible Carlton Thames!

For neither the sea serpent nor the spawn of the sea serpent made an appearance in the next three months!

More than anything else, it was the uncertainty of the thing that was so trying and nerve-wracking. Jim Anthony had the word of a member of the coterie, the word of Nanda Jaini, that Ruric was about to direct his provocateurs, his saboteurs, and his propagandists against this country. Where, he did not know, when he did not know, and exactly how he was not certain.

He knew that the men planted by Ruric and his group would each have the unaccountable strength of twenty men, due to the extracted psythrium of the little *Herr* Doctor Guttmann. The possibilities of such a scheme were unlimited! A solitary agent planted in a munitions factory could literally wreck intricate machines with his hands alone. A solitary man, inspired by the master mind, Ruric, and filled with psythrium, could be turned loose at the base of a bridge and the result would be—destruction.

Somehow, someway, Jim Anthony knew he must get to the base of things, which was the sea serpent. Somewhere in the waters edging the United States, the great submarine monster, that marvel of mechanics, was lying in wait, ready for the moment to spew its spawn of the devil, to release them to their work of destruction.

Every possibility was run down in the next few months. The coast guard was warned. They ran down a thousand rumors. They found smuggling coves and a thousand small violations of the law, but they found no sea serpent, and no trace of one. It had to have headquarters somewhere. There was not an island off the West Coast, no matter how tiny, that was not searched well and thoroughly. And at last Jim had to face the possibility he dreaded—that it might be possible, this late in the game, for the serpent to have rounded South America and come into Atlantic waters.

Jim Anthony's father was really responsible for The Pueblo. As a matter of fact the elder Anthony had been the first white discoverer of the oasis in the middle of the desert. True, there had been many Indian tales concerning the existence of such a place, and one group of Hopis called it their Heaven. It was to them like the Valhalla of the Norsemen. Years ago, when Shean Boru Anthony had been searching this same desert for a fabulously rich lost mine, he had heard the tale. The story of a place, miles from nowhere, surrounded by acres and acres of burning sand where no man, plant, or animal could exist. And that place, according to the Indians, was Heaven, the richest oasis the world had ever known.

There were springs the waters of which held eternal youth. There were tall palms, too old and too tough to be killed by the sun. There were lush grass and tinkling brooks, and beautiful birds. And maidens. There the maidens were the beloved of heaven, beautiful, straight and sturdy of limb, flashing of eye, full-hipped and full-breasted, fit to be the mothers of many sons.

Much of these qualifications and enticements, Shean Boru had discounted. But oddly enough, the fact of the oasis, he kept. Other desert travelers, old prospectors and the like, laughed at him. Mirages, they said sagely, and let it go at that. But Shean Boru Anthony set out in search of the oasis—and found it!

He had found, as he had been certain he would not, no beautiful maidens to mother his many sons. But he had found the palms, and the cool grasses, and the brooks, and the flowers. He also found a great rock, and on that rock the remains of an oasian civilization, not large, true, but well advanced. There were no inhabitants, and no remains of corpses. He never learned what happened to the tribe.

Jim Anthony and Fawn Johntom Anthony, Jim's mother, had accompanied Shean Boru to the oasis, which he had named The Pueblo. He showed Jim why the place had never been found for the past few hundred years, why even the towering purple rock had gone unnoticed. The desert dipped into a valley at this point, and the valley sheltered the oasis. Underground springs fed it, irrigated it, and whenever white men did notice something unusual in the distance, on those few occasions when they passed this way—they shrugged it off, plodded on toward civilization, saying through dry, burned lips, "A mirage, a mirage!"

As Jim Anthony grew to manhood, as he learned about planes and the great work planes can do, he became more and more interested in the oasis, although with his customary secrecy, he kept it to himself. It was Pete Brand, with whom he had attended school, who had the idea. For Jim, flying from Los Angeles to New York with Pete as a passenger, passed over the oasis, pointed it out, interested Pete, and landed. In less than a year's time The Pueblo was unveiled to a cheering West Coast. A resort city, a city of pleasure, set in an oasis in the middle of the desert, accessible only by plane!

The West Coast movie people had taken it up first, only to be followed by the rich of the East. Visiting royalty always made it a point to stop at The Pueblo. It was more widely known than Catalina Island or Palm Springs! Jim admitted that Pete Brand had done a wonderful job. The Pueblo itself, built in the sides of the purple rock by a forgotten people, had been converted into a modern hotel, with all modern conveniences. There were swimming pools and golf courses, short but tricky, there were modern shops and stores, theaters, ball rooms, everything the modern playboy or playgirl could possibly want to amuse himself in a vacation paradise.

When Jim and Tom had left San Rosario and Jim sent word for Dolores, Linda, Dawkins, Mephito, and Carlton Thames to meet them at The Pueblo, it was for one reason alone. The Pueblo was not many miles from the Gulf of California. And sticking in the back of Jim's mind were the words of the Hindu, Nanda Jaini, spoken when the false Perez was holding a gun on Jim's head and thought he was in full control. He had said something about turning north and following the coast, something about having three thousand miles ahead of them!

Which meant, Jim figured, that their destination, then, was somewhere in the Gulf of California. And, The Pueblo being the nearest place to the Gulf that Jim controlled, he had centered on it as headquarters. Now, the Gulf of California had been searched meticulously—and there had been no trace of the sea serpent. And, because he had brought headquarters of his organization to The Pueblo, Jim continued to use it as a base, even though it necessitated many lengthy airplane flights.

Carlton Thames, man of destiny, sat across from Jim Anthony on a balcony of The Pueblo, and gazed out at the lush verdure of the oasis. Neither man spoke. Jim was taut and drawn, having just returned from a flight to the Antilles, where he had investigated rumors of the appearance of a sea serpent—and found the serpent to be the product of liquor and a school of porpoises—to his great disgust. Carlton Thames, too, was tired. He was high in political circles and ever since July had been engaged in a whirlwind campaign to convince the voters that the head of his party was the man they needed for President. Not only had he carried on his political work, but, at Jim's request, had led his own organization of ex-G-men and G-men in the search for Rado Ruric and his nefarious crew.

A soft hand was laid on Jim's arm, he turned, smiled at Dolores Colquitt who was looking down at him anxiously. She wore a brief two-piece swimming suit of yellow, which enhanced the golden glow of her sun tanned skin. The dark robe hanging loosely from her shoulders served as a background to bring richly svelte curves of her lissome figure, the firm, youthful bosom, the small waist and gently flaring hips.

Beside her stood Clive Trent, the movie star, grinning cheerfully and appreciatively as he waited. She said, "Jim, won't you come for a swim with us? You and Mr. Thames? It'll be refreshing for you both; you look so tired."

He nodded in greeting at Trent, noted with the approval of one athlete for another that the man's shoulders were wide without being too bulky, that he looked fit and in shape. To Dolores he said, "We've much to talk about, much to do. Suppose you run along, we'll join you at dinner." She patted his cheek and turned away. He said, "How's Tom feeling? I haven't seen him since I've been back."

Her answer was a giggle and a flash of mischievous eyes. "You're liable not to, either," she laughed. "Poor Tom is so much in love with little Linda that he's in a daze, poor dear!"

"Why 'poor dear'?"

She looked at him oddly, the laugh died away. "Poor dear, because he hasn't got a chance and he's beginning to realize it." And with that she and Clive Trent walked toward the elevator that was to deposit them on the street level. Jim shook his head. The one thing he couldn't figure out was a woman.

The swimming pool was magnificently constructed of black onyx, so that the water took on the appearance of cool ink. At this time in the afternoon it was fairly well occupied, trunk-clad men and scantily clad women either disporting themselves in the water or lounging on the edges of the pool. Out in the middle, on a float fashioned like an inverted top, two people were talking. Those people were Linda Tabor and Tom Gentry.

Tom looked like a sick man. His brow was corrugated, his eyes were shot with red. Never before, in all of his career, had Tom Gentry been in love. Now, peering from the corners of his eyes at Linda, clad in a black silk suit that revealed altogether too great an expanse of white velvety skin, it was all he could do to keep his hands off her. And Linda? She liked Tom. But she thought that was the extent of her feelings.

Bitterly he said, "What do you keep watching that balcony for? Hoping to get a sight of him, I suppose!"

She didn't answer. She patted his hand. But she couldn't keep down the wave of red that flooded upward over her neck and onto her cheeks. He went on, more bitterly than ever. "It isn't enough that he has more millions than he can count, more notoriety than a man could hope for! No! He has to have you, the woman I love!"

She said, "Please, Tom, you don't understand!"

"That's it, I do understand! Jim Anthony and I have been pals for seven years. Oh, he's been good enough to me, I'll be truthful. He's thrown me the crumbs, the things he didn't want." He paused there for a moment; perhaps his conscience was assailing him, for he knew in his heart that his statement wasn't true. "God knows he's drained the best out of me in return. Listen, Linda, listen to reason. You're young and romantic, but you aren't brainy enough to mix up in this organization. Beautiful, yes, and that's what Jim wants with you—your beauty!" As he talked, he became more and more bitter. "He'll find a way to use that beauty of yours, Linda, I know, and when he's used it, you'll be tossed aside, he'll be finished with you!"

Slowly she answered, "I know, I know what you're going to tell me. You're going to tell me how he used a Spanish girl named Maria Flores, a woman who loved him. How he used her, how she killed herself. But that doesn't matter, Tom. I love him, I'd admit it to his face. If it hurts you, I'm sorry. But I'll be truthful with you, always!"

Without a word Tom slid off the float and made for the shore with long, strong strokes. He climbed out of the water, blindly, started for The Pueblo. Dolores Colquitt laid a hand on his wrist, said, "Tom, guess who's here?"

He didn't even look at her. He snarled, jerked his wrist from her grasp and hurried toward The Pueblo. He wanted, most of all, to see Jim Anthony. He was going to quit!

On the balcony, Jim Anthony finally turned to the granite-faced Carlton Thames and spoke. He spoke slowly, and he spoke grimly. He said, "It won't do, Thames. Not at all. I've been to Seattle, I know what happened there, and yet you tried to keep it from me."

Thames had nerve. His eyes narrowed slightly, his lips set a bit more grimly, but he spoke evenly. He said, "All right, Jim, I didn't want you to know. But it's true. We found the man like a Moro gone amok, practically wrecking the shipyard with his bare hands. We had to shoot him. I knew you wouldn't like it, so we kept it out of the papers."

Tiredly Jim answered, "Have there been others?"

"Three others," admitted Thames. "One in Chicago, two in Hampton Roads. The same thing happened. They couldn't be held, so they were shot, and the thing hushed up."

"We'll never find out anything from dead men," snapped Jim. "It's come to this, Carlton. You're going to play it out alone, or you're going to shoot square with me. You have a larger organization than I have. But I don't believe it's as capable. You're letting your political ambitions sway you, putting them before the good of your country."

Thames smoked on in silence, his face more granite than ever, for he knew it was the truth. He wanted Jim Anthony's help, felt that he needed it, but knew the man who got credit for breaking up this ungodly ring could ride to glory in a blaze of popular acclaim. And Carlton Thames was an ambitious man.

The waiter's name was Carl. He was tall, slightly stooped, blonde, with red cheeks and blue eyes. He was a good waiter. He moved discreetly and silently to take the glasses from the table between the two men. Jim nodded at him. He was new at the hotel, but already he had called himself to Jim's attention by his dexterity. And by the fact that he was deaf. For, right before his left ear he wore the small blade button that was an acousticon.

As he moved away, Thames made his decision. He said, "I guess you're right, Jim. This country is facing a crisis with things the way they are all over the world. It's more important that we scotch the snake that threatens us than that Carlton Thames becomes Mr. Big. If you'll come up to my room, I'll show you everything I have." He arose. The waiter, Carl, was returning with fresh drinks. Carlton Thames said, "Never mind. You can bring them up to my suite."

The Thames suite was adjacent to Anthony's personal suite. There were no stairways in the hotel, but ramps, instead, corrugated crosswise to make easy going. There were elevators, of course, but Anthony and Thames took the ramp to the fourth floor of The Pueblo. On four, as they went down the hall, the elevator door opened, a man in swimming trunks plunged out and hurried past them, nearly bowling Thames over.

Jim called, "Tom. Tom Gentry!"

Gentry turned a face as black as a thunder cloud, did not answer, but went plunging on toward the suite he shared with Jim Anthony. Anthony shrugged. He'd see about that later.

They entered Thames' suite. Dawkins, the cockney valet of Jim Anthony, was straightening the room. Thames looked at Jim. Jim said, "Dawkins likes to look after my guests personally, Carlton. That'll be all now, Dawkins."

Dawkins finished his task and departed on noiseless feet. But he stopped at the door and looked at his master, gave him a look that was hot with suppressed excitement. Dawkins, evidently, had something of importance to communicate to Anthony.

For twenty minutes the two men went through the papers and reports possessed by Carlton Thames in regard to sabotage in three cities of the United States, sabotage that brought death to its perpetrators. He told him of various so called religious cults which had been broken up by FBI men because they were found to have been subversive.

Only once were they interrupted. That was when, after a discreet tap on the door, the waiter Carl entered with the drinks they had left on the porch overlooking the oasis. He fussed about a minute, Carlton Thames went on talking. After a moment he left. No one notices a waiter.

"There you are," said Carlton Thames, sitting back, his arms folded on his chest. "Now you know as much as I do. What else is there?"

"There is this." Thoughtfully Jim tapped with his fingers on the desk. "I have the names of the three men who were killed. Has it struck you that there was anything odd about them?"

Thames answered, "Only this, each of the three had been in this country but shortly. However, each came in under his country's quota. This man here for example." He tapped one of the dossiers that lay on top. "He was a Swede, named Larsen. Swedish sailor who entered in San Francisco. There was this lad Dovak. He was a Hungarian, legitimate entry—and then Morales, the Mexican."

"And they're all dead, and all buried!" Jim shook his head. "I wish to God I could have seen them, each of them."

Thames looked puzzled. "Their prints were checked, none of them had a record, Jim. What could looking at them do?"

"How about photos? No, that would hardly do, either. Might help." He arose, slapped the table with his open hand. "I've got to go to Seattle. You get on the phone and you get an order to exhume the Swede, Larsen, who tried to wreck the shipyard. I want it waiting for me when I get there."

Carlton Thames didn't ask why. He knew Jim's mind was resolved on a plan, and that he would keep that plan to himself until it was working out.

He simply said that he would do as Jim asked, and sat staring at the door as it banged behind Jim.

The truth of the matter was that Carlton Thames, just as Jim had hinted, was allowing his political glory to come ahead of anything else. He wanted his man to be president! He knew if he had a hand in solving this thing, that the presence of the serpent submarine and its crew of foreign paid scientists would catch the public fancy and sweep his candidate into the chair.

He went to the door, opened it, looked out, saw that he was unobserved, that Jim had gone. Then he went to the phone and made a call. "Miss Lamington? This is Mr. X. Suppose you come to my rooms this evening, say at six? I have the money for you. You have what I want?"

A husky voice, answered, "I have it, I'll be there."

Hardly had he hung up the phone when a tap at the door signalled the arrival of Carl, the waiter, his washed-out blue eyes beaming, his thin lips smiling as he cleared away the mess.

Thames stood at the window humming and singing, smiling to himself. Jim Anthony was a great guy, all right. But he solved things scientifically. Thames was old fashioned. He believed in baiting traps with sugar, he believed in stool pigeons, and the third degree. For example, while Jim Anthony flew off to Seattle to exhume a body, he, Carlton Thames, would, at six o'clock, lay fifty thousand dollars in front of a beautiful actress, recently from England. She would pick up the money and go. But she would leave a list. A list of names—and addresses—and one of those names would break under pressure! Would lead to the—serpent!

CHAPTER XII
A Man Unmasked

Now that day was to prove a momentous one for Jim Anthony and his cohorts, for the canker of jealousy and its companion germ of resentment had crept into his organization. For once, Jim's inherited foreboding failed to function, he did not see into the immediate future. Before he left, Mephito, his ageless grandfather warned him that danger overhung the oasis and The Pueblo. How Mephito foretold these things only the old Indian knew. But Mephito knew, Mephito knew, and tried to warn his grandson.

But Jim Anthony was too intent on the corpse of a Swedish sailor named Larsen, now buried in Seattle. Hardly had the big plane risen into the air until he set the robot pilot and retired to the efficiency apartment. There, from built in cabinets various instruments made their appearances, and Jim settled to work. He had several hours free before arriving at the Northwest city, and in those several hours he meant to accomplish much.

Back at The Pueblo, Tom Gentry sulked in a chair, drank too much, and found his love-inflamed mind turning more and more to a resentment of his chief, Jim Anthony. He did not have to close his eyes to picture Linda Tabor; she was too fresh in his mind. Before him always danced the vision of her lithe, curved body, so utterly desirable. But worst of all—though of course he had never seen it—he could picture her in Jim Anthony's arms! Jim, having her, too, when he already had so much! By God, it wasn't fair! He arose, pulled out his bags and began viciously throwing his clothes into them. He was so engaged when the worried Dawkins found him.

Dawkins said, "So 'e left without s'ying h'anything to me!"

Over his shoulder Tom Gentry snarled, "And I hope he crashes!" He didn't, of course. Should Jim get into trouble, Tom Gentry would have been the first to go to his assistance. It was simply his accumulated jealousy speaking.

Slowly Dawkins turned an accusing eye on him, his jaw set grimly, his blue little eyes seemed to blaze. "O, h'I've seen h'it coming, Tom, you bloody, blasted fool! H'I know what you mean and h'I know the reason. Women! Leave them alone, take a fool's h'advice, the h'advice of a man that knows! Leave them alone!"

Now here was grist for Tom Gentry's mill. Here was something on which to vent his anger, a something close to Jim Anthony, too! Tom's black face turned blacker, he sneered. "Just what would you know about women, you Cockney fool?"

Neither man saw Mephito enter, both were so intent. The old Indian entered like a shadow, slid in on noiseless, soundless feet, sank swiftly to his haunches and regarded the two men with intent, black eyes, his hands beneath his blanket.

"What do h'I know? You h'ask me that! Listen, h'I know this, h'I know that a bit of my past 'as caught h'up with me! H'I know the most dangerous woman h'in the world is 'ere, 'ere at the Pueblo. And h'I know she means no good, she's never meant no good! That's why h'I wanted to tell Master Anthony! Why, rawther than let 'er cross 'im h'I'd kill 'er with my h'own bloomin' 'ands!"

And afterward he was to regret those words!

Gentry grinned at him, tauntingly. He couldn't imagine Dawkins, thin, skinny Dawkins mixed up with the most dangerous woman in the world! Any more than he could credit Dawkins with the ability to kill anyone at all, let alone that same dangerous woman. His face must have said so.

For Dawkins began raging, "You traitor! Packing to go, when you're needed. H'all over a bit of a tramp that h'ain't worth the fingernails of Master H'Anthony's 'and!"

The word "tramp" was too much for Tom Gentry. With a bellow of rage he leaped for the smaller man, he grasped the front of his shirt and dragged him toward him. He crashed his right fist into the unprotected jaw and let the little man fly through the air and come up with a thud against the far wall.

"Damn you, damn you," he roared, "how dare you talk about her like that? How dare you? I'll take you apart!" He advanced on the thin little valet, while Dawkins, like a stunned dog, crouched on his hands and knees and shook his head. Suddenly Dawkins straightened, and Tom Gentry froze in his tracks. For the ugly nose of a small flat automatic was pointed at his heart.

"This was for *'er*," said Dawkins bitterly, "but h'I'll use h'it on you, s'elp me! Stop!"

They were poised like two birds of prey, waiting to spring.

Mephito said, "Ugh! Fight no good! Jim Anthony spank two of you. You, small man, put gun away; you, big man, vamoose!"

For the first time they noticed him then, and noticed that he was pointing the great horse pistol that was his favorite weapon at the pair of them. And both knew the same thing, both knew this old Indian, whose years were over a hundred, would not hesitate to press the trigger of that big gun! They could read it in his black obsidian-chip eyes, in every wrinkle and line of his face.

There was nothing else to do. Tom Gentry wheeled on his heel, turned and lumbered through the door into an adjoining room. Dawkins put the gun out of sight, straightened, went into the bathroom and washed his jaw, which already was red and swollen where Tom Gentry's fist had crashed into it.

Mephito went across the room to the fireplace. From beneath his blanket he took seven sticks, laid them in a peculiar pattern. He set a small flame to them, he took various charms and dried leaves from his buckskin pouch and added them. The smoke swirled upward in vague, uncertain streamers. After a while he grunted, pushed the sticks into the black maw of the fireplace and trotted soundlessly out the way he had come.

Dawkins moved back into the room and began straightening the various articles out of place. In the next room, with only a small hall intervening, Tom Gentry dressed—and drank. Already he had more liquor than he had ever drank before. He did not reel, he did not stumble. But before his eyes danced the desirable, lithe figure of the girl he loved—the girl who loved Jim Anthony. He heard the buzz at the bell of the main room. Curiously he tiptoed across the hall and listened at the door. And what he heard so surprised him that he sank to spying. He knelt. He opened the door a bit, he peered in breathlessly.

Elaine Lamington had to close the door herself, for Dawkins, white of face, had fallen back before her as if she were a venomous serpent coiled to strike. She was smoking, holding the cigarette loosely between her red, red lips, so that a veil of caressing smoke lingered about her face and head. She said, "Hello, Alf. Surprised? Well," she advanced toward him as he fell back step by step, "well, aren't you glad to see me?"

The table stopped him.

He said, "No, not glad to see you, Elaine. I saw you this morning, on your arrival and knew this couldn't be put off. But I'm not glad."

He talked without the trace of a cockney accent! His shoulders, too, had lost their tired droop, he stood straight and erect, so that he had to look slightly down into her mocking eyes, so close to his own. She leaned over, put the cigarette in an ashtray on the same table, and as she did so, the soft flesh of her upper arm touched his momentarily. He smelled the seductive fragrance of her hair, and with an effort, dragged his eyes away from the cool gleam of white breast revealed by her lacy negligee.

He said huskily, "You shouldn't have come here dressed like this, Elaine!"

She reached out and patted his cheek, swayed boldly against him, pouted her red, moist lips. "Why? After all, Alf, we're still married!"

It was then that he broke away and stumbled across the room, then that her taunting laughter followed him. "Afraid of me, Alf? I still affect you like that?"

"God help me you do, Elaine!"

She swayed across the room toward the white leather divan, her hips a taunt and an insult and a dare. She sat down, crossed her knees with a flourish that accented the long, breathtaking curve of knee to thigh. "Well, darling, can't you offer me a drink?"

He mixed her a drink, there was nothing else to do; but he chattered protestingly all the time. She took it, drank from it, leaving a faint red half-moon of lipstick on the glass rim. Succinctly she said, "Nuts. If anyone yells, there are a couple of things we might tell them. We might tell them the truth, that we're man and wife, who haven't seen each other for eight years. Or we might just tell them I dropped in to see Jim Anthony, your boss."

"What do you want with him?" Dawkins eyes were wild, the muscles of his jaws were like white walnuts. She laughed, waved her hand, adjusted the transparent negligee over her rounded shoulder.

"Not what you think. Don't worry, Alf. I won't tell him about you, I won't tell him you did four years at Dartmoor for espionage, that all over Europe you were known and marked as a successful spy."

"He knows about that, knows it's all behind me. He doesn't know about you, Elaine, doesn't know that I took a rap for you, and that you let me take it. Now what do you want with him?"

Her eyes narrowed. She put the glass down empty, patted the divan beside her. Dawkins was torn two ways. She still possessed an enormous physical attraction for him—so much so that he was afraid to come close to her. On the other hand, how could he find out her wants, what she intended doing, unless he acquiesced? Slowly he sat down. She put her arm carelessly about his shoulder. Her soft hip was warm against his.

"Sweet," she said, "you were a fool to drop out of the racket. I'm still a saleswoman—a seller of information." He tried to think of how she got that information she had always been so successful in obtaining—how she used her beauty, her body and her sex, for years and never hesitated for a pitying thought of what happened afterward to her deluded victims. But he kept still. She went on.

"I'm here now on call," she said. "I won't mention any names, but I've got a list your boss would like to have—your boss as well as the party who summoned me. It's worth a lot of money, Alf. You can help me make a lot more." Her arm tightened, she drew herself close to him, pressed herself eagerly against him. "This information I have to sell," she whispered, "was obtained from a man close to—Rado Ruric! Suppose I had information to take back that was valuable to—Rado Ruric. Double profits!"

That had always been her way, both ends against the middle. All information had sale value.

"Ruric fears," she whispered, "that Jim Anthony has lined out a campaign in connection with Carlton Thames. You can open Anthony's safe. Suppose we search it—darling!"

Her lips were soft against his cheek. Blood flowed hotly through his veins. Before he could stop himself, he turned and kissed her, found her lips parted and demanding, moist and warm. How long he kissed her he did not know. Nor was he but faintly conscious of her long nails at the back of his neck, moving, leaving little red marks behind them. . . .

The glass fell from the table, shattered in a thousand pieces on the floor. That tinkling broke the spell. He fought his way to his feet, looked down at the disarrayed woman on the divan who was still his wife; saw the slotted, enigmatic eyes, the petulant quivering mouth, the white skin of her bared shoulders and upper bosom, the sleek length of her thigh shadowed by the clinging sheerness of her negligee.

He remembered the past, remembered the hours of love spent together, when both of them were purveyors—and sellers—of information—to the highest bidder. And he remembered Dartmoor, how she had been willing for him to stay there four years, when a word from her would have freed him. He remembered the goodness of the past few years, trusted and respected by Jim Anthony. And it didn't take him long to decide.

He fumbled for the little flat gun with which he had menaced Tom Gentry. His voice was harsh. He said, "Elaine, get out of here. Go to your own suite, pack your clothes and get off the Oasis. Jim Anthony wants nothing to do with the likes of you. You're all that's foul and bad in a foul, bad world. Whatever you have, he doesn't need to buy. He can find out without dirtying his hands fooling with you."

She arose now, tried to come close to him. He backed away. "Don't come any closer, Elaine. And if you're not gone from here by morning—so help me God, I'll kill you!"

She spat, "Fool! You're not kidding anyone. You'll kill me to keep from telling Anthony who you really are. Don't tell me he knows your past! Well, I'm not afraid of you. I've got a good layout. I'm an accepted actress on the West Coast and no little dummy like you is going to ruin my setup. Understand?"

"Live and let live. Until you come around Jim Anthony, Elaine. Then it's—death, and you've never known me to fall down."

She turned and hard-heeled across the room. The door clicked shut. A second later Dawkins left the room as well. In the bedroom he found Tom Gentry sleeping—apparently sleeping, at least.

CHAPTER XIII
MURDER!

HERE IN THE OFFICES OF CARLTON THAMES, all was in readiness for Jim Anthony's arrival at Seattle, though there was much disgruntled comment by the local police force. Nevertheless, the Thames influence was enormous—they complied with all requests. Hardly an hour after Jim's arrival, the body of the so-called Swede, one Axel Larsen, was stretched on an autopsy slab in the city morgue.

The big plainclothesman said, "See, here's nine bullet wounds, any one of which should have proven fatal. Me, I been a copper twenty years, and never did I see such a tough monkey."

But Jim wasn't looking at the bullet wounds. He was carefully arranging various surgical instruments on a table, instruments he had brought in the plane with him. The big detective's voice went droning on and on, telling how this Larsen had run amok in the shipyards, how, using only his bare hands he had smashed precision machinery and giant presses, how he had battled with and overcome a crew of tough shipyard workers, how he had battered a riot squad, oblivious of their clubs, and at last had been killed, shot down by police bullets.

Now Jim was arranging a series of what appeared to be common flashlights, beside the instruments on the table. Almost idly he said, "Look, this yard where he was killed, what's their contract?"

"Cruisers and torpedo boats, English, I believe."

Jim nodded. That fit in with his theories. At last, drawing on a pair of rubber gloves, he turned to the body. He said, "Better leave me alone, mister. Orders." The detective shrugged, paused long enough to light a cigar, and left the room.

Jim Anthony went to work with the instruments. He took one of the lights, turned it on. It burned with the brilliance of twenty ordinary lights, casting a glow as white as burning magnesium. Very cautiously he extracted three blond hairs from the man's head, used tweezers to extract three blond whiskers. These he placed on the slide of a powerful microscope and examined.

He was breathing hard when he had finished, his eyes shining. With a great magnifying glass he examined the man's scalp, he probed the bone structure of the cheekbones and the nasal passages. His next move almost nauseated him, but in the interests of the country he loved, he went to work, first turning the cadaver on its stomach. The scalpel flew. Moments later, still a bit sick, he put a piece of parchment-like substance in a shallow pan of chemical solution.

A moment or so later a detective with an oversized bump of curiosity peeped through the keyhole. He went back to his fellows to report that the damned Indian had about sixteen different colored lights turned on the stiff. Outside of that, he had nothing to report.

At about the same time, Tom Gentry was saying hotly to Linda Tabor, on the second floor veranda of the Pueblo, "He's not nearly as infallible as you think! He isn't perfect! He's not the knight in shining armor on a white horse! Even his methods aren't the pure holy things they're cracked up to be!"

She turned to him, wide eyed. "Just what do you mean? Tom, knocking Jim Anthony isn't going to help you with me."

But he was too far gone with his own thwarted passion and jealousy to draw back now. He said, "I'll tell you what I mean—I mean he's got a bunch of thugs and criminals working for him that he keeps in the background! Take that guy Dawkins, the one he calls his valet! He's been an international spy, a man who'd obtain and sell any information for hire! That's the type Jim Anthony employs!" His bitter voice went on and on. He'd had too much to drink. And the more he repeated the vague stories—and some were not so vague—the more he grew to believe them himself.

Three people overheard—three who were sitting on the veranda. And a fourth. Dolores Colquitt sat talking to Gibbons, the tall and gangling editor of the New York *Star*. Carlton Thames was on the other side of a pillar. All heard. It was Gibbons who got up, took off his glasses, walked around the pillar and said coldly, "Gentry, you're drunk. Get up to your room before I beat your head off."

Gentry liked that. He was spoiling for trouble. He unfolded like a steel spring. He threw his left into Gibbons' stomach, caught him flush on the jaw with his right and knocked him, skidding on his shoulders, a full twenty feet across the veranda.

He turned, swaggering to the girl who had leaped to her feet at the first sign of trouble. He said, "Should we go in and have a drink?" And, when she held back, swept away by his own arrogance, "If Jim Anthony were here, I'd do him the same way!"

Linda Tabor said, "Go away! I hate you! I hate you!"

Carlton Thames was already propelling his athletic body up the ramp toward the room where he was to buy his information. He was grinning. Thames was a good man, he was a big man, and he was almost sure to land on top in the coming election. Because he was so strong, he resented strength—perhaps he was jealous of it—in others. For years the Anthony organization had been almost infallible. Now, it seemed to be cracking up, and it pleased him immensely. For there was this about it. He thought of a certainty that he was about to come into a list of the leading Fifth Columnists of this country, men who were responsible for at least ninety percent of all the subversive associations and organizations in operation, traitors who directed all the gnawing from within. And because Anthony's organization was showing signs of breaking down—well, he, Carlton Thames would not have to share the glory with anyone at all!

He whistled as he rounded the hall corner and headed toward his own palatial suite. He had left the door open purposely, expecting the woman, Elaine Lamington, who was to sell out the Fifth Columnists. He knew she would be there waiting. He opened it softly, smiling as he noted the light burning. A few more minutes and Carlton Thames would be well on his way to political fame and fortune. The man who saved the United States from the Fifth Column! He could almost visualize the caption beneath the picture of his own smiling countenance.

Almost instinctively he sensed something wrong. A heavy table stood in the center of the room. The overhead chandelier was lighted, but the lamp that had stood on the table was lying down, broken, on its side on the floor. The drawer barely hung in position, and a great mass of papers lay scattered over the thick rug. Now, those papers were hardly of any definite importance to Carlton Thames—but they did denote the presence of a marauder!

He leaped into the room with an oath, scurried for the bedroom—where the wall safe, especially installed for his own use, was behind the mirror of his dresser. And as he leaped, he dragged the .32 automatic from his pocket that he had carried since the time he was a G-man.

The mirror of the dresser had been swung aside. The safe was open. The top of the dresser, and the floor before it was covered with papers, papers whose safety had meant life and death—not only to Carlton Thames—but to dozens of other people. The safe had been looted!

For a split second, he stood there staring at that open safe. Then, from behind the end of the dresser a man raised up swiftly. In one hand he bore a handful of papers which he had plucked from the floor. In the other was—a gun.

Carlton Thames fired. The bullet plowed a furrow across the little man's scalp, knocked him back against the wall. Consciousness and understanding faded from his eyes, his mouth slacked open, blood from his plowed scalp trickled like a blind red worm across his right eyebrow. Carlton Thames fired again. Dust seemed to leap from the lapel of the little man's coat. He moaned once and hit the floor with a thud. With smoking gun and hot eyes Carlton Thames stood over him.

Behind him he heard hurrying footsteps, uneven, but direct. He whirled, his finger tight on the trigger. The newcomer was Tom Gentry. Gentry was, suddenly, sober. All he could see was the victim's feet and legs protruding from behind the dresser.

"I heard the shot—" he managed, and stepped closer to see who the man on the floor might be. "By God, by God, it's Dawkins! Dawkins! Why'd you shoot him?"

"It's obvious, isn't it?" snarled Thames, his gun making a circular gesture that took in the suite. "I only hope to God I got him before he—" He was about to say "learned too much," but thought better of it and bit his lip. What was Gentry saying?

Gentry lost his head. He said, "I knew it, I knew it. After I saw that woman, after I heard her try to persuade him to loot Jim's safe! Find the woman and—!"

"What woman?"

"I don't know how she's registered, but she's really Dawkins' wife. She came into our suite looking for him just this evening." His cheeks flushed a bit, he licked at his lips. "I happened to overhear them," he finished lamely.

"Well, don't stand there like a dummy!" Thames was used to command. "This place is air conditioned and soundproof. If I hadn't left the door open you'd not have heard the shot. Hurry, man, get a wet towel!"

And, as Gentry scurried toward the bathroom, Thames knelt quickly over the valet of Jim Anthony. Practised fingers went through him, and he found, to his astonishment, that the pockets were not filled with papers as he had thought. He took time enough to note that the man was shot in the shoulder as well as the scalp, then began scrambling through the debris and papers on the floor. A voice quavering with excitement floated out frantically from the bathroom:

"My God, Mr. Thames! Come here, quick!"

There was so much terror and horror in the voice of Tom Gentry that Thames reluctantly postponed his search for the moment and went for the bath. There was no doubt in his mind as he hurried across the room. Dawkins must have taken the letters and papers he could so ill afford to lose and passed them to a confederate, probably his wife, then come back—?

By now he was at the door of the black and chromium bathroom. Tom Gentry pointed to the tub. There were no words spoken for long seconds, for the scene was one of horror.

Elaine Lamington lay on her back in the sunken bath. There were no marks of violence on her. The only way they could tell so instantaneously that she was dead was that her face was looking directly upward into their faces. Her head was literally twisted into reverse on her lithe body. Her hair was as perfectly waved and set as if she had just come out of a beauty shop. She still wore the same negligee Tom Gentry knew she had worn when she came to visit her husband that afternoon. And the long folds hung in perfect array.

Hoarsely Gentry said, "He did it, by God he killed her, just like he promised her he would!"

A thousand things leaped through the ambitious mind of Carlton Thames in split seconds. For a moment he listened to the upset Gentry as he babbled the threats he had heard Dawkins make to this woman that same afternoon. And he suddenly thought of the list she had been going to sell him, suddenly thought of the money he had for her. It had been in the safe, too!

He snapped, "Beat it in there and look around by the safe for money, a lot of money."

Tom trotted out. Thames didn't care so much for the money. He had ample backing, he was rich in his own right. But he did care for that list of Fifth Columnists! He managed to heel the door shut, dropped to his knees beside the lovely corpse, and in the space of moments searched her completely.

She didn't have the money. It wasn't in her stocking tops. It wasn't anywhere at all about her—nor was the so important list that would sweep him to the heights. He stalked out of the bathroom just as Dawkins shook his head weakly, groaned, and sat up, clutching his wounded shoulder.

Dawkins sat in a chair, tried to keep himself from toppling out. There was a plaster over his furrowed scalp, a strip of towel was bandaged about his shoulder. The bone had not been touched, nevertheless the ravages of intense pain were visible in the deep lines of the little Englishman's face.

"Cut out that accent," snapped Thames. "Gentry tells me you can talk as well as anyone."

The feverish eyes of the Englishman flashed to Gentry, who reddened and looked away.

"I've been trying to tell you for five minutes that it's all a mistake. Mr. Thames, you know as well as I know that Master Anthony instructed me to care for you personally during your visit. I simply came in—"

"How'd you get in?" It was time for bluff, rough and tough.

"I have a passkey. However, it was not necessary, the door was open." He paused, as if waiting to see if the big man, Thames, believed him. Then he went on. "The lights were on. There wasn't anyone in the living room, but the table had been searched. I—I—usually carry a gun—" His eyes couldn't meet those of Thames at that remark. "—and thinking the marauder or thief might still be here, I drew the gun and came in to this room. You know the rest. I was picking up, straightening up the papers and you came in. I guess I'd forgotten to lay the gun down. You thought I was about to shoot you—and you shot me instead!"

Thames glared at him, snorted in disbelief. "You know a woman named Elaine Lamington." A flicker of fear passed over the little man's face. He started to shake his head, thought better of it.

Thames didn't let the words get out of his mouth. He leaned forward, so that his face was but inches from that of the wounded man. "Don't lie. She was your wife. Both of you have been spies all your lives! Gentry overheard her proposition to rifle Anthony's safe! You must have gotten together and figured there'd be more loot in mine."

"No, sir! You're right, I wouldn't question Mr. Gentry's word, sir. But I told her this afternoon if she mixed in Jim Anthony's business, I'd kill her myself!"

Carlton Thames glanced significantly at Tom Gentry. He could be very suave when he wanted to be. He smiled. He said, softly, "And you meant it? You'd kill your wife if she did anything untoward to Jim Anthony—or a cause of Jim Anthony's?"

"Jim Anthony gave me another chance, sir. He's been father, mother, sister, and wife to me. Should I let her interfere? I would kill her first!"

Thames sighed as he reached for the valet's arm. He gestured for Gentry to take the other, but Tom, already ashamed of his part in the affair, hung back. So Thames took the shaky Englishman across the room to the door of the bath. He leaned him against the wall. He drew the curtain of the shower to one side like an art dealer might whisk aside the curtain covering a masterpiece.

Dawkins gasped at that masterpiece of murder. He stared, as if unable to tear his eyes away, gasped, his Adam's apple weaving. "Elaine, Elaine," he said brokenly, and sank to his knees beside the corpse of the woman who had been at once his Circe and his Nemesis.

"You fulfilled your threat," snapped Thames. "You did it. Look, Dawkins, at the scratches on your neck, the mark of nails. You'll never get out of this, you wife-killer! Analysis will show the skin from your neck beneath her nails, where she scratched you as you twisted her neck. No one but a husband, an ex-lover, would have rearranged her clothing, fixed her hair so lovingly in that tub. You killed her, Dawkins, rather than split with her. You have, somewhere, a list that she was bringing me. You have concealed, somewhere, a great amount of money I had to pay for that list."

"No, no! I didn't! Not Elaine! I threatened, but I didn't do it!"

Thames led him from the bathroom, put him back in the same chair. Breeze from the palmed oasis blew through the window, tossed his damp hair down into his eyes. "Shall I tell you why you came back? She told you of the list, she told you of the money. You got them both, killed her, went out and concealed your loot. Then thinking there might be other papers of value, you came back, you fool!"

"No, no!" The moan of a stricken animal.

"Dawkins, I'll be reasonable. There were lists, affidavits and the like in that safe that I don't want to use. Keep the money, return the documents, and I'll give you an hour's start."

"No, I didn't do it. Tom Gentry, call Jim. Get him here. He won't see this thing pinned on me, I tell you."

A hand reached around the door. A forefinger touched the light switch. The lights went out. There was a sudden commotion in the room, the sound of hurrying, scurrying bodies, the thud of a heavy man hitting the floor, the scream of Thames, "Catch him, catch him, he's getting away!"

Jim Anthony sat back wearily in the huge employment agency at Seattle. He surveyed the group of eager faces, faces of men he had just hired. "Your pay," he said tiredly, "will be more than you have ever made before in your life. I have shipments of the material we need coming into town via fast plane. You will live and eat on the job. Some of you are electricians, some lens grinders, some X-ray technicians. Three days of this intensive work should clear it up. If there is any man among you who cannot absent himself from home and friends for that length of time, let him drop out."

No one dropped out.

Later, from the direct radio in his plane, Jim spoke to the hotel, The Pueblo, that was the oasis. Linda Tabor turned on the mechanical contrivance that recorded his voice. The message was for Carlton Thames, and as it was recorded, she could not help but hear it.

"In the three cases you withheld from me, Thames, you named the saboteurs as Swedish, and various other nationalities, all of them entering the U.S.A. under their own quotas. An examination of the corpse of Larsen, the supposed sailor, scientifically proves to me that he is not a Swede. The man is a Hindu."

He paused. The little record went on and on, unheeded. Linda Tabor was all ears.

"Some special blend of herbal preparation, doubtlessly perfected by *Herr* Doctor Guttmann, has been used to bleach the hair as well as to take the pigment out of the skin. Super strength was achieved by the drinking of psythrium, which is based on *yerba mate*, and whose action can be explained again for you by Tom Gentry. Delicate surgical operations were performed to change the body structure of the skull, the nose, the chin, and so forth. No doubt a similar examination of the corpses of the other men caught sabotaging and the like will prove them also to be Hindus."

Linda thought: "How tired he is! How utterly worn out his voice sounds." He went on.

"The serpent-submarine of Rado Ruric is at this moment lying offshore the United States, discharging its remade Hindus into this country. We have learned from the man Nanda Jaini, before his decapitation, that Hindus were willing to help Ruric in return for his promised aid in their own country. No doubt this could have been discovered sooner. To dig out these subversive workers, I have worked out a formula for a Z-ray eye-glass lens which I have called WEZ7X for identifying purposes. I am now working with a full crew on the production of thousands of pairs of spectacles containing Z-ray lenses. I intend for the immigration officers at every port of entry in our country to have a pair, so that the remade Hindus may be swiftly detected. The Z-ray spectacle, turned on every face, unbeknownst to the owner of that visage, causes remade skin—such as that de-pigmentized by Ruric on the man called Larsen—to glow with an orange fluorescence. I also want every member of the FBI to have a set of these glasses. Every man investigated for subversive activities can thus be clarified, as working on his own hook, or being in the pay of Rado Ruric and a foreign power. Some of these rats, once captured alive, captured before they can drink the strength making psythrium can be forced to talk. That is all for the present. In three days I return."

He flipped off his set, and the receiver at once broke into voice. "Jim Anthony, Jim Anthony, Carlton Thames speaking. An emergency has arisen. A woman agent of the powers of which you speak has been murdered in my own suite. Various monies and papers have been stolen from me. This was done by one of your own men, Alfred Dawkins, who has been an international spy for years. The woman he killed was his own wife! While I was questioning Dawkins, the light was suddenly turned out in the room and he disappeared. I immediately grounded all planes, the man will be captured. Advise your movements under the circumstances."

Jim's voice came back to Carlton Thames. It was as grim as ever. "It will take me three days to manufacture and distribute the correct number of Z-ray spectacles. I will be at The Pueblo at the end of that time. I tell you this, Thames, Dawkins killed no one. And I promise you this—if you capture him and harm one hair of his head, you'll answer to me. That is all. Three days from now I will be with you."

The machine clicked off.

CHAPTER XIV
HOAX OR REALITY?

DAWKINS' WIFE, ELAINE LAMINGTON, had met her death on Tuesday night. By Wednesday noon the first of the Z-ray spectacles were being rushed via fast plane to their destinations. By Wednesday night they were being turned out with precision and quickness in the Seattle factory taken over by Jim Anthony and his newly hired crew. But not until Friday did Jim slow down and take stock. A careful check of his records of production showed that hundreds of pairs of the glasses, with their attached batteries, etc., had been distributed to the FBI men. All immigration men at all ports of entry were provided with them. Police chiefs of various larger cities, particularly those cities that were railheads, or possessed immense factories turning out war supplies, received a set, along with detailed instructions as to their use.

Not until Friday, when the work had been successfully completed, did Jim think about what had occurred in The Pueblo. His mind was like that. Through long training he had enabled himself to think of one important subject at a time, concentrating to the limit of his great ability, with no outside interference, no worries and cares induced by other objects. But now, circling the flying field at Seattle in his great Douglass, heading back toward The Pueblo, he began thinking and figuring.

Shortly he set the robot pilot and went into the great cabin of the plane. His fatigue showed plainly on his face. His shoulders drooped wearily, the whites of his eyes were shot with tiny red veins. Yet, tired as he was, he knew there was no rest for him. He must do two things. He must plan to catch the real murderer of the woman—and he was convinced that that murderer was not Dawkins—and he must prepare for Rado Ruric's next move.

He opened the door of a compartment and revealed a great spool of the same sort of plastic cord he wore in the mechanical belt about his waist. He pulled on the end, again and again, until the gut like stuff made a pile at his feet. He dropped on a couch, took what appeared to be a big, wooden crochet hook from its place, and began to work.

An ordinary observer might have thought the great Jim Anthony was taking up crocheting, or tatting! For his fingers flew nimbly, though his mind was far away at The Pueblo. Bit by bit the plastic cord grew into a thing that looked like a fishnet. On and on sped the plane through the deepening shadows. After awhile Jim reached up and switched on the radio phone. Presently he had The Pueblo, and, in answer to his request, the soft, magical voice of Linda Tabor filled the exquisite cabin of the great plane.

For three days Jim Anthony had been out of touch with the world. He had not seen a newspaper, he had not heard a newscast. Now all fatigue seemed to fall away from him as Linda's modulated voice told of his success.

"This is an excerpt from the New York *Star*," she breathed, and began reading. Jim had the grace to flush. Gibbons, the editor, had gone to town, and because he worshipped Jim Anthony, he placed credit where credit was due.

"—not only," continued the article, "did Anthony solve the ways and means of the Fifth Columnists, but he figured a way to detect them, to single them out, to find each and every member of Rado Ruric's dangerous organization. These men, as he has explained and proven, are Hindus! Men whose skin has been de-pigmentized, whose hair has been bleached and re-colored, through the botanical genius of *Herr* Doctor Hans Guttmann, formerly of San Rosario. These men, according to Anthony, who has seen it work, are given cocktails of a drug called psythrium, which makes them not only practically impervious to pain, but endows their bodies with inspired muscles, makes them as strong as twenty men!"

There was silence for a minute. The modulated voice dropped to a whisper. It said, suddenly, "Jim Anthony, Jim Anthony, listen quickly, I am all alone!"

He quit work, sat bolt upright, tuned his radio louder.

"Dawkins did not kill the woman, Jim Anthony. I have no proof except my own instinct. He is a trusted friend of yours, and I know your trust would not be misplaced. I overheard that awful Thames browbeating him, so I flipped off the lights. I have him con—"

Silence! Silence! Jim fiddled quickly with the dial. Suddenly the radio broke in again, as if Linda Tabor had never passed along the information!

"Through the use of the Z-ray spectacles, invented and distributed by Jim Anthony, already nineteen members of the Ruric organization have been discovered. Each was detected before he had an opportunity to drink the small vial of psythrium with which each is provided. Two of these men have already broken under questioning and admitted all details, verifying facts as released recently by Jim Anthony. Members of the FBI are jubilant. They claim that it is a matter of hours only before Rado Ruric is brought to justice and the most feared criminal these States have ever known returned to the death house to pay for his crimes against society."

Jim flipped off the radio. He even shook his head at the foolishness of the FBI in underrating Rado Ruric. He knew the capabilities of the man's mind, knew that he, like Anthony himself, never entered into a thing without planning for all eventualities.

He folded the net he had constructed, stored it away, began on another. He thought of Linda Tabor, smiled, thinking of her loyalty to a chief she hardly knew. It troubled him a bit. But he thrust the thought resolutely aside. Presently the radio broke in again. And this time, when he answered, it was Dolores Colquitt.

She said, "I want to tell you all that has happened concerning Dawkins and the murder of his wife. She was his wife, Jim, there's no doubt about that." And she repeated, in great detail, all that had been made public concerning the killing and the disappearance of Dawkins. When she had finished, another voice said, "This Mephito. Mephito know much, too. Mephito see Tom Gentry and Dawkins have fight—mostly because Tom Gentry love-mad over Tabor squaw. Tabor squaw love Jim Anthony."

Jim gasped, reddened. Behind Mephito he could hear Dolores Colquitt's giggle. He listened carefully while Mephito went into great detail concerning the working of a lovesick man's mind, and Mephito knew a lot! And suddenly Mephito's cracked old voice ceased. There was silence. Jim said, "Hello, hello, Mephito. Go ahead, I'm listening." But the voice that came back, bitter and broken, was not that of Mephito.

Tom Gentry said, "It's true, it's all true enough, Jim, all that Mephito has told you. If I hadn't been crazy jealous, I wouldn't have helped Thames pin this on Dawkins. I don't think Dawkins did it, not for a minute. I was wrong, Jim, all wrong and I feel responsible. I'm going away now, I've done enough damage."

"Tom, you fool! In a couple of hours I'll be there, and you're in full charge until I arrive, do you understand? You can't dump me now! You're going to stay!"

Tom snapped, "Just a minute, Jim, there's a newscast coming in. Tune your regular radio. Let's get it."

Jim didn't have to tune his regular radio—it was already set at the proper wavelength, as usual. A newscaster made his introductory speech, spoke briefly of toothpaste and began reading comments and communiqués from England, and China and the Mediterranean. Impatiently Jim started to turn back to his phone, but hesitated.

"Authorities are unable to determine," said the pleasant voiced announcer, "whether the following report is a hoax or not. Three Los Angeles men, all a bit the worse for drink and fright, have reported sighting the sea serpent early this morning some forty miles south of Craigville. According to these men the serpent was nonchalantly headed for the desert. They paused to see no more. Planes have been searching for it all day with no success. It is thought the serpent was really crawling out of a whiskey bottle rather than across the desert."

Back on the phone Anthony snapped, "Now you'll have to stick around, Tom. There's much for you to do. I'm inclined to think the report is authentic. What has Ruric got to lose? Suppose he's jived his Hindus all up with psythrium and stuck them in the serpent. They're headed for The Pueblo, desperate because their plans have all gone wrong. It's Ruric's dying effort, his last convulsive effort! He's after me, he's after Thames. Now listen closely, and make these preparations.

"Get everyone off the Oasis that can be packed aboard the transport planes. All the guests, everyone you can possibly load. But there'll still be some of you left. Issue the thin light gas masks to everyone that stays behind. Go to the cupboard, the east one, in my laboratory and open it carefully. You'll find what looks like a stack of brown saucers. Handle them carefully, Tom, if you value your life! From the report, the serpent approaches from the southwest. Go out in the desert, southwest of The Pueblo, and scatter those bombs around, for that's what they are, Tom, my own type of tank bombs. They're dangerous, so dangerous I couldn't dare make them pressure bombs, but they are radio controlled. Do that as quickly as possible, Tom. That is all."

He cursed a bit beneath his breath because he had not had time to construct more nets of the plastic cord that was so phenomenally strong. But that was behind him now. He hurried to the controls of the big plane, cut in another engine, watched the hand of the speedometer pick up slowly, slowly. The plane was making almost half a thousand miles an hour.

He stood in the center of the cabin with his head bowed in thought. The secret of Jim Anthony's success was his ability to make preparations, to meet all obstacles as they were thrown in his path. He was asking himself: what if the serpent comes in from another direction? He did not underestimate Ruric's cunning. He opened a cabinet and took out a four foot bar of what appeared to be glass, a bar hardly thicker in diameter than an ordinary pencil. Would it work, or wouldn't it? It was still in the experimental stage, this stuff he called Corghion. Yes, it looked like glass, it was transparent and frail and light to hold, but it had a dozen times the strength of steel—perhaps more than that, for Jim Anthony had never so far had sufficient opportunity to give it real test.

He grinned at that thought. Certainly here was a time for the test, but he wished it could have been made under more auspicious circumstances. He laid the rod of Corghion with the fishnets of plastic, extracted a small box that was filled with radio apparatus from the cabinet and put it with the other stuff. Then he opened the sliding hatch in the bottom of the cabin and looked carefully down at the small thing resembling a miniature plane, anchored beneath the giant Douglass.

Yes, Jim Anthony believed in preparation. When he had left The Pueblo for Seattle he had taken the serpent and its clouds of chemical dust into consideration! The small plane riding on the landing gear of the Douglass was not a plane at all.

It was a glider!

CHAPTER XV
List of the Dead

Luckily, Tom Gentry got exactly what he needed to cure him—action. And Tom Gentry was equal to the emergency. There were, perhaps, including the staff and guests, some five hundred people on the Oasis. In less than an hour's time he had nearly all of them safely loaded aboard planes and headed for the West Coast and safety. He opened the cabinet, as directed, and stared suspiciously at the stack of brown saucers in the corner. They were not so much like saucers, he decided, as they were like the thin pads often distributed in beer gardens, on which a stein or bottle of beer is set. Gingerly he took an immense armload, took a small tractor car out into the desert southwest of The Pueblo and distributed the tank bombs as Jim had told him to do. He reported all this via radio phone, laughing as he reported.

"Mephito," he giggled, "has his horse pistol in his hand and is patrolling the streets. He thinks he is the equal of any serpent that ever existed. A couple of the waiters refused to go, Thames stayed on with the two men who are his bodyguards, Linda and Dolores wouldn't leave. Any more instructions?"

"Just that you stay masked, all of you. The serpent is no doubt so well camouflaged that it can't be spotted from the air. I—"

"Look, Jim, you said those tank bombs were radio controlled. I gather from that you intend exploding them yourself. All right, if the serpent is so well camouflaged, how are you going to spot it?"

"Don't bother your head about that. As a matter of fact, I've got a set of ultra-violet ray spectacles with me. I'll—good grief, what was that?"

For floating over the ether came the sound of a woman's shrill hysterical scream, a scream of horror and fear. Jim heard Tom's excited voice calling, "Dolores! Calm down! What is it, Dolores? Dolores!"

He could hear Dolores' voice explaining something in the background, could hear the patter of running feet—then silence! He jeered again at the speedometer, estimated that he would reach the Oasis in less than an hour. Then, Tom's voice again.

"Jim, are you there? There's been more killing here, Jim! Both the fellows, the bodyguards that stayed with Thames, both of them, dead in the bar. The bar was deserted, you know. Dolores went down for brandy and found them.

Both with their necks twisted, exactly like the neck of that woman, Elaine Lamington. Jim, you don't suppose Dawkins—?"

"Nonsense! How could the little man get strength enough to—?"

He quit at that. For both he and Tom Gentry were having the selfsame thought. Little, yes, Dawkins was a small man. But—? Tom and Jim both remembered the skinny *peons* in San Rosario, who literally lifted and carried a Ford truck down the street. Could Dawkins have somehow obtained a drink of psythrium? Had he gone suddenly insane, crazy for revenge, a mad killer? Perhaps he was trying to get at Thames, and knew those bodyguards stood in the way!

"Where's Thames?" roared Jim.

And the heavy voice of Thames, panting with excitement, came to him. "I'm here—by the skin of my teeth! Jim, that damned serpent is about twenty-five miles due southwest, ambling right along toward us! I never saw such a thing in my life! I took my plane out to do scout duty, saw what looked like a stretch of sand moving, dove over it and was damned near killed for my pains." Jim knew! Chemical dust! Thames went on. "I had to make a forced landing when the motor conked out, and had to run nearly three quarters of a mile! Whew!"

"Could you estimate their speed?" snapped Jim, observing his own speedometer anxiously.

"Couldn't be doing over forty. Some kind of tractor appliances as far as I could make out. How far away are you?"

Jim grinned like a wolf! He was going to make it! He'd get there in time to intercept the mechanical monster! "Not long," he sang out exultantly. "*I'll be there! In time!*"

It was the longest twenty minutes Jim Anthony ever spent in his life. For once, the ability to turn his imagination on or off like water from a faucet refused to function. *He had to get there!* He knew no one on the Oasis possessed the ability to stop the superstrong Hindus. He put himself in Ruric's place. Suppose he made the oasis, what would he do? He'd loose immense clouds of that chemical dust, scatter it with fans, all over the Oasis. Why, the stuff was so powerful that the mechanisms of every gun it reached would be ruined almost instantaneously.

Gas? If he estimated the cunning and ability of Rado Ruric correctly the arch criminal would be well prepared for gas! He could picture those man-made Samsons running amok through the deserted streets of the Oasis town. Pulling it down in ruins about them, uncaring whether they lived or died as long as they destroyed and killed! This would be Rado Ruric's revenge. Full payment for the spectacle rays that ruined his plans for Fifth Column activities.

He had to get there in time! And then, with his glasses adjusted, peering out of the window of the plane toward the south, he saw it! Through the glasses it was purple, a purple snake humping and weaving its way across the desert! Quickly he looked to his left—the bomb field, sown by Tom Gentry at his command, glowed purple through the glasses! A series of tiny purple flares, it appeared. And the serpent was headed directly for it!

Quickly Jim climbed in the Douglass! He needed altitude for this! Far below him he saw that he had been spotted, for the serpent began spouting greasy clouds of the chemical dust, not from its mouth alone, but all along its body! Jim grinned in delight, as he noted that the glasses enabled him to see through the smoke as if it were not there, still enabled him to make out the serpent itself and the deadly bomb field ahead of it.

He gathered the paraphernalia he had assembled, opened the hatch and climbed down into the sturdy little glider. First, of course, he set the mechanical robot, to bring the plane down in a dead stick landing a little farther on. He did not want to risk the engines of the Douglass.

At five thousand feet he cast off the glider, went soaring down toward the desert in the engineless plane. The radio control was in his hand! Below him, through the pall of smoke he saw the serpent, crawling, crawling, toward that field of purple fluorescence that meant mines! Exultantly he threw his voice into the breeze, "Goodbye, Ruric, I've got you now!"

Four thousand feet. The serpent moved relentlessly as the hands of time. Now the nose of the thing was in the field of purple light! Down went Jim's forefinger on the radio control! The glider rocked and swayed in the blast that followed! With difficulty Jim kept it on an even keel, while he watched over the side.

What was that! The head of the serpent was no more, the head and a section of the body! But what was that? Look at the tail! The tail detached itself, the section ahead of the tail, and the section ahead of that! And suddenly Jim understood. The serpent was made of separate sections, just as a giant liner is made unsinkable through the use of bulkheads closing off many sections! Now below him Jim saw a series of sections spread out fanwise, like the *panzer* sections of a *blitzkrieg*. He banked the little glider so sharply that he almost went into a spin, and at that, did go into a steep glide. Up and down he worked the radio lever.

Explosion after explosion resulted in the minefield! Sections of iron and fragments of flame shot by him! The left wing of the glider, struck by a piece of steel I-beam, suddenly crumpled. Jim had just time enough to bail out and pull the cord of his parachute. The black blossom that was his chute brought him up with a jerk. He peered down through the chemical dust. How many of those tanks had gotten through? Had any—and then he saw them! Two of them plunging straight ahead toward The Pueblo! Another scuttling rapidly to the right at a tangent! Three had gotten through!

Grimly he tugged at the shrouds of his parachute. He had to get ahead of them, had to get in between them and the unprotected people on the oasis. As the tugging on the shrouds released the air from the chute, he hurtled faster and faster to his right. He had to risk it, had to risk a speedy landing!

As it was, he made it. Fifty yards ahead of the oncoming tanks. But he landed so hard that momentarily he was stunned. It was hard for him to breathe through the transparent envelope of his gas mask, but he dare not lift it on account of the chemical dust. He tried to move, found his left leg either numb from the fall, or sprained. And through the dust he saw the first tank, bearing down on him! He summoned every muscle, summoned all his will power, and as he rolled, he saw that he was observed, for the tank altered its direction to run him down!

To die now, when so much depended on him? He drew the bar of Corghion from his belt, gathered all his muscles for a final effort and waited. It loomed nearer and nearer now, a streamlined tank, weighing tons, its great treads eating up the distance across the sand! Now!

With a magnificent effort Jim rolled swiftly aside. The tread missed him by inches! He took the bar, thrust it into the caterpillar tread and into the side of the armored tank itself! He dug his heels into the sand, grasped the bar with both hands and strained his back into it. For a moment it felt as though the veins would burst in his head, the tendons pop in his throat. His very jaws hurt with the effort. But he was rewarded! For with a great crackle and crash, one at a time the sections of the caterpillar tread began breaking out! The Corghion worked! It was stronger than the tread on a tank.

Suddenly he withdrew the bar, thrust his hand into his belt again. The tank, with its tread disabled, and pushed by that on the opposite side, began going around and around in a circle. He caught a glimpse of a goggled and masked face peering through a slot at him. Then, staggering to his feet, Jim took the object he had taken from his belt and hurled it at the face! The face disappeared. The object flew into the tank, and Jim Anthony turned and ran as he had never run before—in the direction of the second tank. Behind him he heard the blast of the explosion resulting from the grenade he had tossed into the disabled tank. It threw him flat on his face.

Half blind, his ears ringing, he stumbled to his knees. And saw that the second tank had turned and was headed for him! Could he do it again? Did he have enough strength left to break the tread of this one?

He was never to find out. For the tank stopped. A door opened. A masked figure stepped out of the tank, leveled a gun at Jim Anthony and squeezed the trigger. All the animal instincts of a thousand years, all the primitive instincts of his primeval ancestors helped Jim Anthony then. For no sooner had he glimpsed the gun than he started rolling. Once something burned across his left shoulder, but that was the only time he was hit.

He counted to seven, seven shots in the automatic, then got to his knees. The masked man dropped the gun, started toward Jim with his bare hands. Jim waited, grinning. The man wasn't large! He wasn't so big. And then Jim remembered the so-called Larsen, how it had taken nine pistol bullets to stop him! Larsen had been full of psythrium! And this man, small or not small, was the same!

Often, afterward, Jim thought about what followed with a thrill of horror. Often he dreamed about it. For Jim Anthony, master fencer, used that thin pointed stick of Corghion like an epee. The man moved slowly, it was easy to do—but horrible to do! Three minutes later, bleeding from at least twenty wounds he was still moving in on Jim like an automaton. Jim was panting, perspiring as much from the unspeakable horror of the thing as from the exertion. Grimly he waited, en garde again. The automaton put out a hand to brush the weapon aside. Jim feinted, the man lunged, and the point of the Corghion blade plunged through his heart and a hand's breadth out behind the Hindu's body. He staggered. Jim leaped back. The man fell on his face on the sand.

Jim wiped away the sweat with his forearm. A man in an Anthony envelope mask staggered through the pall of chemical dust toward Jim Anthony. It was Tom Gentry. "Jim, Jim, are you all right?"

Jim nodded, staggered a bit himself as he went to meet his friend. "I think we got them all but one. One tank made off to the right. Didn't you pass it?" Tom shook his head. The chemical dust was beginning to disperse, now.

And suddenly another man came into a clear spot. His features were obscured, not by an envelope mask, but by one of the black masks used by the men of Rado Ruric! He plodded along with his head down, like a robot, and over his shoulder he bore a half nude woman!

"It must be Thames," gasped Tom. "He started out here. And it's Linda! She's probably hurt!"

He started forward. Suddenly Linda Tabor seemed galvanized into life. Long, lithe legs kicked and flailed as she writhed and struggled and beat at her captor with her clenched fists. She screamed, "Stay away! Stay away, it's the killer!"

Tom Gentry dove forward. The man in the black mask threw up his hand. It met the charging Gentry, knocked him down in the sand. Relentlessly the man came on, bearing his precious burden. He said no word, he simply plodded toward the desert, as if he expected to walk all the way to the Coast! Tom Gentry, half stunned, got to his feet. He started forward again.

Linda cried, "Tom, no! No! He'll kill you! He's killed—!" The robot knocked him twenty feet, plowed over his inert body as if he were so much rubbish. Jim Anthony fumbled at the cords of the plastic net he had made aboard the Thunderbird II.

Ten feet away the robot stopped, the great eyes of his mask seeming to glare at Jim Anthony. Suddenly he raised the girl, hurled her screaming through the air. Jim could not dodge in time. Linda caught him directly across the chest, knocked him backward, half stunned him. He got to his feet, conscious of her fragile white body on the dark sands, conscious of Tom yelling hoarsely in the distance. Then the robot had him, raised him, gripped him in a great bear hug!

Anthony gave to that hug, knowing any stiffness would allow his spine to be broken like a matchstick. He gave, but he thrust both thumbs deep into the hollows below the robot's ears. So great was the pressure he exerted that he actually felt his thumb nails break the skin and dig into warm flesh.

For the first time the robot emitted a noise. He roared, like a wounded gorilla. He raised Jim as he had raised the girl, cast him headlong through the air. Jim Anthony's training came in good stead. Like a cat he twisted in the air, so that he alighted softly on his hands and feet. And the second he lit he was again fumbling with the cords of the plastic net. He wheeled quickly.

Mad eyes peered through the slots of the black mask. Two streams of blood gushed from below the robot's ears. But hands extended, emitting strange noises, on he came. Like a gladiator of old, who entered the arena with a fishnet and trident, stood Jim Anthony.

With a bellow the drugged man charged. Anthony stepped aside lithely and tossed the net. It fell over the robot's head, his feet became entangled in it, he stumbled and fell. In and out ran Jim Anthony, pulling a cord here, another there. Single strands of plastic had failed to hold the pair of *peons* in San Rosario, but the net, each strand reinforcing the other, was successful. Bit by bit the robot became more and more entangled, but never for a second did he cease the mad struggle.

One at a time the others joined them. By now the battered Tom had been revived by Linda Tabor, who had come out of her faint. They were fifty feet away, oblivious of the others. For Linda at last realized the depth of Tom's love, realized that with his bare hands he had attacked the monster who was bearing her off to—what?

The dust was almost entirely dispersed, though, being but slightly lighter than air, it hung above them like a black cloud. Dolores was with Jim, binding up the shoulder where the bullet had nicked him. Mephito was there, as inscrutable as ever, and Dawkins as well, who had been concealed for three days by Linda Tabor.

Entangled in the net the robot's struggles grew weaker and weaker. A shadow passed overhead. Jim looked up, gasped, "My motor ship! One of them made The Pueblo and stole my motor ship!"

For it was undeniably the motor ship, waggling its ailerons with derision. Then, suddenly, out of the ship itself plunged a figure! Head over heels it tumbled for split seconds, all eyes upon it. A parachute blossomed above it and the fall was arrested. Serenely it settled, the inert body of a big man, swinging like a pendulum, totally devoid of clothing. They started running toward the spot where it would land.

Later, sorrowfully, they returned to where the women awaited. To Dolores, Jim said, "Poor Thames. That was Ruric in the plane. His was the one tank that got successfully through my amateur minefield. There was a note pinned to Thames' body with a knife." He handed it to Dolores, gazed at the drugged man in the net, whose struggles had almost entirely ceased.

"That's Carl the waiter. At least that's what he called himself here. According to Ruric's note he was Mahatma Garda. But read the note."

She read aloud. "Anthony: You win again, Anthony, but there'll be another meeting. I'd hoped to get to the Oasis before you could return from Seattle. You were lucky—maybe not so lucky next time. Do not expect Garda—the man whom you knew as Carl—to talk. I saw that he had a lethal dose of the drug, he will die from shock. Another conflict and you pay in full! Rado Ruric."

Jim leaned over the man in the net, used a tiny pair of special clippers he always carried to cut the net away from him. Blue eyes that once had been black opened.

Weakly the man said, "I die—for India! Ruric will carry on!"

"Ruric gave you a lethal shot of the drug, Garda. Ruric has deserted you."

The blue eyes peered up suspiciously, but in Anthony's eyes they read only truth. The dying lips formed words. "So, I knew he was not to be trusted. May he—die a thousand deaths!"

Jim leaned closer. "You're dying, Garda, betrayed and deserted. Don't you want to tell me about the woman, about Elaine Lamington? An innocent man may suffer."

"The truth?" Fainter and fainter the words grew. "I killed her. I overheard. Somewhere she obtained a list of Ruric's agents. She was going to sell us out." His eyes protruded, his breath came in gasps, his chest heaved. His last words were, "Ruric! May—he—burn—in hell! God save India!"

So died Mahatma Garda, the dupe of Rado Ruric.

Jim, with his arms about Dolores' shapely shoulders, gazed about at the desolation caused by the mine field. He shuddered, thinking of all the deaths, thinking of Thames, and all the others. Dolores understood. Reassuringly she said softly, "It was worth it, it had to be, to destroy Rado Ruric's work. Without this—this destruction, Ruric's Fifth Column would be carrying on its work of sabotage and destruction today! Twenty deaths are infinitely better than—twenty thousand! Maybe more!"

Arms about each other Tom Gentry and Linda Tabor were walking back across the desert toward *The Pueblo*. Jim pulled Dolores to him, started following them, plodding somberly through the sand. He knew that somewhere, someday, he and Rado Ruric would match wits again. And he knew in his heart that next time—or the next—he would be successful in wiping out the man himself, as well as the man's fiendish work.

Sometime—

www.ingramcontent.com/pod-product-compliance
Lightning Source LLC
Chambersburg PA
CBHW030338030726
47499CB00003B/827
9780978683696

Super-Detective!

In the late-1930s, Culture Publications was the leading producer of salacious, under-the-counter pulp magazines like *Spicy Mystery* and *Spicy Detective*. And then the comic books happened. Culture Publications, after having redefined "culture" as "creamy bosoms exposed by torn, lacy undergarments," added a new neo-wholesome imprint, Trojan Publications, and gave the comic-book fans a reason to stay with the pulps. The reason was *Super-Detective*, introduced in 1940, a (near) monthly pulp featuring the novel-length adventures of Jim Anthony, detective extraordinaire, written under the house name of "John Grange." But Anthony was no mere sleuth. He possessed phenomenal physical and mental abilities. Patterned after Street & Smith's Doc Savage, and with the aid of his far-flung Anthony Legion, he battled super-villains bent on the destruction of the United States—no mere whimsy as the dark clouds of World War billowed.

After ten amazing adventures, we may conclude that the comics won the battle for the super-enthused readers, for *Super-Detective*, while retaining its title, transformed the Jim Anthony novels to a hard-boiled detective-story mode. The criminals were less ambitious, and more susceptible to guns and fists. But the stories were no less entertaining.

Here, in this *Super-Detective Flip Book*, a joint presentation of Off-Trail Publications and Reverse Karma Press, are two Jim Anthony novels, one from each phase of Anthony's career. Flip the book and read the other novel. Also included are introductions that explore the dual worlds of Jim Anthony, and the authors who brought him to life. John McMahan introduces "Legion of Robots" (November 1940), from Jim Anthony's high-adventure period, and discusses the author, Victor Rousseau, and the factors that went into creating the series. John Wooley introduces the hard-boiled "Murder's Migrants" (March 1943), and explores the working collaboration between its authors, Robert Leslie Bellem and W.T. Ballard.

SUPER-DETECTIVE

Flip Book

TWO COMPLETE NOVELS

featuring

LEGION OF ROBOTS

Introduction by John McMahan

MURDER'S MIGRANTS

Introduction by John Wooley

A JOINT PRESENTATION OF

Off-Trail Publications

&

Reverse Karma Press

Acknowledgements

The editors are grateful to John DeWalt, John Gunnison, Don Hutchison, John Locke, Stephen Mertz, Will Murray, Phil Nelson, Jerry Schattenberg and Al Tonik, for assistance and invaluable research.

SUPER-DETECTIVE FLIP BOOK: TWO COMPLETE NOVELS

ISBN-10: 0-9786836-9-2
ISBN-13: 978-0-9786836-9-6

OFF-TRAIL PUBLICATIONS
2036 Elkhorn Road
Castroville, CA 95012
offtrail@redshift.com

Printed in the United States of America
First printing: March 2008

The Second Coming of Jim Anthony, Super Detective

By John Wooley

In his introduction to the first novel in this Jim Anthony double-header, John McMahan gives us the lowdown on the Super Detective's early years, when the resemblances between him and the wildly popular pulp hero Doc Savage, the Man of Bronze, were, well, pretty much intentional. Like Doc, Anthony was a superb physical specimen who coupled scientific knowledge with near-supernatural powers. Also like Doc, he had his own cast of recurring characters—including his mystical American Indian grandfather, Mephito; a lovely, spunky fiancée, Dolores Colquitt; a freckle-faced aviator pal, Tom Gentry; and a butler named Dawkins—as well as a penthouse headquarters in New York City and a secret lair (Anthony's was called the Teepee, located deep in the heart of the Catskills).

That's the way Jim Anthony rolled during his first 10 appearances in Trojan Publishing Corp.'s *Super-Detective* magazine—as a kind of Native American version of Savage, a red man (technically, half-Comanche) as opposed to a bronze one. And, like Doc, his adventures tended to have a science-fictional quality, as demonstrated by our flipside novel, the wild "Legion of Robots."

That all ended with the December 1941 number of *Super-Detective*, which introduced readers to a Jim Anthony who was more detective and less super than he'd been just a couple of months before. Gone was the Doc Savage-esque high-adventure superheroism, replaced by more realistic settings and characters—or, at least, the kind of realism portrayed in the hard-boiled detective stories of the day.

These new and more "adult" Jim Anthony tales jettisoned all his supporting characters but Gentry, who became a bit more of a horndog, brandishing his little black book and forever trying to set himself and Anthony up with dates. He smoked and drank a considerable amount as well—as did his crime-busting pal. Sometimes he and Anthony would even have brandy in the morning, with their coffee and cornflakes.

And while Anthony wasn't constantly on point for the ladies like his running mate, it quickly became obvious that, in his new incarnation, the

Super Detective had a deep appreciation for a pretty face. In August 1943's "Curse of the Masters," for instance, our hero is so taken with a female character's looks that he lets her get the drop on him:

> Jim was too busy admiring her somber beauty; the eerie loveliness of her waxen face, the vivid scarlet of her lips, the glossy blackness of her hair enclosed in a white satin turban that seemed to complement her darkly glowing eyes.
>
> Then, finally, he saw the weapon. . . .

Chances are good that Doc Savage would've seen the weapon first—not to put too fine a point on it.

This new version of Anthony percolated for a few issues, but it didn't really arrive in all its full-bodied flavor until it was taken over by a couple of veteran detective-pulp writers, Robert Leslie Bellem and Willis Todhunter Ballard. Records unearthed by the invaluable pulp researcher Al Tonik indicate that Ballard and Bellem took over the series with "Hell's Ice-Box," in the October '42 issue of *Super-Detective*, and continued to the end of Anthony's run in the mag, which came with October '43's "Pipeline to Murder," a yarn concerning nefarious doings among some oil-rich Native Americans in Oklahoma. (Bellem had spent time in that state in the early '20s, working for the since-deceased afternoon newspaper *The Tulsa Tribune* long enough to meet and marry his lifelong wife, Blanche "Bebe" Washburn, sister of one of Bellem's co-workers.) Following Bellem and Ballard's ten Anthony yarns, *Super-Detective* became a straight, non-character, detective-fiction number (to which Bellem occasionally contributed) until its demise—seven years after "Pipeline to Murder" came out. That was in October 1950, a year that saw tons of pulps bite the dust, outgunned by newer diversions like television, paperbacks, and comic books.

As John McMahan writes in his introduction to "Legion of Robots," it's pretty certain that the science-fiction specialist Victor Rousseau Emanuel wrote the first three Jim Anthony adventures. After those, however, there's a long stretch of Anthony stories whose authorship remains a mystery. A full dozen, from "Bloated Death" (January '41) to "Mark of the Spider" (August '42), are still open to speculation, although author and pulp expert Will Murray wrote us recently that he assumes the writer continued to be Emanuel, until he left—or was fired—and Bellem and Ballard took over.

McMahan agrees with Murray, especially when it comes to authorship of the first ten stories, all cut from the same larger-than-life cloth. He's not as sure about the five that came next, which were more detective-styled tales, beginning with December '41's "I.O.U. Murder" and ending with "Mark of the Spider," after which Bellem and Ballard took over.

Why did Anthony metamorphose from kids' superhero to being an amateur sleuth for grownups? It seems pretty clear that the folks at Trojan Publications threw that switch, probably because the hero pulps weren't doing as well as they once had, their mostly youthful audience eaten into by the fast-growing and less mentally taxing comic-book industry. And once the Trojan powers-that-be made the decision to go more "adult," it follows that they would've soon concluded Robert Leslie Bellem was their go-to guy for the assignment.

Bellem had been a reliable and prolific talespinner for the company since the early '30s, and, in 1934, had created what would become the outfit's most enduring character—a flippant, cocky, and sometimes near-oafish Tinseltown lug named Dan Turner, Hollywood Detective. As the first-person narrator of his own adventures, Turner became famous for relating his tales in an incredibly stylized form of American English that can still make jaws drop. He might, for instance, say something like, "Behind me, a roscoe sneezed *kachow* and a lead pill split the ozone next to my noggin. I ankled the lot hellity-blip, my back pockets dipping gravel."

Translation: Someone shot at him and he ran.

Since this introduction is about Jim Anthony and not Dan Turner, we'll let it go at that, with a suggestion that those interested in more Dan can have their curiosity slaked by *Roscoes in the Night* (Adventure House, 2003), which presents a baker's dozen of the best Turner tales along with an introduction by yours truly. The point here is that it was undoubtedly Bellem who originally landed the Anthony gig, since the folks at Trojan knew him and his work. Bellem, in turn, brought his writer chum W.T. Ballard in on the deal.

Ballard, like Bellem, was best known at the time for a Hollywood-detective character. But while Bellem's Dan Turner appeared in pulps issued by the rather disreputable Trojan Publishing Corp. (which, as Culture Publications, perpetrated the *Spicy* line of pulps, whose sexual content often forced them under the counter at America's newsstands), Ballard's Bill Lennox ran in the legendary *Black Mask*, the pulp magazine generally credited with birthing the hard-boiled school of detective fiction.

The Lennox stories, all set within the movie industry, had begun in the September '33 *Black Mask*, with Bill Lennox becoming the first of the hard-boiled Hollywood detectives to appear in a pulp series. Immediately popular, the character would show up regularly in the title through May '42, and then make the jump to books. The last Lennox adventure, *Lights, Camera, Murder*, came out as a Belmont paperback in 1960.

(For a great selection of Lennox stories, along with excellent material from editor James L. Traylor and Ballard himself, check out *Hollywood Troubleshooter* [Bowling Green Popular Press, 1985].)

The resumes of Ballard and Bellem, as you might imagine, stretch well beyond the tales of their most famous two characters. Both were busy fictioneers who, during the '30s and early '40s, produced somewhere around a million words a year, knocking them out and shoving them into the insatiable maws of a variety of pulp publishers, who—ideally—shot back checks in return. The pulps' per-word rate may have been low, even for proven scribes like Bellem and Ballard, but if a person could crank out those words quickly enough, there was a decent living to be made.

As busy as these two were, however, they apparently weren't too busy in the early '40s to turn down new jobs. In an extensive interview with novelist and pulp aficionado Stephen Mertz, which appeared in the winter '79 number of *The Armchair Detective*, Ballard remembered meeting fellow pulpster Bellem "sometime in the mid-1930s." Not long after that, he said, the two rented "adjoining offices in an old corner building on Colorado Boulevard in Pasadena and worked there until I left for Wright Field during the Second World War, in 1942."

If the building still exists, there ought to be some kind of shrine erected outside those two rooms, where a pair of the pulps' greatest scribes labored daily for years, knocking out hundreds upon hundreds of tales. Maybe a hip historical society could even re-create the office interiors, circa 1942.

Then again, a veil might have to be drawn at some point.

"[The] old western pulp writer Walter Tompkins was a friend of Bellem's during the forties," noted Stephen Mertz in a letter from 1980, "and wrote to recall that Bellem's writing office walls used to be plastered with nudie pinups. Also, that the Bellem's apartment in Pasadena was totally nondescript. Tompkins recalls reacting with surprise that a man with such an imagination would have a personal habitat totally devoid of personality."

Maybe Mrs. Bellem had something to do with that. Or maybe not. At any rate, Bellem probably spent at least as much time in the office as he did at home anyway, and in the early '40s, some of that time at work was devoted to collaborations with his pal W.T. Ballard.

According to an essay by Ballard in *Hollywood Troubleshooter*, the mode of operation on the Jim Anthony stories (which continued to be published under the house name of "John Grange") consisted of Ballard telling a rough story into a Dictaphone ("It took me three days," he noted), which Bellem then polished and sent to the publisher.

In the Mertz interview, Ballard elaborated further on his writing partnership with Bellem:

> Bob was always a good word man but had trouble with story, which was my field, and he did not work well under pressure. Frequently, he would blow up, come apart, and throw the thing in my lap. That

> was especially true when the longer pieces became popular. His best work was in short material. He was a pugnacious, small man but easy to collaborate with, never pretentious about his prose, and we edited each other without many battles.

They also appear to have had a little bit of fun, at least based on the inside jokes that occasionally turn up in the Jim Anthony tales. In "Curse of the Masters," for instance, from the August '43 *Super-Detective*, a wealthy art lover found strangled in an apartment is identified as "Mr. Willis Ballard—the retired railroad magnate," while an island mansion is mentioned in passing as belonging to one "Robert Leslie." (In this same story, Anthony has brandy and cigarettes with his morning coffee—behavior Doc Savage would hardly condone for a fellow crimefighter.) And in "Murder Between Shifts," January '43, Dan Turner's long-running friendly nemesis, police detective Dave Donaldson, makes a crossover appearance.

In his *Hollywood Troubleshooter* essay, which had been written for but never published by *Argosy* magazine, Ballard recalled that the Anthony assignment "was a meal ticket worth four hundred dollars a month to each of us." Al Tonik's research at the University of Oregon, which houses Ballard's papers, indicates it wasn't quite that good. Ballard and Bellem each got $260 for "Hell's Ice-Box," their first Anthony, and checks ranging from $210 (for November '42's "Days of Death") to $352.50 (for the series finale, "Pipeline to Murder") thereafter. The difference in amounts probably has to do with the word counts of the individual stories. At the same time Bellem and Ballard were knocking out the Anthonys, they were also collaborating on a series for the Thrilling pulp *Popular Detective*. The Dr. Zeng stories revolved around an Oriental doctor, who was actually an American, and his Chinese helper, who clomped around on a fake leg capable of storing everything from weapons to a radio transmitter!)

Although the checks they got from Trojan were decent enough, they weren't exactly a princely sum. So imagine Ballard's surprise when the IRS asked him why he hadn't reported $35,000 that Trojan had paid him for one year's work. Bellem got a similar message. As it turned out, they'd been the victims of a scam by a couple of Trojan's assistant editors.

Explained Ballard in *Hollywood Troubleshooter*, "They [the assistant editors] had gone back into the magazine's files, pulled stories, changed the names with a lead pencil, rerun them, vouchered them through Bob and me and some other contributors, had the checks drawn, taken them down to their favorite bar, forged the endorsements, and cashed them."

It worked for a while. But, as Ballard told Stephen Mertz in the *Armchair Detective* piece, "Bob Bellem and I combined to send them to Sing Sing for five years each," by blowing the whistle on the larcenous pair to Trojan

editor Frank Armer.

By the time the war ended and Ballard returned from Wright Field—the Dayton, Ohio-based research and development center responsible for the design and construction of many World War II combat aircraft—it was a new era. The pulps were dying *en masse*, and paperback books and TV were coming on hard. Ballard began hitting both of those markets, while Bellem stayed with the pulps until the very end, making what appears to have been a nearly seamless transition to TV scripting. He and his old friend W.T. began collaborating again, this time on television shows like *Death Valley Days*, *Dick Tracy*, and *Cowboy G-Men*, but Bellem found the medium more to his liking than Ballard did. In the '50s, '60s, and '70s, Ballard did far more books than television scripts, penning an impressive number of both paperback originals and hardcovers under a number of different names—including, for his numerous western novels, Todhunter Ballard. Bellem stayed mostly in television, delivering scripts for such well-remembered series as *Perry Mason*, *Superman*, *The Lone Ranger*, *77 Sunset Strip*, and *Tarzan*—up until his death, in 1968, of a heart attack. He was 66.

Ballard, born in 1903—a year after Bellem—lived until 1980. His final book appears to have been the Doubleday western, *Sheriff of Tombstone*, which came out under the Todhunter Ballard moniker in 1977.

Both Robert Leslie Bellem and W.T. Ballard are names still known—and in some cases, *loved*—by those captivated by the swift and exciting prose offered by the pulp magazines of yesteryear. They were solid professional writers who, over long careers, saw their opportunities and took them, to the delight of hundreds of thousands—maybe millions—of readers. The reworking of a Doc Savage knockoff was just one of many challenges they encountered, together and separately, and they did a fine job with it—as you'll see in "Murder's Migrants," the timely-as-today's-headlines story that follows.

And as you read this swift little tale, perhaps at some point you might want to pause and give a momentary thought to the unique guys who created it, working right next door to one another in an old Southern California office building some 65 years ago, writing and editing and arguing and then maybe having a few drinks together before the next day dawned, and they started the process all over again.

SUPER-DETECTIVE

March 1943

They were using Jim Anthony's name and reputation in one of the most gigantic criminal plots in history. But just how was each involved—the fat man, the collegiate reporter, the rhyming photographer, the society girl, and the clever, good-looking secretary?

Murder's Migrants

By John Grange

GRIMLY, DOGGEDLY, THE HUNTED MAN FLED ONWARD through a gathering fog which had subtly deepened into night without bringing him any actual awareness of the change. In the chaos of his tortured brain there was no place for thoughts of time or weather; there was only a constant, gnawing hunger for revenge that goaded him forward like a living automaton.

Long ago he had lost all count of the days, the hours, consumed by his harried journey. Sometimes it seemed as if he had been on this endless trail for years, centuries—ever conscious that he was being pursued; that somewhere on the wet road behind him lurked ruthless killers who had failed once, but who were closing in for a second chance to strike.

He held no hope of escape, for he realized the power of the person he had grown to hate during these past few hellish days with a hatred such as he had never before experienced. He knew that he was doomed to die very soon; but he prayed with all his waning strength that he would be spared just long enough to kill the one who was responsible.

It was a strange sensation to Nick Uvaldi, this burning urge to end another man's life. The feeling was foreign to him; as fantastic as the circumstances in which he now found himself. It marked the bitter finish of what, to him, had always seemed a career of incredibly good fortune.

Where else except here in America could he, the son of an immigrant Greek shoemaker, have been permitted to enter one of the country's leading technical schools? In what other land could he have graduated with honors despite his insignificant, unimportant family background?

This, he told himself, was democracy at work; the liberty and equality to be found only in the United States. And for the privilege of citizenship in such a country he owed a heartfelt debt—a debt he was willing to pay with

his blood, his life. It was a payment he would make willingly; but he was fanatically determined that another man should die with him.

An enemy of America!

Slogging through the darkness, Nick Uvaldi thought again of his academic life after graduation. Still in his middle twenties, he'd been retained by the school to do experimental work in its shining laboratories; and he might have been there yet if it hadn't been for the war.

The cowardly Jap assault on Pearl Harbor had changed everything. He'd tried to enlist, only to be rejected for an unsuspected physical defect. Then he had decided to fight on the industrial front if he couldn't wear a uniform; surely a man of his technical training could find a place in some war plant. He owed it to the land that had given him this training.

By sheer chance, then, he'd stumbled upon a certain employment office on lower Broadway in New York. They'd accepted his application; told him to report at six that same night, ready to travel. Vaguely he understood that he was headed for a California factory which was one of the far-flung enterprises set up by a famous young capitalist to assist a government engaged in titanic battle.

The bus rolled out on time, loaded with men who were being moved across the breadth of the nation to work in war production. Steadily for almost twenty-four hours the big vehicle lumbered westward; and the following evening it happened to halt in a little Pennsylvania mountain town so the passengers could eat in a dingy restaurant—at their own expense, of course, just as each of them had paid as much cash as he could afford toward the cost of the bus trip.

There were two drivers, and they went into the cafe kitchen, leaving their labor recruits out front. Once again it was sheer chance that drew Nick Uvaldi into the plot, allowing him to overhear a disturbing conversation.

"Where you takin' this load?" It was the cook who had asked the question.

One of the drivers chortled dourly. "New Mexico. We dump 'em a hundred miles from no place. It'll be days before any of them get to where they can squawk."

Nick hadn't understood. He pressed closer, listening; and he presently learned that he and his fellow passengers were the victims of an ugly, gigantic hoax. There weren't any jobs waiting for these men on the west coast. The busload of workers—and hundreds more just like it—would be abandoned in the far desert, to make their way back to civilization as best they could!

He lost his head, then. He should have slipped away, returned to New York and reported his findings to the proper authorities. Instead he burst into the kitchen and confronted the two drivers; threatened them with exposure.

It was a foolish move. The cook was behind him—and a blackjack slugged home to Nick Uvaldi's skull. Stunned, he swayed on his feet. Another vicious, smashing blow felled him; and then the bus drivers began using their boots on his unprotected body.

Eventually he lost consciousness.

Darkness had fallen when his senses returned, and the bus had long since resumed its westward journey. But Nick wasn't on it. He was tightly trussed in the cafe kitchen, and preparations were already under way to murder him as soon as a grave had been dug in the cellar to receive his battered corpse.

He still couldn't quite remember how he'd managed to escape. There were gaps in his memory now; blank spots induced by that terrific beating he had taken. Somehow he must have inched himself to a table where butcher knives were kept; must have contrived to cut away his fetters. In his mind, the whole scene was jumbled and disconnected.

He got away, though. That much he knew. And he knew he'd stolen some of those sharp, expensive knives—which he later traded in a pawnshop for the gun that now made a comforting bulge in his pocket; the gun he planned to use on the man responsible for what had happened.

As his bruised, weary legs carried him along New York's riverfront he tried to rehearse what he meant to say when he faced the millionaire he was going to kill. But the words refused to form in his tired mind. They weren't important, anyhow. One bullet was worth a hundred speeches, he told himself. One deadly, well-aimed bullet would do his talking for him.

It was funny to think about murdering a millionaire. Especially *this* millionaire—a man who owned a vast newspaper empire of which the New York *Star* was the cornerstone; who owned the biggest hotel in Manhattan; who owned and directed a tremendous scope of business properties, all of which had supposedly been turned into non-profit organizations for the benefit of governmental war effort.

Non-profit, hell! If the real truth were known, the man was probably fattening his pockets in secret; milking additional millions from his industries at the expense of hard-working, hard-fighting Americans. At least that was what Nick Uvaldi concluded, knowing what he knew.

He thought of the hundreds, perhaps thousands like himself who'd been clipped for bus fare on the fake promise of jobs that didn't exist. Men who were even now being dumped and left to shift for themselves in the western desert. Lured away from their homes to be ditched, maybe even to starve to death! Was that a millionaire patriot's idea of benevolence, of serving his country? Faugh!

And they talked of the man's amazing abilities in other lines of endeavor: his scientific discoveries, his mechanical inventions, his charities—and

his astounding feats of detection in the field of amateur criminology. Why, unquestionably, the fellow himself was either a criminal or a sadistic madman! How else could you explain his recruiting of labor for imaginary war work? Labor that was being chiseled for paltry dollars and then shipped to nowhere?

Pain-wracked and not quite sane, thanks to the punishment he had undergone, Nick Uvaldi had made up his mind to put an end to such things. Long ago he'd dismissed all thought of asking the law for help. The brutal beating inflicted on him had distorted his sense of proportion, destroyed his confidence in orderly police procedure. You couldn't depend on the cops, he told himself. They were crooked, corrupt—all of them. If you wanted justice done, you had to arrange it yourself. Well, he was ready for the grim task.

Provided he lived long enough, of course. His escape from that cafe in western Pennsylvania had resulted in relentless pursuit; more than once he had barely eluded the murderers who were trailing him to shut him up. His flight had been reported, he knew; because a dozen traps had been set and waiting for him on his long trip homeward.

Luck and a certain crazed cunning had enabled him to avoid those pitfalls, however. Thus far he had fooled his enemies. And now he was back in New York, prepared to serve the country he loved by executing a man whom he considered to be nothing better than a monster.

After that they could lynch him or electrocute him or do as they pleased. But first he must accomplish his purpose; and it would require careful strategy, for his proposed victim would be well guarded. He already had a scheme to get past those guards, though.

As he trudged onward he patted the gun in his pocket; *the gun with which he intended to kill Jim Anthony!*

CHAPTER II
DEATH'S DINNER-GUEST

THE SUPPER ROOM OF THE WALDORF-ANTHONY HOTEL was ablaze with lights, filled with the hum of conversation and the melodic under-current of music from a big name orchestra. And at a gleaming table in the very center of this tastefully furnished hotel restaurant sat the man who owned it; the man whose very name spelled the magic of accomplishment.

Jim Anthony.

Impeccably attired in white tie and tails, Jim made a striking figure against his opulent background. He would have been equally notable against any background. Tall, lean, muscular, his broad-shouldered body a dynamic reservoir of strength, he sat with the lithe ease of a finely trained athlete. From his swashbuckling Irish captain-of-industry father he had inherited this superlative physique along with one of America's greatest fortunes; and he had developed his physical perfection to the topmost limits, thanks to constant exercise—just as he had likewise developed and expanded his financial empire far beyond its original scope, thanks to his brilliant mind.

But it was his face that attracted and held your attention. Sun-bronzed under sleek black hair, the nose jutting, the cheek bones high, the dark eyes hawk-like and penetrating, it was a face that reminded you of some American Indian chieftain—which was natural enough, for Jim's mother had been a full princess of the Comanche tribe.

From her, perhaps, had come his instinct for the hunt; an instinct which had turned his many-sided abilities toward the biggest game of all—the tracking down of wrongdoers. As a manhunter Jim Anthony had no equals; his fame as an amateur scientific criminologist was world-wide. Detection was his hobby, his avocation; countless were the mysteries he had solved, the murderers he had brought to justice after the police themselves had failed. In consequence, the mere mention of his name was enough to strike terror into the heart of any transgressor.

Tonight the millionaire criminologist had two dinner guests. The first was his lifelong friend and boon companion, the freckled, happy-go-lucky aviator, Tom Gentry. Earlier in the day, Jim had gone into conference with the skylarking flyer.

"I'll leave the ordering of the dinner to you, Tom," he had said. "Eating is one of your delights, so I'm depending on you to arrange an impressive spread."

"With girls, pappy? I've got three pips in my address book. Knockouts, no less. The kind you dream about on rainy Sunday afternoons. If you want to impress this frog—"

"Frog isn't a very polite term for a man as important as the one we're entertaining," Anthony grinned. "It would probably be a shock to him if he heard you call him that."

Gentry shrugged. "Okay. Frenchman, then."

"Free French. Remember, Dr. Montclair barely got out of Paris ahead of the Nazi occupation. If they'd caught him, he'd have been stood against a wall and shot."

Tom sighed with mock resignation. "So all right. Dr. Montclair, Free Frenchman. Former industrialist and efficiency expert in French war-material production. Now a refugee, staying here in the hotel. Joining up with you in an advisory capacity to help increase the output of your plants. Have I got all of it so I can show the right amount of awe?"

"I think so," the wealthy detective had to laugh in spite of himself. "You make it sound spectacular."

"Yeah. So the guy's a big shot. So he's still human, ain't he?"

"Quite."

"Then why don't we invite these three cuties I mentioned? I mean Montclair would have to be deaf, dumb, and blind not to get a kick out of them. We could make a night of it."

"Sorry, Tom. You're thinking more of yourself than of Montclair, I'm afraid. And he has more important things on his mind than girls."

The aviator bridled. "What's more important than girls? Name two!—Okay, okay, don't hit me. I give up. We'll dine stag if you say so." Then, ducking his millionaire pal's playful punch, Gentry went searching for the chef.

Now the three men were quietly enjoying a meal on which that chef had outdone himself. There was Jim Anthony, there was Tom Gentry, and there was Dr. Francois Montclair—a dapper little man whose prematurely grey hair and deeply wrinkled features betrayed more than a hint of the perils he had undergone in those dark days when his native land had fallen into the hands of invading enemy hordes.

At this particular moment the wealthy criminologist and his guests were between courses. Anthony was deep in conversation with Montclair and they were speaking French—which could have been Sanskrit as far as Gentry

was concerned, for he couldn't understand a word of it. Bored, toying with his silver, the genial aviator was secretly wishing he'd disobeyed orders and invited at least one girl to the feast. Then he would have had somebody to talk to, anyhow.

His roving gaze strayed over the big room, pausing now and then to admire some particularly lovely and beautifully-gowned woman. Then, suddenly, he tensed.

A strange figure had appeared through the service doorway and was making its way toward the Anthony table; a youthful but battered-looking fellow whose hair was disheveled, whose face bore the marks of savage bruises, and whose eyes held a curious glitter. He carried a tray and wore a busboy's uniform jacket; but it didn't fit very well—which struck Tom Gentry as odd, because any employee of the Waldorf-Anthony Hotel whose duties required the wearing of livery always had that livery tailored to his exact measure.

Moreover, this oncoming chap's appearance had other peculiarities. Beneath the ill-fitting coat his trousers were dirty and torn, the cuffs frayed and mud-spattered. His shoes, too, were muddy and shapeless, as if he had just come from a long hike through rough terrain. He walked with an unsteady gait; the unmistakable evidence of complete fatigue—or complete drunkenness. Yet he didn't seem drunk, aside from this. There was something cold and sober and purposeful about him.

Gentry let out an astonished exclamation. "Gosh, pappy, I wish you'd look at the new style in busboys!"

At the words, Jim Anthony abruptly broke off what he'd been saying to his French guest; stared in the direction of the genial aviator's gesture. And as he narrowed his hawk-like eyes, he felt a subconscious premonition of danger inching through him; a warning sensation such as he always experienced at the approach of peril. This weird sixth sense was another of his heritages from his Indian mother; it had never failed him in the past and he could not ignore it now.

The short hair stirred at the nape of his neck when he saw that ragged figure in the uniform jacket, making for his table. Simultaneously he observed that the captain of waiters and the maitre de hotel had also spotted the strange intruder and were angling toward him, trying to intercept him. Shocked stupefaction was scrawled on their faces, for nothing like this had ever before occurred within the four walls of the famed Waldorf-Anthony Hotel.

They were too far away to do anything about it, though. By now the newcomer had almost reached the millionaire criminologist's table. Nick Uvaldi had timed his arrival with cunning cleverness; there was nobody

between him and his intended victim. His lips began to move soundlessly. Then he swung aside the empty tray he was carrying—and revealed the pawn-shop revolver clenched in his fist.

"Look out!" Tom Gentry squalled as he caught sight of the ugly snub-nosed weapon. "Duck, Jim! It's a hold-up!"

"No. You will not move," the battered man's voice was as implacable as the mask of hate that twisted his features. "Be still, or I'll kill you right now. And I don't want to do that. Not until you know why you're to die."

Tom froze and so did the Frenchman, Francois Montclair. But Anthony had an appearance of complete relaxation; of utter indifference to jeopardy. Beneath this counterfeit calmness, however, his splendid muscles were invisibly taut and ready to erupt into surging motion at the first opportunity.

"All right, my friend," he said easily. "Tell me why I'm to die."

Throughout the great dining room a hush had fallen; a frightened, shivery silence as hundreds of eyes watched the unbelievable drama unfolding before them. In this silence, Nick Uvaldi's answer rang with the clarity of a bell.

"Your death is atonement to the little men, Mr. Anthony. The workers who are your dupes, your victims. The poor deluded fools you shipped to nowhere after stealing what money they had. I am their hand, striking out to punish a rat who thought himself too big to be touched."

The speech was meaningless to Anthony. All this talk of shipping workmen to nowhere after stealing their money—it sounded like the ravings of a demented person. Just the same, a crazy man could shoot you as quickly as a sane one; and for less cause. It wasn't a pleasant prospect.

Mentally Jim judged the distance between himself and the gun that was aimed at him; weighed his chances of lunging sidewise out of his chair and going for the flat automatic which he himself carried under his left armpit.

And then, before he came to a decision, there came the thunderous crash of a pistol's report. And at the same precise second, every light in the room was switched off.

The windows were shielded by heavy drapes to prevent any inner glow from seeping to the dimmed-out street; and now the drapes performed a reverse service by cutting off any possible light that might have sifted into the room from outside. In the solid darkness that ensued, Jim Anthony hurled himself to the floor and whipped out his automatic.

"Tom!" he called. "Dr. Montclair! Are you both okay?"

"*Oui, Monsieur*," came the Frenchman's answer. And then Tom's gasping blurt of relief: "Jeepers cripes, pappy, did he manage to plug you?"

"No. Be quiet." This time Jim's voice sounded from another direction, for he had crawled Indian fashion on his belly away from the position he occupied when he first spoke. Thus his assailant couldn't draw a bead on him

by listening for the source of his words.

As it turned out, the trick proved unnecessary; there was no more gunfire. Rustles of whispering began to sweep across the restaurant like sibilant surf as dinner patrons stirred and gave voice to their excitement. A scowl darkened Anthony's unseen countenance at this; for the whispers drowned out what he was straining his hypersensitive ears to hear—the possible slither of movement marking his attacker's location.

He resorted to a Hindu trick he had learned years ago from a yogi in Calcutta; dilated the pupils of his eyes to abnormal size by sheer muscular control. By means of this trick he was enabled to see clearly in darkness where ordinary vision was useless. Crawling forward again, he peered ahead.

"By God!" he whispered.

A man's form lay sprawled before him, gun in hand. But the stiffening fingers would never pull the weapon's trigger. There was a bullet hole through the back of the man's skull. He'd been shot from behind, the slug traveling from some spot on the far side of the room.

The millionaire criminologist stood up. "Lights!" he called grimly. "Somebody get to the master switch."

In an instant his command was obeyed and brilliance once more filled the fashionable eating place. Nearby, a woman moaned; another screamed hysterically. Tom Gentry leaped to his feet, registering amazement as he saw Anthony standing over the limp body of the fake busboy.

"Guard the doors," Jim said tersely. "See that nobody leaves. Send the house detective to me and telephone police headquarters. This man has been murdered."

CHAPTER III
SHAKEDOWN SET-UP

THE EDITORIAL OFFICES OF *FOCUS* MAGAZINE occupied a musty set of rooms in an old building in the Forties. In the largest of these offices a fat man sat at a battered desk; but instead of the galley proofs and photograph prints you might have expected to find on an editor's work-table, the green blotter was covered by a tray on which reposed one of the biggest porterhouse steaks ever seen in Manhattan.

Nobody could say this steak was actually raw; there were a few slight evidences that it had come into contact with a broiler—but briefly. Crimson juices ran from its seared edges, and a delicious aroma arose from the heaps of French-fried potatoes which flanked it. There was another plate nearby containing two whole heads of lettuce liberally doused with mayonnaise; steaming coffee rich with cream filled a cup to the brim, and a dozen rolls were stacked alongside, dripping melted butter.

The desk's owner had a napkin tucked under his multiple chins, and he was attacking the steak with all the vigor of a man who'd been starving on a desert island for the past six weeks. Aside from his appetite, though, he showed no signs of starvation. He wasn't just fat; he was almost obscenely gross.

His three hundred pounds literally overflowed his creaking office chair in all directions; his face was moon-like and puffy; and his eyes, although large enough by ordinary standards, were almost lost in the purses of flesh that pocketed them. Just now they glittered with childish pleasure as he popped the first tremendous morsel of meat into his mouth.

The mouth was like a slit; a trap that snapped shut so that no trace of the food's flavor could escape. And somehow, despite the man's well-tailored clothes and infantile gurglings of pleasure, you got the impression that he himself was a trap—a deadly snare awaiting any unwary prey that came too close.

Feasting, he paid absolutely no attention to the girl who stood across the office and watched him. To an outsider, this might have been somewhat puzzling; for Lana McBride was eminently worth looking at from the crown of her

beautifully coiffed yellow hair to the soles of her small, opened-toed pumps. As a private secretary and editorial assistant she was not only decorative, but efficient as well.

She proved this by remarking with disapproval: "You'll eat yourself into the grave one of these days, Gabe. That wouldn't be very good for business."

He twinkled at her fondly, but he did not stop chewing until he had swallowed the mouthful and washed it down with a gulp of fragrant coffee. Then, when he finally did condescend to answer, he had a curious manner of talking that omitted all unnecessary words—as if each syllable were a silver dollar he hated to part with.

"Glorious death," he grinned. Then he went back to his meal without offering to share it.

Lana McBride viewed her employer with a cross between amusement and disgust. For three years she'd been a slave to the various magazines published by L. Gabriel Stope, none of which had lived very long; and sometimes she wondered why she remained with him. For all his other faults, though, he had imagination coupled with a complete absence of ethics; and there was always the chance of making a financial killing by staying in his service.

Take his current publishing venture, for instance: this *Focus* magazine. He was launching it as a nickel pictorial weekly in competition with the established ten-cent picture publications; with any sort of financial backing it might be a huge success. But lack of money had delayed the initial issue week after week, and Lana McBride wasn't feeling too hopeful.

"If Higgie Smith doesn't bring home the bacon, I'm not even sure you can afford enough steaks to kill yourself," she retorted tartly.

"Bacon. Steaks. Got *you* talking food now." He waved a piece of lettuce at her. "Stop worrying. You saw Higgie's wire. Got the goods. Flying home. Should be here now."

As if on cue, the office door opened and two men crowded into Stope's musty sanctum. The first was round, chubby, but not fat; he wore Kollege-Kut Klothes at least six years out of fashion, a pork-pie hat with the brim turned up front and back, and he carried a portable typewriter whose scarred case slapped him on the knees when he walked. This seemed to cause him perpetual surprise; but beneath the naive exterior of Higgins Smith, sole and only reporter on the staff of *Focus* magazine, lurked shrewdness as sharp as a scalpel.

"Hi, Toots," he said to Lana. "You look gorgeous tonight." Then he turned to the fat man, who had not paused in his eating. "We're in, boss. But definitely! I don't know how you got your tip-off, maybe you had a crystal ball. All I can say is, you hit it smack on the nose."

"Of course. But did you?"

Higgie Smith was not disturbed by the fat man's cold voice. "Sure. Wait until you get a load of the interviews I got from a dozen of those poor devils in the Arizona badlands. And the pix Rhymer snapped. Show him, Rhymer," he said to the cadaverous individual who had followed him into the room.

This tall, skeletal caricature of humanity was Rhymer Koenig, *Focus* magazine's only photographer, and his loose suit hung on him like the threadbare garments of a scarecrow. As he unslung his battered camera case, his beady eyes wolfishly surveyed that steak on Stope's desk. Then he cleared his scrawny throat.

"A hunk of that I'd like to eat. And then I crave to take a seat. Because, you see, my dogs are tired. I'd ask for dough but I might get fired."

Higgie made disparaging sounds. "There you go spouting poetry again. Skip it, bub. Let's have those prints."

From an inside pocket, Rhymer produced an envelope and dumped a series of pictures on the desk. With the same movement he shagged two sections of fried potato and lifted them toward his mouth.

Stope hit him on the fingers with a spoon. "Lay off."

"For you I do not like to work. You've crippled me, you dirty jerk!" The scarecrow nursed his hurt hand. He dropped the potatoes, however.

"I'll break your arm if you touch my food again," the fat man growled. Then he looked at the snapshots. "Good."

"You like 'em, do you?" Higgie Smith asked.

"Yes."

Higgie gathered them up, stowed them in his pocket. "We're glad to know it, Rhymer and I. You can have them when you kick in with our back salaries."

"Hold-up, eh?"

"Sort of. Remember, when you had us sign up with that employment agency, you gave us only enough cash for plane fare home. I didn't see any eating money."

"Airline feeds you," Stope said.

"This one didn't. The stewardess had tough luck with her buffet; spoiled all the grub. The other passengers ate at various way stations when we came down for refueling. Rhymer and I were broke. We had a doughnut apiece for breakfast. For lunch and supper we played like we weren't hungry."

The fat man opened the top drawer of his desk and put both hands in it. His left hand came out with a dollar bill. "Here," he said. "Take this. Buy hot dogs. Give me pictures."

"Oh, no. Not for any lousy buck."

Stope's other hand appeared. It had an automatic in it. "Not for a buck.

For this."

"Gabe!" the startled protest came from Lana McBride.

He cast her a frigid glance. "Quiet." Then, to Smith and the startled photographer, "Fools. I don't plan to publish those pix and interviews."

"What?" Higgie stiffened. "After all the trouble we went to, getting them? Why, you said yourself they'd create a sensation. Our circulation would hit half a million with the first issue!"

"Take too much time. Printer would get most of the gravy. I have a quicker way. Hell with half million *circulation*, I'll get half million *dollars*. Cash. Maybe more."

Lana McBride lifted her eyebrows on an indrawn breath. "Explain that, Gabe. We're just ignorant dopes."

"Yes," Stope agreed. "Jim Anthony. Millionaire. Controls a hundred factories. Threaten him with exposure. Publish the evidence; labor recruited, then dumped. Unions would call strikes in every Anthony plant."

The girl's eyes sharpened. "Blackmail!"

"Ugly word. Don't like it. We sell him *Focus* for a million dollars. Lock, stock, barrel. He suppresses story and layout. We retire. Rich."

"It's still blackmail," Lana said. "But it's a knockout. Put away the gun. Give him those pictures, Higgie. Let's all go call on Mr. Anthony."

L. Gabriel Stope twinkled affably, but his mouth had as much mirth as a snake's. "Knew you'd see it my way," he said. "Scram while I finish my steak."

CHAPTER IV
PHONY FOUNDATION

JIM ANTHONY'S LIVING QUARTERS took in the entire penthouse on the roof of the Waldorf-Anthony Hotel. Here, in his luxurious living room, he now faced Lieutenant Trotter of the New York homicide department.

Nearly three hours had passed since the lights had been doused in the hotel restaurant and the misguided, unfortunate Nick Uvaldi had met death in the ensuing darkness. In those three hours many alleys of investigation had been opened—and found to be blind.

First Jim himself had been bluntly accused of the killing. "In self defense, of course," Trotter had reluctantly stipulated. "But you're the one guy with a logical motive."

"How so?"

"He pulled a gun on you. He claimed you were mixed up in some labor beef. He was going to plug you—so you beat him to the trigger."

Anthony had smiled faintly. "I'd have to be a contortionist. I was in front of him; the bullet entered the back of his skull. Don't be absurd."

"Okay, then. He was drilled by one of these two guys at your table. Gentry or Dr. Montclair."

"They were in front of him, too. Why not give us the paraffin test and see if any of us discharged a firearm?"

This was done; and the results had shown negative. Tests were then made on the hands of every other person in the supper room, employees as well as patrons—all of whom had been detained by Jim's orders pending an investigation.

And again the results were uniformly negative.

There was only one plausible answer. After firing the fatal shot, the murderer must have escaped in the darkness; his moves had been covered by that concert of excited whispering which had prevented Anthony's abnormally acute ears from hearing any sound of receding footfalls. At this point the police had been temporarily stymied; forced to release all the witnesses after the formality of taking their names and addresses.

Now, three hours later, Lieutenant Trotter had returned to the hotel for another interview with the millionaire criminologist. And the homicide

official looked definitely unhappy about the whole thing.

"I don't get any part of it," he rasped around the fragments of a frayed cigar. "Something tells me you're holding out on me. In fact, I feel sure of it."

Jim wasn't particularly startled by this remark. He and Trotter had locked horns on many a previous occasion, and there was little love lost between them. Or at least Trotter showed truculent traces of animosity whenever his duties brought him into professional contact with the wealthy amateur detective. Perhaps it was jealousy; time and again Anthony had solved cases through sheer scientific ability where the police department had failed. Trotter seemed to resent this, although he usually received a lion's share of the credit.

Now the crusty homicide lieutenant was singing the same old tune, hinting that the sun-bronzed millionaire knew more than he was telling.

"Why should I hold out on you?" Jim asked calmly.

"That's what I'd like to know. For instance, what was your connection with this Nick Uvaldi?"

"Nick Uvaldi? Never heard of him."

"He's the guy that got bumped." Trotter made an impatient gesture. "We've been checking on him. He was a graduate of a big-time technical school; worked in their research lab afterward. He quit to enlist but was turned down."

"And—?"

"So then he applied for war industry work through your foundation office on lower Broadway."

Inwardly, Jim Anthony tensed with surprise; although none of it was revealed on his impassive countenance. "My foundation office? Afraid I don't follow you."

"Look, pal," Trotter lifted a lip. "Don't make with the mysterious stuff. It won't buy you anything. We did a routine check on that outfit when it first opened, two weeks ago."

"I still don't follow you."

Trotter aimed a menacing finger. "Are you trying to tell me you aren't connected with this so-called Foundation For The Redistribution Of War Manpower?"

"It's all news to me," Anthony said.

The homicide official puffed his reddening cheeks. "Don't pull that stuff! You're *behind* the thing! You and a lot more rich guys. Listen. If you say you don't know Dorothy Dawson Carradyne, you and I are going to tangle."

"Yes, I know Miss Carradyne," Jim admitted. "I've met her a few times. Quite a striking woman."

From his seat across the room, Tom Gentry remarked: "That's an

understatement if I ever heard one, pappy. Striking? She's a wow!"

Trotter ignored the interruption; kept right on talking to the millionaire criminologist. "Okay. So you know her. How much do you know about her?"

From the amazing catalogue of his mental index file, Jim Anthony produced an instantaneous *dossier*. "Dorothy Dawson Carradyne," he said. "Last surviving member of an old New York family. Well established in society. Parents were wealthy but died penniless; bad investments. Dorothy was educated in Europe; had post-graduate work in Berlin until her own funds ran out. Came back to America a few years ago; plunged into social service activities."

"Yeah. And that's why you hired her. On account of her experience finding jobs for down-and-outers."

Jim shook his head. "I never hired her."

"Don't give me that!" Trotter bellowed. "I just talked with her less than thirty minutes ago. I routed her out, made her go down to her office. She looked through her records and identified this Nick Uvaldi guy who got killed while threatening you. He signed up with the Redistribution Foundation last week and shipped out with a busload of other workers for one of your California plants."

Anthony's hawk-like eyes glittered. "My California plants have all the men they need. We're not hiring extra help until our expansion plans are complete."

"Nuts! I asked this Carradyne jane who she was fronting for. At first she wouldn't talk except to say some of the biggest capitalists in the country were furnishing funds out of their own pockets to help relocate labor; guys who didn't want their names mentioned."

"Did you learn any of those names?"

"Finally, yeah. And yours is at the top of the list as chairman. She showed me your personal letter asking her as a favor to take the job of running the outfit."

"I wrote no such letter."

Trotter made a bitter mouth. "Naturally you'd say that, after what happened. You're trying to get out from under. Here's a man, Nick Uvaldi, that's hired through a labor-exchange you organized. He ships out on a bus to work in one of your plants. A few nights later he shows up again, back in town, and for some unknown reason threatens to blast you. But he gets blasted first, before he's able to explain what's eating on him. If you were anybody else but Jim Anthony, you'd be in the clink this minute—and you might land there yet if you don't tell me the score."

"Sorry. I don't know the score. I intend to find out, though." The

millionaire criminologist's tone was bleak.

Lieutenant Trotter's heavy features grew apoplectic. "You refuse to talk, hunh? Okay. Maybe I'll come up with some way to make you whistle. Just wait. And look out! This is one time I won't be taking any of your shenanigans." Whereupon he strode stiff-legged to Jim's private automatic elevator, entered it, closed the door and viciously punched the *down* button.

In the penthouse living room, Tom Gentry built three generous drinks; one for himself, one for Francois Montclair, and a double jigger for his wealthy friend. "After that little session I have an idea we need these," he said.

The dapper but haggard-looking French refugee made a wry face as he sipped. "*Mais oui!*" he agreed. "But what does it all mean? It is of a strangeness I do not comprehend, this talk of labor relocation foundations and letters one did not write! At the first I thought the poor devil who was killed must have been insane, a victim of persecution complex. But now one wonders if there is a deeper significance!"

"I'm sure of it," Anthony frowned. "And I'm going to dig until I find the answer—"

He was interrupted by the melodious bell of his private telephone, and there was annoyance in his manner as he uncradled the instrument. "Anthony talking."

From the lobby came the voice of a desk clerk. "Sorry to intrude, sir, but there are four persons down here demanding to see you. Three men and a lady. They decline to give their names, but insist that you receive them at once."

"Give them my regrets. I'm very busy."

There was a pause; then the clerk came back on the line. "I am asked to tell you they're calling to confer with you on a matter of vital importance. The transportation of labor."

When he heard this, Jim Anthony stiffened; a cold gleam came into his slitted eyes. He had planned to leave the penthouse at once and go see that Dorothy Dawson Carradyne who was allegedly in charge of the mysterious Foundation For The Redistribution Of War Manpower. But Miss Carradyne could wait a while, now; because apparently someone else had turned up who might be a source of unexpected information.

He spoke into the phone. "Four people, you said? Three men and one lady?"

"Yes, sir."

"All right. Send them along in my elevator."

Tom Gentry stared. "Now what pappy?"

"I don't know," the wealthy investigator said as he rang off. "But we'll soon learn."

CHAPTER V
CLOSE CALL

MANY CURIOUS-LOOKING CHARACTERS had stepped out of Jim Anthony's elevator into the foyer of his fabulous penthouse; but never had there been an odder assortment than this present delegation representing *Focus* magazine.

Of course, Anthony didn't know, at first, that they represented this publication. In fact, he was not even aware *Focus* magazine existed—which, actually, it didn't, since its initial edition had not been issued.

Lana McBride emerged first; and Tom Gentry emitted a soundless whistle of admiring appreciation when he caught a glimpse of her blonde loveliness. He frowned, though, when he saw the fat man who followed her.

This individual was forced to squeeze his three hundred unattractive pounds of flesh through the doorway of the cage, and his ponderous gait resembled the waddling of a monstrous, overfed duck. He, in turn, was trailed by one of the tallest, thinnest men Gentry had ever seen; a scarecrow carrying a camera in a battered case slung to his shoulder. Last to appear was a chap with apple-dumpling cheeks and naive blue eyes; an individual whose pork-pie hat and Kollege-Kut Klothes made him look like a fugitive from some obscure campus.

"A circus side-show, no less!" Gentry whispered to Francois Montclair. "The living skeleton, the ton of blubber, the shimmy dancer and the press agent!"

Oblivious to any such whispers, the fat man made directly for Jim Anthony and shoved out a pudgy hand. "Pleasure, Mr. Anthony. Nice to meet a fellow publisher. Introduce myself. Owner of *Focus* magazine. L. Gabriel Stope. These," he indicated his companions. "My staff."

Anthony's eyebrows lifted imperceptibly and he seemed not to see the fat man's extended hand. "You wanted to see me regarding labor transportation, I believe you said?"

"Ah. Get to the point. No lost time. Like to do business on that basis." Stope moved to a table and spread a layout of snapshots. "Look. Interesting."

Jim cast a glance at Tom Gentry, which the aviator missed because he had drawn the blonde girl aside and opened a conversation with her. She

seemed calmly pleased at having gained the attention of such a fast worker, particularly when he was the best friend of a famous millionaire.

Her companions, the tall photographer and apple-cheeked reporter, stood as silent as museum statues; while Francois Montclair sat in a corner wearing the expression of one who suddenly finds himself in a madhouse without understanding how he happened to get there. Anthony, too, experienced a momentary sensation of being in the presence of a group of escapees from a lunatic asylum; then his uncanny sixth sense began to function, warning him that although these people might appear crazy, they were in reality as dangerous as a time bomb.

Jim turned to study the pictures which L. Gabriel Stope had placed on the table-top. The first showed a doorway in front of which stood a cluster of men. The door itself bore the lettered legend:

FOUNDATION FOR THE
REDISTRIBUTION OF WAR MANPOWER

Anthony scowled. That blasted foundation again!

The next photograph was of a large bus crowded with passengers. Some of these men were recognizable as having appeared in the first snapshot; but the principal point of interest was the canvas sign on the side of the bus: *Anthony Enterprises.*

Once more he scowled, for he knew of no such vehicle in his industrial empire!

There were several other snaps, most of them not quite as sharp as the first pair. They revealed the same bus halted and silhouetted against a barren desert background. The passengers were huddled beyond, their faces angry, while the uniformed bus driver held them at bay with a threatening gun.

"Nice, hah?" Stope said. "Rhymer Koenig. Good photographer. Miniature camera inside his vest. Snapped pix through his buttonhole. Driver didn't suspect."

Jim faced the fat man. "What's the gag?"

"No gag. Don't pull innocent act. Evidence all against you. Obvious. Can't figure your purpose, but you've been recruiting workers on east coast, promising jobs, shipping them west, then stranding them."

The millionaire's nostrils quivered, flared. "So that's it! Now we're getting somewhere."

"Sure. Suppose I publish pictures and story in *Focus* magazine? Big expose. Make you mighty unpopular with American labor. Unions may act. Call strikes in all your plants. Complete breakdown of war production. Government might step in. Anthony the hero becomes Anthony the heel."

"Do you intend to publish this exposé?"

Stope smiled unpleasantly. "Depends on you."

"I see. Blackmail."

"Nasty word. Don't like it. You're a publisher. Own a chain of newspapers. Why not own a picture magazine too? Sell you *Focus* including title, good will, editorial material on hand. Including labor relocation pix and story. You can suppress the layout then if you like. Do as you please. Your own property."

"And the price?" Jim purred silkily.

The answer came, surprisingly enough, from the lips of that tall, skinny figure who carried a camera. "No matter how or where you look, you see we've got you on the hook. Your reputation's not worth shucks, unless we're paid a million bucks."

"Quiet, Rhymer!" the fat man snarled. Then he waddled close to the scarecrow photographer and deliberately hit him in the mouth. He was smiling again, though, when he turned back to Anthony. "Wrong. Not one million. *Two* million."

"That's pretty steep."

"No. Cheap. Just buttons to a man as rich as you."

The millionaire pretended to consider this. Presently he announced: "I'll let you know by noon tomorrow."

"Noon. Very good. One minute later, deal's off. We print a complete exposure. Understood?" He pivoted like a cumbersome pig, gestured to his staff. Silently they trailed him into the elevator and the cage wafted them downward.

The instant they had vanished, Francois Montclair leaped to his feet. "Criminals! *Cochons!* They will make you the most hated man in *les Etats Unis!*"

Anthony's stoic face was grimly expressionless. "I'm afraid I may be that in any event, if someone has been using my name in connection with the fake recruiting of labor. Provided those pictures were true, there's at least one busload of workers already stranded somewhere in the west. Maybe scores more. Once those men manage to get back to civilization, hell's going to pop."

"Yeah," Tom Gentry said sourly. "Strikes, government investigations, maybe a Federal indictment—gosh, Jim, what do you plan to do?"

"Move," the wealthy criminologist answered. "Move fast, before the storm breaks. You get on the phone, Tom. Contact this Dorothy Dawson Carradyne woman either at her home or the Foundation office. Ask information for its number. Tell her we want to see her at that office within the next half hour."

Gentry leaped to obey.

Meantime, Jim drew his French associate aside. "Listen, Dr. Montclair. In France you were an industrial efficiency expert. That's why I invited you into my organization. Now I need your abilities."

"*Oui, Monsieur Anthony*. I am at your service."

"Good. I'm giving you carte-blanche authority; placing my entire resources at your disposal. I want you to start sending out telegrams to every city, village, and hamlet west of the Mississippi River. Notify all police stations, sheriffs' offices, state constabulary posts to be on the lookout for migrant workers who've been dumped from busses bearing my name."

"And—?"

"Spare no expense. Have searching parties sent out. Pick up every last man who may have been victimized. See that each one is given a hundred dollars cash. Plus a ticket to California on the first available Pullman. And the guarantee of a job in war industry, with salary commencing from the time each man left his home. Got that?"

"I comprehend."

"Okay. Then get busy!" And Anthony saw Montclair to the elevator; despatched him down to his own suite on the fifth floor of the hotel.

By that time, Tom Gentry had finished phoning. "I talked to the Carradyne cookie, pappy. Boy, has she got a voice that makes your ears tingle!"

"Never mind her voice. Was she at the office?"

The freckled flyer nodded. "She said the cops had pulled her down there and hounded her with questions until she was worried sick. Claimed she was on the point of trying to reach you for instructions when I called. She's waiting for us."

"Fine. Let's go."

"Hey, wait. Don't you want me to phone the garage and have your car brought around?"

"We'll take a cab. It's quicker," Jim said.

In this, he was both right and wrong. He might save time in a taxi; that was true. But the decision came very close to costing him his freedom.

The attack came with vicious swiftness. It was a Yellow that Anthony and Gentry had chosen; and as it circled the block to get headed in the right direction for lower Broadway, another cab pulled abreast. Something small and white, like a pellet or thumb-sized capsule, was hurled from this second taxi into the tonneau of Jim's conveyance. The instant it landed, it burst with a tiny puff. Billowing fumes arose.

Simultaneously, a shot was fired and Anthony's cabby lurched forward over his wheel. He died instantly with a bullet through his brain—and the Yellow went out of control.

Tom Gentry yowled: "Damnation—!" and then, as he sucked in his breath

to yell again, the billowing fumes engulfed him. They entered his mouth, his nostrils; sifted stranglingly into his lungs. He choked, moaned; streams of unsolicited tears began to spurt from his eyes. "God—" he gasped.

"Don't breathe!" Anthony spoke just the two words; wasted no more of the precious air with which he had filled his own mighty chest a split second before the pellet had burst. Meanwhile his cab, which fortunately had been rolling along in slow second gear, was slanting over toward the far curb with the murdered driver's body slumped on the steering wheel, cramping it.

And that other taxi was crowding in.

The millionaire criminologist moved with the speed of lightning. His eyes were smarting now from the effects of the gas that drifted around him; his nostrils felt inflamed as if by a myriad stinging needles. But he controlled his lungs, held his breath; and with the butt of his automatic he smashed the glass partition between himself and the front compartment.

Then he reached through the jagged aperture, stretching until he found the ignition switch. He flipped it off. Braked by the compression of a dead motor, the cab slowly halted.

The second car also stopped. Its driver bounced to the street and two more men erupted from the tonneau, wearing masks and carrying guns. They deployed to Anthony's taxi, yanked its door open. "Come on, chumps. Out!"

Jim Anthony obeyed—but a lot faster than they anticipated. Like a surging streak of motion he flashed into view, using his automatic as a blackjack. A clubbing blow sent one of his assailants reeling backward, stunned. A second smashing impact dropped another masked thug to the street, unconscious.

"Boy!" came a whining bleat from the driver of the murder-cab. "The guy breathes tear gas an' *likes* it! I don't want no part of snatchin' anybody like that!" And he scuttled to his machine, slid under the wheel, clashed his gears.

As the vehicle roared forward, the first hood made a desperate grab for it; the thug Anthony had slugged groggy but hadn't quite felled. He caught a hand-hold, leaped to the running board and clung there as the taxi gathered speed.

Anthony could have drawn a bead on him, picked him off with one shot. But it would have been the same as cold-blooded homicide and he couldn't bring himself to kill a defenseless man—not even an outlaw. Moreover, the police could be depended upon to capture the two fleeing gunsels sooner or later. Particularly since they'd left the third member of their trio stretched out senseless on the street.

Unfortunately, the thug clinging to the escaping cab must have thought of the same possibility; for as the machine rocketed around the next corner

he snapped a bullet backward. It hit the prone gunman with deadly accuracy; tore a tunnel all the way through his heart.

Which made two murders in as many minutes: the innocent driver of Anthony's cab, and this masked thug who would never again regain consciousness to squeal on his companions.

CHAPTER VI
FORGERY'S FILES

ANTHONY CATAPULTED BACK TO HIS YELLOW; wasted no time on vain regrets or useless oaths. He hauled Tom Gentry out into the open air.

"God, pappy . . . my eyes . . . my lungs . . . on fire . . ." the aviator sobbed without meaning to, any more than he meant the tears that streamed down his freckled cheeks.

"You'll be okay. It was just tear gas." From his pocket, the millionaire criminologist extracted a flat black kit which he always carried; a kit compactly packed with a varied and sometimes startling assortment of scientific equipment.

Opening the kit, he produced a vial of colorless liquid which he spilled on a clean handkerchief, soaking it. Then he used the handkerchief to sponge Tom's face and nostrils, carefully squeezing a few droplets of the fluid into each of the flyer's watery eyes. Then, finally, he wadded the cloth over Gentry's nose and mouth.

"Breathe in. Deep. Through the handkerchief's folds. Inhale as much of this volatile stuff as you can."

Tom obeyed; and in a moment he began sputtering in amazement. "I—I'm okay again!" he exclaimed. "I ain't weeping! And I can take a breath without it burning like hell!"

"Right," Anthony said. "I used a special neutralizing chemical of my own formula; works only on tear gas. Now let's get out of here. I think I hear a mounted cop coming and we haven't got time to answer questions."

The genial aviator looked around, shuddered, started loping with his wealthy friend. "Gosh—two stiffs! We might be just as dead if you hadn't—"

"I don't think so. Had they wanted to kill us, they could have shot us down the way they did our cabby. Instead, all they used on us was gas, hoping to put us out of action so they'd have no trouble kidnaping us."

"It was a snatch?"

"So one of them said, accidentally."

"But why, Jim?" Then Gentry snapped his fingers. "I've got it! That fat guy from *Focus* magazine! He wanted to make sure you wouldn't run out before he could collect!"

"Possibly, although I doubt it. I'm beginning to see something deeper in all this mess. Maybe somebody doesn't want me to investigate this Manpower Relocation outfit."

Tom beckoned a cab and they piled in. "Say!" he whispered. "That's right! I *did* tell the Dorothy Dawson Carradyne quail we were coming to see her—!"

"And we still are. In fact, here's the address," Anthony remarked a few minutes later. "Let's go."

The office of the foundation was on the building's second floor. A sign on the wall by the staircase pointed upward; but the elevators didn't seem to be running, so Jim and Gentry took the stairs.

The door they wanted was directly opposite the stair-head, and they entered a big waiting room lined with bare wooden benches. Then an inner door opened and Dorothy Dawson Carradyne came forward to greet them.

She was tall, graceful, completely feminine in spite of her man-tailored suit. Her jet black hair was also cut man-fashion in a short bob that shaped to her head like a raven cap, accentuating the patrician quality of her chiseled features. She wore low heeled shoes; the sensible kind. But her stockings were of sheer nylon.

"Mr. Anthony!" she said, her voice rich and throaty. "Thank goodness you got here."

"Did you think maybe we wouldn't, babe?" Tom Gentry popped off, his light tone masking suspicion.

"Why—why, no, of course not. I knew you'd come, sooner or later. You phoned, you know." With this she dismissed the flyer and returned her attention to Jim. "I can't understand all the things that seem to have been happening tonight, Mr. Anthony. The murder of that Uvaldi man, and the—the police asking me so many questions—"

The wealthy criminologist made a wry grimace. "There are a lot of things I don't understand myself. For instance, Lieutenant Trotter tells me you're under the impression that I'm backing this labor relocation foundation."

"Under the impression?" she stared at him. "And why shouldn't I be? I have your letter asking me to undertake the work."

"May I see that letter?"

She nodded, conducted him to an inner office and produced a thin sheaf of correspondence from a file. "All your communications are here, together with those I've received from other members of the board. Naturally I've never spoken to any of you personally about the work; I was given to understand that you were all very busy, which was why you placed me in charge. I—I've tried to do a good job. I rented the most inexpensive offices I could find, kept my costs to a minimum—"

"Where did the money come from?" Jim interrupted her.

"Why, from the bank account you set up in my name."

"You used that money for bus-charter as well as office rental?"

Her puzzled frown grew deeper. "But Mr. Anthony, you know I had nothing to do with the transportation end. I was merely notified by letter to have so many workers of certain types ready to leave at a certain date and hour. I had them here, the bus would arrive, and that was all there was to it."

"How many loads of men have you shipped?"

She looked at a paper on her desk. "Thirteen the second week. None at all the first week. And only one this week."

"You've been operating three weeks, then?"

"We've been open that long. But operating for only ten days, actually. It took time to get established." Then she added casually: "Of course I don't know how many busloads have been shipped west from Philadelphia and Baltimore and—"

"Snow on a mountain, pappy!" Tom Gentry burst out. "They got *branches!*"

Presently the millionaire detective began inspecting the correspondence which he was supposed to have written. All the letters were on Foundation stationery, with a list of sponsors printed along one side: names that represented the ownership and management of some of the nation's greatest industries. Anthony's own name headed the list in larger type, just as his purported signature was boldly appended to many of the communications.

Beyond doubt, it was his genuine signature; no forger could possibly have made such a clever copy. As he leafed through the letters, though, a curious fact struck his eye. In each instance, his name had been signed in exactly the same way as the last; no slightest variation could be found.

He called this to the attention of Gentry and the Carradyne girl. "No matter how carefully a man writes his name, he never does it quite the same way twice," he remarked. "There are inevitable discrepancies. Ask any handwriting expert."

"Meaning what?" Tom asked.

For reply, Jim again had recourse to his flat, compact kit of scientific equipment. From a stoppered glass tube he spilled a few drops of chemical on one of his suppose signatures; then added a smear of jelly-like substance from a tiny plastic jar. The reaction was immediate and astonishing. As if the "James Anthony" had been scrawled with acid, it ate through the paper and vanished, leaving in its place the signature's silhouette sharply cut like a stencil.

Dorothy Dawson Carradyne muttered a guttural: "*Herr Lieber Gott!*" and then flushed with embarrassment. "Forgive me for lapsing into German.

After all, I spent so many years as a student in Berlin . . . and your experiment was so startling—"

Jim's well-schooled features betrayed no expression as he politely accepted this glib explanation of her slip. In fact, he ignored it and pointed to the letter.

"One of the cleverest forgeries I ever encountered," he announced quietly. "Accomplished by a new method. This was not an ordinary ink."

"Then what was it?" Gentry demanded.

"Somebody procured a copy of my autograph and made a photoengraving of it. These letters were not signed by hand. An impression of my signature was struck in some sort of small printing press—exactly the way counterfeit money is engraved!"

The brunette woman's eyes widened. "But—but why?"

"That's something I'm not yet prepared to answer. However, I think you must realize by now the obvious fact that I had nothing whatever to do with this so-called Foundation."

"It—it w-would seem so," she admitted reluctantly. "Although I can't understand why anyone would go to all this trouble just to make a f-fool of me!"

Anthony faced her. "Disregard yourself for a moment. Consider the others who've been duped; the hundreds of men who were shipped out of town in my name and then left stranded."

"Stranded—?" she recoiled, as if this had been an angle unknown to her previously. "Then your California factories had no jobs waiting for those men?"

Jim nodded grimly. "That's the story. I'd like to see your records on Nick Uvaldi, the murdered man."

"Of course." She thumbed through an index box, withdrew a card and handed it over.

He studied it, noting the date and hour of departure of the bus on which Uvaldi had been a passenger. Then he made a hasty mental calculation as to approximately how far west the vehicle might have traveled before the doomed man left it to come back to New York in time for his appointment with death.

After a moment Jim returned the card. "Thanks. And now, if you don't mind, I'd like those letters for police inspection. I want expert opinion on them."

Surprisingly enough, she refused. With a swift gesture she snatched up the sheaf of correspondence, thrust it in a drawer of the steel file by her desk, closed the drawer, locked it and then quickly unfastened her tailored jacket. Dropping the file key into a pocket of her blouse, she rebuttoned the coat.

"Sorry, Mr. Anthony," she said firmly. "This whole affair has placed me in an extremely awkward position. Those letters are all I have to indicate that I was acting under your authorization; or rather, that I thought I was. And while I have duplicate records and photostats of the letters in my bank safety deposit box, I prefer to keep the original correspondence in my possession until I've had time to consult an attorney."

If her action angered the wealthy detective, he revealed no hint of it; nor did he show the merest sign that her stubbornness had aroused his suspicions. Instead, he smiled. "Very well, Miss Carradyne. I can understand your feelings."

She seemed to lose some of her tension. "Thank you. If you have f-finished with me, I'd like to go home. I—I'm somewhat tired."

"That's understandable too. But I wish you'd stay here for just a little while longer. I have an errand to do, then I want to come back for one final look-around. It won't take long, I promise."

"We-e-ell, all right."

Jim moved toward the door and Gentry followed him. "What comes next, pappy?" the flyer asked in a low tone. "Could that fat Stope jerk and those other screwballs have schemed up this mess just to blackmail you?"

"Possibly. But it certainly cost them a terrific financial outlay to put their plans in operation."

"Not so terrific compared with the two million they're asking," Tom pointed out sagely. "If they stick you for that much dough, it's been a good gamble." Then he added: "Where we going now?"

"*You're* not going anywhere."

"Hunh?"

"You're to stay here, see that Miss Carradyne doesn't make a getaway with those letters. Keep your eye on her. I'll hunt up Lieutenant Trotter and bring him back with me. An official police request will make her part with that key."

Tom said: "Maybe I can get it without a police request." But his millionaire friend was already striding from the room and didn't hear the speculative remark.

As it turned out, Tom now found himself alone with the lovely Dorothy Dawson Carradyne; and he lost no time putting his strategy into motion. "Did anybody ever tell you how gorgeous you are, toots?"

She looked astounded. "Why—why, I—"

"You're wasting your life in this social service stuff, kitten. You ought to be behind footlights or something. Maybe the movies. You've got what it takes."

"Really?" she drawled, smiling a little. Her amusement didn't indicate displeasure, though. She was just the same as any other cutie, Tom told

himself. None of them could resist flattery.

He moved closer to her. "Sure. Take me, for instance. I ain't very often impressed by beautiful women." He wondered if heaven would strike him dead for the outrageous lie.

"Aren't you?"

"No. But you do things to me."

"Such as . . . what?" she purred.

"Well, like making me want to kiss you." Audaciously he slipped an arm around her waist and pulled her to him; put his mouth on her lips.

At that moment the ceiling fell on him.

Jim Anthony hailed a cruising cab and had himself driven to that side street where his first taxi had been attacked by those three thugs. Having left the corpses of two murdered men there—his original hacker and one of the masked gunsels—he had a hunch he would now find Lieutenant Trotter on the scene investigating the twin killings.

And he was right. The homicide official and a squad of his underlings had the street roped off to traffic while they bayed through the block like bloodhounds on a false scent. The bodies had been removed to the morgue by this time, although the wrecked Yellow still rested at the curb.

Trotter spotted the millionaire criminologist. "You!" he growled bitterly. "What are you doing here? Haven't I got enough grief on my hands without—?"

"I know, I know," Jim said in the tone of one who soothes a petulant child. "If you'll hold your temper, I'll try to give you a line on the two corpses you just found."

"*What*?" Trotter shouted. "You mean you know what happened to them? Why they were plugged?"

"I was here." And Anthony explained the attempted kidnaping, the manner in which he had frustrated it, and the subsequent escape of two of his thwarted abductors.

The headquarters man looked dazed. "I might have known you were mixed up in it somehow. Any time trouble begins cropping up in bunches I can figure you've got a finger in it." Then, a trifle more calmly, he asked: "Have you any idea why they tried to snatch you?"

"There are two possible theories."

"Well, spill them! Or is it a secret?"

Jim smiled bleakly. "First, someone may have wanted to put me out of action for a few days until a certain labor scandal breaks wide open. Second, it may be that somebody hoped to prevent my inspection of that relocation foundation's files."

"What about the files?"

"Those letters you saw were all forgeries. And now Miss Carradyne

refuses to give them up. I'd like you to go back to her office with me and demand the forged correspondence."

Trotter announced that he would be glad to do this. "But as for a labor scandal, I don't get your drift."

Briefly and concisely, Anthony furnished a resume of all he had learned, without revealing his sources of information. "You can see the possibilities," he concluded. "Hundreds of workers dumped on the desert in my name, left penniless and jobless after being promised employment—why, hell, it could cause strikes and walkouts in every plant I own. And a single day's stoppage of production would be a serious blow to American war effort at the rate we're turning out the goods."

"So that's why they tried to snatch you!" Trotter breathed. "To get you out of the way until it'd be too late to repair the damage!"

The millionaire criminologist inclined his head. "It's probable—although it wouldn't have done them as much good as they thought."

"Why not?"

"Because I already have my French associate at work. The man you met: Dr. Montclair. He's busy right now, setting the machinery in motion to rescue the stranded men and give them transportation, money, jobs."

"Smart enough," Trotter approved. "But who was behind this caper?"

Anthony's lips thinned. "Think it over a minute. Who'd gain by promoting disunity in this country? Who might have the biggest reason for fostering a rift between American capital and labor? Even though we mended that rift later by exposing the truth, we still would have lost thousands of man-hours that could never be made up."

"Good God; You mean—?"

"Yes. Axis agents. Saboteurs. A nation-wide plot to throw a temporary monkey wrench in our machinery," Jim said.

Trotter was appalled. "But who's responsible?" Then his big face darkened. "Say, that Carradyne woman was educated in Germany. And when I grilled her she accidentally used some German gab. Do you suppose—?"

"She spoke German to me, too. I've already thought of that. Which is why I'm asking you to go with me and have a showdown," Anthony reminded him.

"Yeah. What are we waiting for? Here's my car. Come on!" A vast impatience seemed to fill the homicide lieutenant as he realized they were wasting precious time.

But for all his sudden haste and the breakneck speed with which he presently sent his official sedan careening down Broadway, it developed that he might just as well have saved the effort. For when they finally burst into the offices of the fake Foundation For The Redistribution Of War Manpower,

he and Anthony discovered that Dorothy Dawson Carradyne was gone. Her files were looted and empty. And Tom Gentry lay sprawled on the carpetless floor of the inner office, as unconscious as a man who had been hit by a battering ram. In fact, from the appearance of the bruise on the back of his skull, it must have been a pile-driver that had bludgeoned him.

CHAPTER VII
REVELRY AT MIDNIGHT

"I KISSED HER," GENTRY MOANED when first aid measures eventually brought him back to his senses. "I kissed her just once. Pappy, did you ever kiss a girl and have it kick you into the middle of next week?"

Jim Anthony was in no mood for humor. "It was a blackjack, not the kiss, you idiot. I thought I left you here to guard her! Instead, you laid yourself wide open for an attack from behind. Won't you ever learn that crime and flirting don't mix?"

"Some day, maybe," the freckled aviator's tone was contrite. He rubbed the swelling on his scalp. "Anyhow, I'm certainly being educated the hard way."

Across the room, Trotter made irate noises. "Are you sure you didn't dish yourself that lump just to make the set-up look good?"

"Now, that's a lousy thing to say," Tom complained. "Why would I try to beat my own brains out?"

"It could be a cover-up," the homicide official peeled back his lips. Then he glared at Anthony. "I'm not forgetting that Uvaldi guy who got creamed in your hotel restaurant, my friend. He apparently had something on you—and he died. Whatever it was he knew or suspected, it was in connection with this Relocation Foundation."

The wealthy criminologist said: "Well?"

"Well, nuts! You've been feeding me a lot of baloney on forged letters and Axis saboteurs and melodramatic poppycock. How do I know any of it's true? Maybe you really *are* backing this relocation racket. Maybe it was some stinking scheme you hatched up to ship a lot of labor out west, strand them and then hire them at half-pay—which they'd be forced to accept, because they were stuck," Trotter theorized inelegantly.

"And the disappearance of Miss Carradyne? The missing files of records?"

"Yeah. A neat gag when you saw you'd overstepped yourself. The dame drops out of sight and takes all the organization papers with her. So now nobody can prove or disprove your connection with the outfit. Gentry bumps himself on the conk to make it smell sweeter—but it's still got a stench as

far as I'm concerned."

From past experience, Tom Gentry realized that the animosity existing between his millionaire friend and Lieutenant Trotter was one that could never be fully erased. It arose from deeply rooted differences in their natures, their habits of thinking, their training. Trotter had been schooled for direct action—the law of the nightstick, where every man is considered guilty until proven innocent. Anthony was the man of science, modern methods, rationalization. Between two such individuals friction was inevitable.

All the same, Tom couldn't restrain his temper as he heard the homicide official making his absurd insinuations. "Dizzy as I am, I've got a good notion to shove a few teeth down your throat!" he grunted at the headquarters man.

Anthony held up a warning hand. "Take it easy, Tom. If Trotter thinks I'm involved, that's his privilege. It's also his privilege to prove it—if he can."

"Is that a challenge?" the lieutenant asked.

"You may call it that."

"Okay. From now on, I'm breathing down your neck. Make one wrong move and I'll nail you, understand? And don't be coming to me with any more baloney about foreign spies. Don't look to me for help in chasing down blind alleys that you yourself arranged in advance. I'm after you and I'm going to get you, Mister Jim Anthony."

Then, snorting and muttering, Trotter tore out of the room in a towering rage.

"Hey, Jim," the freckled flyer said plaintively. "What did drizzle-puss mean by foreign spies?"

Anthony explained his saboteur theory. "The worst of it is," he ended, "I need those office records. First to prove my signature was forged; second, for the names and addresses of the men who were shipped west, so I can make amends."

Tom frowned. "But you've got Montclair working on that. The expert touch."

"He's shooting blind; putting out feelers in the dark. Chances are he'll miss connections with a lot of those fellows."

"What about Fatso from the picture magazine, Jim? Could he or one of his pals have bopped me, taken the files, and snatched Miss Carradyne? Or could she be in cahoots with the outfit?"

Anthony paced the floor. "Perhaps. Stope may think I'll pay off quicker if he offered me the foundation records along with his photos. If so, there's one flaw in his reasoning."

"What flaw?"

"The time element." Jim didn't elaborate on this. Instead, he said: "Let's take a look through his publishing office, Tom. We might find something." And they went down to hunt a cab.

Ten minutes later they stood before the musty suite in that dilapidated building in the Forties which comprised the headquarters of *Focus* magazine. The corridors were dark, deserted; no lights could be discerned through the door's frosted glass panel, and the door itself was locked.

This didn't daunt Anthony, however. From a secret pocket in his coat he drew his prized steels, those famed implements with which he could work the cleverest lock ever invented. In a brief moment the door swung open. He and Tom entered.

But their visit proved fruitless; they found nothing remotely resembling the files of the labor relocation foundation. "If I only knew Stope's home address!" Jim whispered.

Astonishingly, Gentry came up with a possible solution. "We might get it from his blonde secretary. I can tell you where she lives. She gave me her address and phone number when I talked to her in your penthouse."

Anthony's lips pulled back in a quick, dark smile. "So that was why you fastened onto her. I believe if you were heading for the electric chair and passed a girl, you'd get her number."

"Why not? Maybe the current would fail, pappy."

Lana McBride's apartment seemed to be the scene of unexpected revelry when the two friends arrived. At least you could hear conversation, merriment, the clink of glasses filtering through the door as the millionaire criminologist knocked.

It was the tall, skinny photographer who opened up. Like a slightly tipsy scarecrow he blinked at Anthony and Gentry, while in the room behind him a hush fell upon L. Gabriel Stope, Higgie Smith, and the McBride girl.

Then the cadaverous Koenig bowed drunkenly. "You find us in a celebration, drinking premature libation. Noon tomorrow is the deadline, or you'll be in every headline. Welcome to this little stash; I hope you brought two million cash."

CHAPTER VIII
Bullet Trail

Oblivious to the rhymed greeting, Jim Anthony strode forward until he was face to face with the publisher of the picture weekly which didn't exist. "Now, then, Stope."

"Ah. Twelve hours ahead of time. Good. Shows excellent judgment. I'm ready to complete the deal if you are," the fat man's slitlike lips were scissors chopping off the words.

"There'll be no deal. Not on your snapshots, anyhow."

"Wha-what?"

"They're worthless for blackmail purposes. They aren't exclusive," Jim announced.

"Crazy talk! Sure they're exclusive. Got my first tip twelve days ago. Overheard two men in saloon. Said they were signing up, shipping, out. Gave me a hunch. I had Higgie and Rhymer apply at foundation office. Accepted. They went with first busload. Dumped in Arizona. Other men broke. Not Higgie and Rhymer. Hired a rancher to drive them to closest town. Airport. Took plane back to New York. No other reporters and photographers on job. Course our pix are exclusive."

"Temporarily," the millionaire criminologist agreed. "But not for long. Even if I paid you blackmail to suppress your findings, the news is bound to break in a day or so; maybe sooner. The minute the first stranded workers reach civilization they'll talk—and the story will become public."

Stope seemed to deflate. "True. But—"

"So why should I pay you for a silence that can't possibly last more than a few more hours? You were hoping to stampede me for a quick settlement. I don't stampede worth a tinker's dam."

Higgie Smith moved forward, flanked by Koenig and Lana McBride. "What is this, an act?" he demanded suspiciously.

"No act," the fat publisher looked sheepish. "Tried to pull a fast one. Anthony too smart."

The blonde girl made a bitter mouth. "Maybe you're both too smart. Maybe you're still pulling a fast one—on us. Perhaps Mr. Anthony has already bought you off, and this little scene is to make us think the scheme

failed. Listen, Gabe. If you've already collected and think you can squeeze us out of the gravy—"

"Don't try it," Higgie Smith growled. "For a chisel like that I'd put a bullet through your fat gut."

Stope seemed genuinely scared. "No payoff. Word of honor. I wouldn't hold out on you." He turned to Anthony. "Tell them," he pleaded.

"It's true," Jim said quietly. "I haven't given you any money. But I might pay a reasonable figure for those records of the phony foundation."

Higgie Smith, Rhymer Koenig, and Lana McBride looked bewildered; apparently they didn't know what Anthony was talking about. But Stope's expression was crafty rather than surprised. "Files missing, eh?" Then he shook his head. "Sorry."

"Meaning you haven't got them?"

"Right."

"You don't know what happened to Miss Carradyne?"

"Who's she? Oh, the foundation secretary. No. Can't tell you a thing. Wish I could."

The millionaire detective touched Gentry's arm. "Come along, Tom. We're wasting time here." And they left the apartment, followed by the sounds of bitter argument as the conspirators hurled recriminations at each other for the shakedown fortune which had slipped through their fingers.

Downstairs, Jim drew his aviator friend into the shadows of an areaway. "You realize what I've done?" he asked the flyer.

"Sure. You caused a falling out among thieves."

"More than that, I've let them know I'll pay cash for stolen property. Stope may have been lying. He may have those files. If so, he'll probably do what his pals accused him of doing: pull a double cross, try to sell the files to me and keep all the money for himself."

Tom blinked. "Gosh, pappy, then that gang of vultures would really blow their tops!"

"Exactly. And in the process, one of them might accidentally let something slip."

"Such as—?"

"The possibility of them being in the pay of the Axis to foster industrial disunity in this country. With the blackmail game as a sort of sideline."

"So now what happens?" Gentry asked.

The wealthy criminologist smiled bleakly. "I have a hunch Mr. L. Gabriel Stope will be going home shortly. I want you to trail him. If he digs up those files, get them. Even if you have to do it with brass knuckles."

"That would be a pleasure."

"Then we'll drop a hint that he sold the stuff to us for pay. His friends will

do the rest when they hear that."

Tom chuckled with anticipation. "But what about you, Jim?"

"I'm starting out to hunt for Dorothy Dawson Carradyne," the sun-bronzed investigator responded. "I intend to find her if I have to turn New York upside down. Should that be necessary, we have just the organization to do it!" And he pivoted, made off into the night.

Tom Gentry knew what his friend meant by organization. In every strata of Manhattan society, from newsboys and lowly char-women up through the middle classes of white collar workers and even reaching as far as bankers, sportsmen, and capitalists, you could find secret membership in the legendary Anthony legion—a fabulous regiment of the adventurous whose allegiance and devotion could always be counted upon in time of stress. Into the ordinary every-day humdrum of their lives, Jim Anthony had carried the occasional thrill of battle against lawlessness; they were his undercover shock-troops, a heterogeneous army of modern Vigilantes banded together to fight crime.

And on those infrequent occasions when Jim called them into action, hell always spilled over!

Gentry grinned to himself as he lurked, alone, across the street from the entrance of Lana McBride's apartment house. He knew matters would soon be coming to a head, and he took grim delight in having a hand in the game. The action couldn't start too soon to suit him!

Presently he tensed as he saw two figures emerging from the building, one tall and thin, the other chubby. The genial aviator recognized them as Rhymer Koenig and Higgins Smith; and for an instant he was tempted to loiter along behind them; find out where they went, what they did.

Then he remembered his instructions. He was posted here to flush out bigger game, so he remained reluctantly in hiding and allowed the ill-assorted pair to pursue their course unmolested. He wished, though, that he might have been twins for the next couple of hours. . . .

"Oh-oh!" he whispered to himself. "*Stope!*"

It was true. The fat man had appeared and was now furtively moving toward the far corner with haste in his waddling walk and a leather brief case in his hand. The brief case seemed heavy, bulging.

To Tom Gentry, that leather bag was deeply significant. Maybe Stope had the foundation records in it. Maybe they'd been in Lana McBride's flat all the time, unknown to Rhymer Koenig and Higgie Smith. Possibly Stope and the McBride blonde were working together, planning a freeze-out which would leave Smith and Koenig minus their share of the proceeds.

"We'll soon see!" Tom told himself. And he began shadowing the fat publisher.

This was not exactly easy, for L. Gabriel Stope seemed worried by some inner fear of a tail. He kept glancing back over his shoulder, forcing Gentry time after time to duck into some darkened doorway. Presently, though, Tom's corpulent quarry scuttled through the entrance of another shoddy apartment house a few blocks distant; and here the chase ended.

Up a flight of stairs the fat man laboriously climbed, unaware of the silent, freckle-faced figure which followed. Then, in the second floor hallway, Stope produced a key, unlocked a door, and entered a flat.

Gentry caught just a fleeting glimpse of the interior before the door was closed. It was one of those old fashioned apartments where the rooms were laid out in a long line, like beads on a string. Access to them was gained by means of an inside hall that ran the length of the layout, the way a narrow passage runs along a Pullman compartment car.

Waiting until he could no longer hear the fat man's footfalls, Gentry tiptoed to the door and tried the knob. It refused him; the latch was snapped. He scowled, swore. What, he asked himself, would Jim Anthony do in a case like this?

He'd use his prized steels, of course.

But Tom had no steels. All he had was a pocket knife with a screwdriver blade. Well, it was worth a try—provided nobody came along and caught him! He set to work, unscrewing the face-plate under the knob.

Eventually it came loose and he made some tentative stabs at the lock proper. He was astounded when this actually brought results. "I burgled it!" he gasped.

And he slipped over the threshold.

Dead ahead, light gleamed pallidly. He made for the illumination's source, making no sound; and then, cautiously, he peered into what proved to be a kitchen.

L. Gabriel Stope stood over a white enameled table, fumbling at the catches of the brief case. There was a childlike expression of contentment on his fat features, an avaricious gleam in his eyes, a snake-like up-curl to the corners of his slitted lips. Now he reached into the bag, fondly.

Watching, Tom Gentry gathered himself to spring. The instant he saw those foundation records he would be ready to pounce and grab; to smack the publisher senseless if he made so much as one protesting yelp.

Stope's two hands came out of the brief case, bearing a cold roast chicken!

Stunned disappointment slugged through Gentry's heart as he realized he'd been on a false trail. Correspondence, hell! This fat slob had merely brought home the main course of the feast which had been broken up at

Lana McBride's place. And now he was carving the golden brown fowl with a kitchen knife, slicing off a juicy slab of the breast, conveying the succulent white meat to his traplike mouth.

Tom's own mouth watered. He suddenly recalled that his last meal had been dinner at the Waldorf-Anthony; a dinner interrupted by the murder of that Uvaldi fellow. Hunger began to clamor in the aviator's belly as he saw Stope munching a vast morsel of chicken and licking the grease off his fingers.

Gloating, smacking sounds came from the fat man's lips. For a single raging second, Gentry considered catapulting into the kitchen to snatch at least a drumstick for himself. And then, suddenly, a shot sounded.

The barking report blammed from the kitchen's open window, a few inches over the sill. There was a swift blurt of orange flame streaking across the room with L. Gabriel Stope as its target. The pudgy publisher screamed, dropped the chicken, grabbed at his left shoulder. Spinning, he collapsed into a chair—which went to pieces under his weight, dumped him floundering to the floor.

Tom Gentry said: "Cripes!" and instinctively launched himself into view; made a flying leap over Stope's sprawled form. Stope saw him and screeched again, wildly. "Murderer!" he yowled. "You shot me—!"

Paying no heed to the accusation, Tom gained the windowsill. There was a fire escape landing just outside, with the rusty rungs of an iron ladder leading downward. Somebody was on that ladder, descending with jerky speed.

The happy-go-lucky aviator didn't even hesitate. He clambered out, started down. His soles smacked the alley pavement just as a thin, slight figure raced away.

"No you don't!" Tom roared. He sprinted with all his might; overhauled the fleeing man at the mouth of the alley and nailed him. "Got you!"

His victim squirmed to face him. "*Monsieur* Gentry—!" he exclaimed.

He was Dr. Francois Montclair.

CHAPTER IX
PENTHOUSE PARTY

STANDING IN THE FOYER OF HIS ROOFTOP PENTHOUSE, Jim Anthony faced two visitors. For the millionaire criminologist, trouble seemed to be coming in carload lots tonight. He'd been home less than an hour, just long enough to get his famous organization moving and to make some startling discoveries; and now he had a new worry to contend with.

Higgie Smith and Rhymer Koenig.

He scowled at them. "I've already told you, gentlemen, that I'm not interested in buying your blackmail pictures."

"We didn't come to sell them to you, sir," Smith answered, a vindictive glitter in blue eyes which were no longer naive. "Although blackmail's what I want to talk about."

"Yes?"

The chubby reporter nodded. "Gabe Stope tried to put the bite on you. How much will you pay us to testify against him? You can send him up for attempted extortion; get even for all the grief he's caused you. All Rhymer and I want is some cash—and a promise of immunity."

Abruptly, Anthony had a feeling that he would like to fumigate the room when he got rid of these two lice. But his bronzed countenance was expressionless as he said: "Sending your employer to jail doesn't interest me. I might pay you for certain information, though."

"Name it then, and if we can, sir, we will try to give the answer," Rhymer Koenig looked pleased with his impromptu doggerel. "Gabe is dirty, Gabe is deep; we hate his guts, the moon-faced creep!"

Jim was not amused. "I want to know who's behind Stope. Has he any foreign connections?"

"Foreign connections—?" Higgins Smith stiffened. "Hell, no. I never heard of such a thing."

"He gets no funds from overseas?"

"Funds! He never has two dimes to rub together. Not for salaries, anyhow. He always manages to buy himself steaks; stuff his bloated paunch. But as for any big dough—nix!"

"You're sure of that?"

Higgie was about to embroider his negative theme, but there came a sudden interruption from the penthouse elevator. The cage opened and two newcomers surged into the foyer: Lieutenant Trotter and L. Gabriel Stope himself, with his shoulder bandaged and his arm in a sling.

Trotter had a satisfied smirk on his face. "Where's Gentry?" he demanded.

"Not here." Anthony's sixth sense warned him that more troubles were about to pile up on those he already had. "Why? What's wrong?"

"Oh, nothing," the homicide official sneered elaborately in Jim's teeth. "Nothing at all. Not a thing." Then he roared: "Except I want him on a charge of attempted murder!"

"*What*?"

The fat magazine publisher chimed in venomously. "You heard right, Mr. Anthony. Your freckled friend tried to kill me."

While this startling announcement was being made, the private lift had silently descended in its shaft, drawn downward by someone pressing the button in the hotel's main lobby. Equally unnoticed, the noiseless car now came back up again to penthouse level and its sliding door whispered open.

From the elevator's streamlined interior stepped Tom Gentry and the haggard little French refugee, Francois Montclair. Tom called: "Hey, Jim! I've been zigzagging all over town, ducking the cop—co—ka-humph! Oh-oh! Wrong floor. Excuse it, please." As he caught sight of Trotter and Stope, the genial aviator attempted to reverse himself and pull Montclair back into the cage with him.

He was too late. The headquarters detective emitted a snarl of triumph and nabbed him. "No, you don't! So you've been ducking the cops all over town, hanh? Well, you picked the wrong spot to duck this time. You're under arrest."

"Who, me?"

"Yes, you."

"What for? What's the beef?"

Trotter feigned a weary sigh. "What's the beef, he asks me! You see this man here, don't you?"

"Man?" Tom looked at Stope. "Is it a man? I thought it was a lump of blubber. Yeah, I see him."

"And you see the bandage on his shoulder."

"Sure."

"Well, that's where your bullet plugged him. The slug you aimed at his heart. Stick out your hands for the cuffs."

Gentry summoned a look of injured indignation and glared at the fat publisher. "Did you go to the law and accuse me of winging you, for cripes' sake?"

"I didn't have to," Stope said. "Law came to me. Neighbors heard the shot, phoned headquarters. Police asked questions. I told them what happened." He didn't seem happy about it, though. His manner indicated he'd have preferred to let the whole thing drop if it hadn't been for Trotter.

Jim Anthony stepped to the fore. "What about it, Tom?" he asked quietly. "Did you shoot him?"

"Gosh, no, pappy!" Then the aviator glowered at Stope. "I want you to answer something, Fatso."

"Go ahead."

"Which way were you facing when you stopped the pill?"

"Toward kitchen window. Eating chicken."

"And which way did the slug go in your shoulder?"

"From—from the front."

"Where was I when you first saw me?" Gentry probed.

"Kitchen door. Behind. But—but—"

Tom spread his hands at Trotter, palms upward. "See? This ape's trying to frame me. What really happened, I saw him get blasted from the window. I leaped for the sill and chased the gunsel down the fire ladder." He summoned a noble expression. "My duty as a citizen, you know."

Trotter was growing more crimson by the instant. "Stow it! Don't preach! What became of the guy with the gun?"

"He got away clean," Gentry lied unblushingly, not risking a glance at Francois Montclair.

The homicide lieutenant swung on Stope and exploded like a cannon cracker. "Why did you try to pin it on this lug? What's the idea?"

"I—I really thought he—" the fat publisher choked out the truth for once in his life, but couldn't make it sound convincing.

Jim Anthony made a suggestion. "Perhaps it was another little blackmail idea."

"Blackmail?" Stope paled. For the first time he seemed to notice the presence of Higgie Smith and Rhymer Koenig; then it dawned on him that they'd sold him out. "You two!" he extended a fat, accusing finger. "Now I get it! *It was one of you that shot me!* You'd made threats—"

Even Anthony had to admit, in secret, that Stope was clever as hell. With an eel's slippery skill he had adroitly eluded a pitfall; and by this new accusation he had managed to put his two staff members in an awkward spot. Any testimony they might offer against him from now on would be vitiated, disbelieved, thrown out of court. A case of the pot calling the kettle black.

Lieutenant Trotter buried his face in his hands and moaned disconsolately. "Ye gods and little gremlins, what've I done to deserve this? Every time I make an arrest it blows up in my teeth like a loaded cigar! Will everybody

kindly get out of my road while I go quietly nuts?" And he stumbled over to the elevator like a man in a horrid nightmare.

Anthony called after him. "Take these vermin with you and turn them loose." He indicated Stope, Koenig and Higgie Smith. "They make the place smell bad."

The atmosphere seemed a trifle clearer when Trotter and the *Focus* magazine trio had departed; but there was still a suspicion of tension. Especially when the millionaire criminologist stared speculatively at his freckled friend.

"You lied, Tom."

"Yeah, pappy, I sure did."

"You lied about not catching the gunsel."

"That's right."

"Who was he?"

Gentry jerked a thumb. "Frenchie here."

"Dr. Montclair? Good God!"

"I fronted for him," Tom said. "After the way he explained things, I couldn't do anything else."

Francois Montclair looked haggard, rueful and grateful all at once. "It is of the truth, *Monsieur* Anthony," he confessed. "I shot that *canaille* of a Stope. I tried to kill him. My aim, she was miserable. I point at the heart, I hit the shoulder. I win no medals for marksmanship, *hein*?"

"But why, in heaven's name?" Jim demanded. "Why should you attempt a thing like that?"

"It is simple, *Monsieur* Anthony. Me, I am a refugee. Driven from my homeland by pigs who would have executed me if they had caught me. I come to America. I am penniless. You take me into your industrial empire, your confidence."

The millionaire made a disparaging gesture. "I need men of your ability. It was no favor. It was business."

"*Oui*. Yet the fact remains. You give me a new chance, a new hope, a new life. Then this so-accursed Stope appears. He makes the trouble for you, my benefactor. He is no better than a Nazi rat. So, *Pouf!* I shoot him." The little Frenchman shrugged as if his act had been the most natural thing in the world.

Anthony began pacing the thick rug. His face was set in a grim mold; lines of worry appeared around the corners of his mouth.

"What's the matter, pappy?" Tom Gentry asked. "After all, I got Frenchie clear. Nobody suspects him. And Stope's in no position to bellyache."

"I'm not thinking about that."

"Then what *are* you thinking about?"

"Two things I discovered after I posted you to trail Stope," the wealthy

criminologist answered heavily. "I returned here to the hotel; started my organization moving. Then, by accident, I found something in this very penthouse."

"What was it, Jim?"

"A dictaphone. It had been planted here to enable somebody to eavesdrop on my private conversations."

The aviator stiffened. "Gosh! Where'd it lead to?"

"An unused trunk room on Five! I traced it there. And then I found Dorothy Dawson Carradyne."

Tom's eyes bulged. "Did you make her talk?"

"She'll never talk again," Anthony said bitterly. "That was why I was upset when Trotter came in a while ago. You see, I've made no report on it as yet; but Dorothy Carradyne was dead when I found her. She'd been dead for quite some time."

CHAPTER X
Focus on Sabotage

Barely a few brief hours before dawn, Jim Anthony finally finished summing up his interpretation of all the ugly events that had happened. Pacing the floor, burning numberless cigarettes, stopping occasionally for a drink, he had steadily given voice to his theories and his convictions.

"I'm positive it's the work of Axis agents," he concluded. "Not just one, but many—with a single clever, crafty, cunning brain leading them. This whole plan springs from Berlin."

"Yeah, Jim?"

The hawk-like criminologist seemed not to hear Gentry's murmur. "A scheme to disrupt the harmony that exists between labor and the Anthony industries. A plot to make all workers reluctant in the future to move from one city to another for war positions. Not to mention the temporary loss of manpower through bickering and strikes because busloads of men were stranded. Even after I get that mess straightened out, the bad taste will linger."

"But look, pappy—"

"I might not have had the slightest inkling of trouble until it was too late—if it hadn't been for that poor Uvaldi fellow. I know now that he got off a bus somewhere in Pennsylvania; came back here to kill me because he thought I was responsible. Someone killed him first, though; someone on the other side of the restaurant, who escaped in the darkness. That murder was for the purpose of keeping me in ignorance of conditions until the storm broke."

"What about Stope's blackmail stunt?"

"A side issue. We're dealing with a master mind, man or woman, who has money, nerve, daring—and plenty of underlings for the actual dirty work. Think of the ramifications. This Foundation For The Relocation Of War Manpower, for instance. Offices in New York, Philadelphia, Baltimore. The bus charters. The gunsel bus-drivers. The bank accounts. The phony letterheads with forged signatures. Masked killers and snatch artists in hijacked cabs. The thing's so big it staggers you."

"Listen, Jim. This Carradyne dame—"

"Poisoned. Potassium cyanide. Instant death."

"Could she have been the brains? And killed herself when she saw you were closing in?"

"I don't know," Anthony said. "She may have been a suicide, or she could have been murdered; brought here to the hotel under duress and forcibly given the fatal dose because she knew or suspected too much. Suppose she saw the face of the man who slugged you unconscious in the foundation office? That alone would have been her death warrant, even if she'd been innocent otherwise; a mere dupe of the sabotage mob. Her corpse may have been left in the trunk room by the dictagraph receiver just to make it appear that she was implicated. I won't be sure until after the banks open in the morning."

Tom stared. "Banks? What have they got to do with it?"

"Everything, I hope. The answer to the riddle—or at least a means whereby I can repair the damage that's been done."

"How come?"

"Well, you perhaps recall something she said when we interviewed her a few hours ago. She mentioned duplicate records in her safety deposit box."

"Yeah, she did speak of that."

"And do you remember where she placed the key to the filing cabinet which she locked in front of our eyes?"

Gentry sighed with reminiscent regret. "Inside her jacket."

"Right. So when I examined her corpse in the trunk room not long ago I found another key in the same pocket. A bank key to a safety deposit box at the Commerce First National."

"Jeepers! You think the duplicates will be there?"

"I'm hoping so," Anthony's dark eyes were shrouded. "But in the meantime, I want you to help me bait a trap."

The aviator leaped to attention at the prospect of activity. "Sure, Jim. What's your plan?"

"You're to go to that blonde girl, Lana McBride—"

Tom choked a protest. "Aw, no, pappy! Not her! You ain't going to tell me *she's* mixed up with Axis agents! She's a little crooked, maybe, but not that crooked!"

"There you go again, letting a pretty face distort your common sense," the millionaire criminologist reproved him. "After all, the McBride girl is Gabriel Stope's secretary; which could be a blind for her other connections. Aside from that, whatever she learns will inevitably get back to Stope—and to his slimy underlings, Rhymer Koenig and Higgins Smith."

Gentry digested this. "By gosh, I wouldn't put anything past that pair of weasels! Even Rhymer's name, Koenig—that's a German moniker, ain't it?"

"Correct. And the character of a poverty stricken photographer would make an excellent disguise for the head of a ring of enemy agents who wished to stay under cover. Which is why I ask you to go to see Lana McBride."

"What am I to tell her that might get back to Koenig or the others?"

"The facts about Dorothy Dawson Carradyne's safety deposit box. Its possible contents. And a tip that I intend to go to the Merchants' Fourth Trust to inspect that box as soon as the bank opens its doors in the morning," Jim said.

"Hey, wait," the aviator checked up. "What's this about the Merchants' Fourth Trust? I thought you told me it was the Commerce First National?"

Anthony smiled bleakly. "I did. That's the trap part. If my suspicions are correct, the saboteur gang will do one of two things. First, they may try to make a getaway out of town when they learn I'm about to get the dope. If they do, they'll find themselves picked up. I'll have every road, tunnel, bridge, and depot under police surveillance."

"Suppose they sit tight, though?"

"In that case they'll probably make a concerted move on the Merchants' Fourth Trust to intercept me and take those records away from me in a daylight hijack."

Tom looked bewildered. "But you won't *be* at the Merchants' Fourth Trust! The box ain't there!"

"Exactly. Therefore, instead of hijacking me, the mob will run into the arms of the waiting cops. Meantime, you and I will go quietly to the Commerce First National where the box is actually located. Nobody will molest us, because we've thrown the saboteurs off the scent and into a trap several blocks distant. We kill two birds with one stone."

Gentry grinned suddenly. "I get it! We'll be picking up the evidence at the Commerce First National while the cops are picking up the Axis gang at the Merchants' Fourth Trust!" He hastened to the elevator. "I'm on my way to see Blondie!"

"Good," the millionaire detective approved. With sudden concern he turned to Francois Montclair. "Forgive me for talking so long. It's nearly dawn and you're utterly worn out; you've had a hard night. I suggest that you get some rest if you want to be in on the finish a few hours from now."

"*Merci, Monsieur*," the haggard little refugee thanked him. "As you say, the night has been of the difficult."

A fitful nap didn't seem to have helped Montclair very much when payoff time rolled around. For that matter, Tom Gentry, too, looked drawn and worn in the morning sunlight. But Jim Anthony, who'd had no sleep at all, appeared as fresh and keenly attuned as a well trained athlete newly

awakened from a full night's repose. His hawk-like eyes were sharp, his clean-shaven face glowing with bronze health, his stride vigorous as he and his weary companions made for the stately structure on Fifth Avenue which housed the Commerce First National Bank.

The massive doors were just opening for the start of the days' business transactions when the millionaire criminologist arrived there with Tom and Montclair. Three armored money-trucks bearing uniformed guards were in the act of parking before the big building, and Avenue traffic flowed smoothly in its accustomed morning grooves: delivery vans, private cars, the usual flood of cabs painted every color of the rainbow. Streams of pedestrians moved along the sidewalks: New York's motley assortment of workers en route to their jobs.

Anthony halted briefly. "Tom, I'm posting you here to wait. Not that it's necessary, but just as a safeguard. Come along, Dr. Montclair. We'll get that box."

Grumbling, Gentry took up his post at the entrance. Traffic, both vehicular and pedestrian, seemed to be thickening. Abruptly the freckled aviator stiffened as he noticed a fat figure crossing Fifth and heading in the direction of Lexington. It was L. Gabriel Stope—and that other bank, the Merchants' Fourth Trust, was located on Lexington Avenue! The bank where a trap had been baited and prepared!

Was the fat publisher approaching this trap, or was his appearance merely a coincidence? If coincidence was the explanation, *then why was he being followed at a discreet distance by Lana McBride, Rhymer Koenig, and Higgie Smith*?

Tom thought about the pre-dawn visit he had made to the McBride girl's apartment just a few hours ago. He had worked that pretty cleverly, he told himself. He'd pretended to be slightly drunk and very much infatuated. He had made a couple of tipsy passes at the golden-haired Lana, which she had repulsed—but not too indignantly. In her manner there had been more than a hint that she might be receptive to his attentions at some other time.

Then, before she persuaded him to leave, he had managed to impart certain false information to her, the way a drunken man might make loose conversation. And now she was headed for Lexington Avenue with Koenig and Smith, trailing Gabriel Stope in the direction of the Merchants' Fourth Trust.

It was entirely possible, of course, that they weren't intending to go anywhere near that bank trap. Maybe they had some other, more innocent destination; errands to perform. They vanished from Tom's view in a surge of traffic that seemed to grow more abnormally heavy every instant.

And then hell broke open.

The deadly action commenced at the exact instant of Jim Anthony's emerging from the depths of the Commerce First National. The millionaire criminologist had a flat green metal box tucked under his arm and Francois Montclair trotting along beside him. Jim saw Gentry standing guard; nodded to him. He tapped the box he was carrying, as if to indicate that everything had gone off without a hitch.

But Anthony's casual manner was a mask covering his actual tautness, his alert realization of danger. Deep within the wealthy detective's subconsciousness his weird sixth sense shrilled a warning. He froze.

Those three armored money trucks were still parked in a row at the curb; and now, viciously, suddenly, their doors flashed open. Uniformed guards erupted to the sidewalk, brandishing automatics and tommy-guns. They weren't guards, though. They were thugs in disguise. Nazi agents.

They closed in on Anthony.

The thing caught Tom Gentry flat-footed. All he could do was goggle at the scene and yell frantically: "Jim—look out! It's a heist!"

And then a seeming miracle took place.

Along Fifth Avenue in both directions, vehicular traffic came to an astounding halt. The broad street was suddenly blocked by a jam of motorcars packed in and wedged from one curb to the other. There were sleek limousines and battered jalopies; delivery trucks and garbage wagons; taxicabs, private coupes, sedans that ranged in size from midget Austins to swanky Cadillacs and Packards. A hellish din arose as each and every machine's horn started bleeping and yowling and braying.

Simultaneously, blurts of charging humanity began appearing from the vehicles. And on the sidewalks, that abnormally thick flow of pedestrians pressed inward, converging upon the uniformed thugs who had leaped out of the armored trucks.

"Gosh!" Tom Gentry gasped. "It's the Organization—Jim's Vigilantes!"

He was right. Scrubwomen and bankers, newsboys and dignified stockbrokers, janitors and society dowagers and stenographers and debutantes, soldiers and sailors and marines on furlough—the crush comprised a thrilling cross-section of America; the embattled citizenry of the United States waging war upon their homeland's enemies!

Guns barked. Fists thudded home. Tommy-guns were torn from the hands of the sabotage mob and used as clubs, with Jim Anthony himself in the thick of the fray, dealing out grim punishment with his battering knuckles.

Panic-stricken, the fake uniformed guards broke in terror and tried to regain the safety of their three armored trucks. It was a useless maneuver, a fruitless retreat. Even had they reached their sanctuary, they could not have driven a single yard—because Fifth Avenue was plugged by halted cars as

effectually as if a solid wall had been built from curb to curb. Horrified, the saboteurs threw down their weapons and raised their pleading hands. From bashed and bleeding mouths came the concerted whine of cornered rats: "*Kamerad! Kamerad!* We surrender!"

Then, and only then, did Jim Anthony draw his own automatic from its shoulder holster. He pivoted, took aim at a furtively scurrying figure which was trying to burrow through the jammed throngs.

He fired just once. He sent a bullet through the escaping man's left leg; brought him down.

"Got you, Francois Montclair," he said quietly.

In Lieutenant Trotter's office at police headquarters, Jim faced the crippled Nazi who had posed as a Free French refugee. "Toward the last, I knew you were the one I wanted; the brains behind this whole rotten plot."

Montclair squirmed, cursed him gutturally in German.

"You see," the wealthy criminologist went on, "I realized it had to be someone fairly close to me; someone with access to my signature, my business methods, my industries. And you were the only newcomer in my confidence. So my suspicions were justifiable under the circumstances."

Again the Nazi saboteur cursed him.

Jim ignored the oaths. "But I couldn't be certain until you made one false move; overplayed your hand. That was when you attempted to murder Gabriel Stope. The fat man was innocent of anything except blackmail; but because of his extortion scheme, he almost spoiled your own game. That is, he told me enough to make me realize I was up against an Axis plot. Therefore you tried to kill him—and sealed your own doom."

"*Schwein!* American dog! You trapped me! It was illegal! It was not according to the rules—!"

"You're a fine one to talk about rules." Anthony's smile was thin, mirthless. "As far as I'm concerned, I'll exterminate vermin with any means at hand. Sure I trapped you. In your hearing, I pretended to be baiting a snare for the *Focus* magazine people. Actually the bait was for you—and you swallowed it, hook, line, and sinker. You thought I would be unprotected when I went after the safety deposit box at the Commerce First National. I intended for you to think that."

"It was unfair!"

Anthony said: "That's according to how you look at it. The main point is, I wanted to capture you; but I was equally anxious to nab your mob of henchmen. The bus drivers. The kidnap thugs. The man in my hotel restaurant who killed Nick Uvaldi. I wanted all of you to pay for Uvaldi's death, and the murder of innocent Dorothy Dawson Carradyne, and the stranding of the duped workers who were dumped on the desert. I knew you'd have your

whole stinking mob on hand to hijack me when I came from the bank; so I arranged a plan to nail them. The plan worked—and now I'm turning the whole lot of you over to the F.B.I. in Washington."

"*Nein*—they'll hang us—!"

"I sincerely hope so," Jim Anthony said. Then he turned his back on the cringing Nazi and strode from the room.

Lieutenant Trotter visited the Anthony penthouse the next evening; faced Jim and Gentry. "Did you get your own affairs straightened out?"

The millionaire nodded quietly. "Every last worker was located, given money and a job. As you know, the newspapers have headlined the story; revealed it as a Hitler plot. Consequently there's no disunity between labor and capital. Our plants are producing faster than ever."

"You know, of course," Trotter said, "I could pinch you for causing a traffic jam and riot on Fifth Avenue."

"Do you intend to?"

"Hell, no. In fact, I'll drink with you if you'll invite me."

Tom Gentry reached for a bottle. "Three snorts coming right up, pappy," he chortled happily.